MILLARD
SALTER'S
LAST DAY

MILLARD SALTER'S LAST DAY

JACOB M. APPEL

GALLERY BOOKS

New York   London   Toronto   Sydney   New Delhi

G

Gallery Books

An Imprint of Simon & Schuster, Inc.
1230 Avenue of the Americas
New York, NY 10020

First Gallery Books trade paperback edition November 2017

GALLERY BOOKS and colophon are trademarks of Simon and Schuster

For information about special discounts for bulk purchases, please contact Simon & Schuster Special Sales at 1-866-506-1949 or business@simonandschuster.com.

The Simon & Schuster Speakers Bureau can bring authors to your live event. For more information or to book an event, contact the Simon & Schuster Speakers Bureau at 1-866-248-3049 or visit our website at www.simonspeakers.com.

Interior design by Davina Mock-Maniscalco

Manufactured in the United States of America

1   3   5   7   9   10   8   6   4   2

Library of Congress Cataloging-in-Publication Data
Names: Appel, Jacob M., 1973- author.
Title: Millard Salter's last day / Jacob M. Appel.
Description: First Gallery Books trade paperback edition. | New York : Gallery Books, 2017.
Identifiers: LCCN 2017014958 (print) | LCCN 2017021408 (ebook) | ISBN 9781507204092 (ebook) | ISBN 1507204094 (ebook) | ISBN 9781507204085 (paperback) | ISBN 1507204086 (paperback)
Subjects: | BISAC: FICTION / Literary. | FICTION / Humorous. | FICTION / General.
Classification: LCC PS3601.P662 (ebook) | LCC PS3601.P662 M55 2017 (print) | DDC 813/.6—dc23
LC record available at https://lccn.loc.gov/2017014958

ISBN 978-1-5072-0408-5
ISBN 978-1-5072-0409-2 (ebook)

To Rosalie, Ruth & Theia

Most things may never happen: this one will . . .

—Philip Larkin, *Aubade*

PART 1

DAWN TO MIDDAY

1

On the day he was to hang himself, Millard Salter made his bed for the first time in fifty-seven years. He struggled briefly with the fitted sheet, but by bracing the mattress against his good knee, he managed to hook the elastic bindings over the corners. Then came the flat sheet, the pillowcases, the silk comforter that his second wife, a dialysis nurse, had received as a gift from an elderly Taiwanese patient. Millard had called it a duvet, until Isabelle—rest her soul—pointedly explained the difference. (Words had mattered to Isabelle: *Pictures are hung,* he could hear her chiding. *People are hanged.*) Finally, he drew the spread over the comforter, letting the fringe hang loose at the foot like a skirt hem, and propped the breakfast pillows and the flanged shams against the headboard. When he'd finished, shortly after six o'clock, the queen-sized bed looked togged up for a fashionable hotel. Only a mint on the pillow was lacking. *I suppose they'll cut me down and lay me out on the covers,* Millard reflected. *And if they assume that I tidied my bedding so fastidiously* every *morning, is that such a crime?*

Soon the birthday wishes would be arriving—from his children, or at least the three who were likely to remember, because with Lysander, you could never tell, and from his baby sister in Tucson (*his baby sister who was now sixty-eight!*), and from Virginia Margold, a high school acquaintance who, post-divorce, had taken to phoning the surviving Hager Heights graduates of the class of 1957 to commemorate their special occasions. Virginia was certain to take poorly the news that solid Millard Salter—or "Salty," as she'd previously known him—had shut his own book at seventy-five. That, fortunately, would not be his concern.

How strange it was, reflected Millard, as he tied his shoelaces—an elaborate procedure since his disc had slipped—that the act of dressing proved no different in its final rendering. Same Lancing tie. Same crew neck cardigan. Same black bag, a gift from his own father at his medical school graduation. Only choosing a belt required reflection. He retrieved his two best belts from the bathroom closet—the closet where Isabelle's used cosmetics decomposed in a water-warped carton, waiting to be discarded—and looped the leather around his fists, tugging each to test its strength. He intended to use one for his slacks, the other for his neck; the last thing he desired was for them to find him dangling in the bathroom with his trousers bunched around his ankles. Besides, he'd read once that hanging triggered erections, and while the prospect of greeting his "rescue" party with an alert member struck him as amusing, sort of like a raised middle finger on steroids, he didn't wish to leave the world with the impression that he'd been angry in life, or even disappointed, because he had not.

Millard claimed the elevator for himself from the ninth floor to the fourth, when Elsa Duransky boarded in a cloud of lavender. She carried an ancient Yorkshire terrier in the crook of one elbow, its tiny black paws scampering through empty air. Her husband, Saul, once a respected endocrinologist, had become another of those unfortunate creatures who dressed for work every morning, impeccable as a military guard, but with no patients to see, doddered from staff meetings to clinical grand rounds to case conferences, leaving behind a trail of tangential, long-winded questions. He was everything, in short, that Millard had determined not to become.

"How's the old-timer?" he asked, meaning the dog. He could never recall the animal's name, which was either Mr. Spark or Mr. Spike or something similar.

"The old-timer was out the door thirty minutes ago," replied Elsa, rolling her eyes, and Millard realized she believed he'd been referring to her husband. Yet she didn't seem offended—and it was one of those misunderstandings not worth correcting. Certainly not during his final encounter with Elsa Duransky, which this was likely to be. No, a clarification now would only sound awkward, insincere. Far better to grin like an imbecile while Saul's wife filled the elevator car with plumes of gossip. ("Grin like an imbecile"—they'd probably fire him these days if he used an expression like that in the hospital—or, at a minimum, make him sit through some pointless online sensitivity training.) He recalled how Isabelle had summed up their neighbor, after a particularly tedious meeting of the co-op board: "Half of what that woman says is true. The problem is she doesn't know which half." Isabelle had possessed a knack for distilling people.

"I ran into Lysander," said Elsa. "Did I tell you?"

The boy's name corralled Millard's attention. Not that you could legitimately call him a boy anymore, not at forty-three. At twenty-five, even at thirty-five, you could get away with such terms, you could speak of him as a good kid with potential, of his early penchant for mathematics and his prodigious imagination—he'd graduated from Wesleyan, after all—but two decades later, Lysander hadn't harnessed that imagination for anything except daydreams.

"In the park," said Elsa. "Walking his dogs."

"Did you?"

"Sweetest dogs he has," said Elsa. "Although Mr. Scratch here might beg to differ."

The terrier glowered at Millard—his snub nose Elsa's, his shaggy cliff of a brow distinctly Saul's, as though the beast had grown into the son the couple never had. The elevator stopped on two, but the corridor stood vacant; someone had given up and taken the stairs.

"We're having lunch," said Millard. "I'll send Mr. Scratch's regards."

Elsa hardly registered his remark. "What are their names?" she asked.

A moment elapsed before he realized she meant the dogs—and then he felt a pulse of anger, uncharacteristic anger, that Elsa cared about something so trivial. Or maybe she didn't care, merely needed to fill the time-space continuum or dormant gray matter. And, dammit, what were the names of those dogs? The car opened and they stepped into the lobby, where a cologne of damp hardwood—an "Old New York" scent—hung perpetually in the shadows.

"Adolf and Benito," he replied.

They'd been the first duo to pop into his head. He could easily have said Abbott and Costello or Sonny and Cher. Not that it really mattered. This was the solace of knowing that you wouldn't live to see the dawn: unabashed irreverence.

Elsa's neck stiffened perceptibly, then relaxed. "Well, in any case, he's so good with those animals," she said. "Maybe you'll make a veterinarian of him yet. . . ."

Maybe, but unlikely. What gnawed at Millard wasn't that his younger son had piddled away twenty-one post-graduate years without a full-time job, or a serious relationship, or even filing his own tax returns, but that Millard, embroiled in extraneous affairs, had let him. Still, in preparing for death, Millard found himself pondering whether a man who hadn't yet amounted to a bucket of warm glue might not generate an artistic or literary masterwork at the age of forty-three . . . or, at least, embark upon a career. That was indeed the purpose of their lunch—their *final* lunch, Millard reminded himself, his last opportunity to steer the boy onto "the straight and narrow," as his own father would have said.

All week—all month—he'd been ticking off his "lasts": his last visit to the public library, his last lecture to the medical students, his last dental checkup, although what a man planning to live ten days wanted with a biannual dental cleaning was hard to articulate. He'd sworn to himself that he wouldn't deviate from his usual routine. So he'd renewed his subscriptions to *Psychosomatic Medicine* and *Architectural Digest*, prepaid his dues at the faculty club, requested an absentee ballot, as he always did, for a primary election in which he'd no longer be alive to vote. That afforded him the opportunity to back out, to reverse course even to the end. Yet as the appointed day approached, rather than fearful, or even reluctant, he found himself resigned—as though, to paraphrase the High Holiday *Amidah*, his name had already been inscribed on the casualty list inside the Book of Life.

Millard's only lingering concern was of method, not purpose. Self-destruction hadn't been designed for the faint-hearted, which explained why most attempts failed. How many patients had he encountered who'd downed a bottle of Tylenol—and, "rescued" by a concerned neighbor or intrusive letter carrier, had awakened to a transplanted liver? No, pills entailed too much uncertainty. With carbon monoxide, one ran the risk of asphyxiating the neighbors. Or, heaven forbid, blowing up the entire building—leaving a legacy of rage and fragmented plaster. For weeks, he'd considered purchasing an unlicensed handgun, but illicit firearms proved hard to come by in his social circle. (Obtaining a legal pistol, even if he could eventually secure one, entailed navigating months of red tape.) He finally appreciated the truth of those Dorothy Parker lines that had merely amused him as an adolescent: "Guns aren't lawful; Nooses give; Gas smells awful; You might as well live." Since living wasn't an option that Millard seriously entertained, a makeshift noose seemed the least-worst alternative. Assuming, of course, he marshaled the nerve to kick the chair from beneath his feet.

"And *you*, Millard?" asked Elsa—as though suddenly realizing his presence. She adjusted his necktie while she spoke, stymieing a quick exit. "How *are* you?"

"I'm good," he said. "Life is good."

Life, on the whole, *had* been good to Millard—probably more generous, he conceded, than he had been in return. With his ex-wife, Carol, a benevolent tyrant, he'd raised three adult children, two of them successfully. The older boy, Arnold, had moved out to St. Louis, where he served as general counsel to a consortium of beer distributors and coached little league soccer. Their daughter, Sally, married a naval architect who'd inherited a lumber fortune, and had twin six-year-old girls of her own. She divided her time between Suffolk County, home to a renovated nineteenth-century farmhouse overlooking Long Island Sound, and a two-story pied-à-terre on Gramercy Square. And with Isabelle, there'd been Maia—striving, crystal-eyed Maia—a magnificent late-life blessing. If not for Lysander . . . "In baseball," Millard had once half-joked to Isabelle, "three out of four is Hall of Fame material."

"Good," said Elsa. "I'm glad."

Yet the woman managed to inflect just enough doubt into her words that, when she vanished through the revolving doors, he found himself wondering if she hadn't meant more—if she'd intended to insinuate that he *wasn't* well, but that she'd be willing to maintain the illusion of his prosperity if he wished her to do so. And was he really in such fine shape? He *was* going to kill himself, after all. Had he been one of his own patients, he'd have phoned 911 immediately. Who could ever say whether a suicide was rational or irrational, justified or unpardonable? A lifetime reading Hume and Durkheim drew one no closer to any defensible truth; one simply had to operate on blind instinct, a visceral sense of right and wrong. He remembered his mother's father, gout-hobbled, emphysemic, escorting him to hunt acorns in Van Cortlandt Park, warning, "One day, Mil, you blink your eyes open and you're an old man." Well, one day, he'd been a married, mid-career psychiatrist enjoying a casual fling with a dialysis nurse—and then he'd blinked his eyes open and he'd had a second family, a daughter two decades younger than her half-siblings, and somehow one of those half-siblings had slipped through his grasp.

"You're a regular Tony Randall," jibed Storch, his late best friend. And, slapping him on his back, "A regular Saul Bellow . . . regular Strom Thurmond." How he missed Hal Storch. Others had called Millard different things, less generous, from a distance. The chatter always looped back to him like a poisonous vine.

That was what they'd talk about at the funeral. Not the desperate souls he'd helped in forty-nine years of practice. Not his passion for German opera, for fishing excursions on Sheepshead Bay. Not that morning five decades earlier, at the butterfly conservatory in the Natural History Museum, when the moment had seized him and he'd proposed to Carol. No, they'd blather in hushed tones about the second family, whispering knowingly that his affair with Isabelle, rather than any intrinsic character shortcoming, had frittered away Lysander's potential. And they'd blame his death on despair, on his two years of widowhood, because who, other than a depressed person, hangs himself in a

Fifth Avenue bathroom—a once luxurious bathroom equipped with mood lighting and solid brass fixtures—on his seventy-fifth birthday? But that would also not be his concern, although he couldn't resist wondering whether Carol, to whom he hadn't spoken since the split, would make a cameo at the graveside. She'd surprised him with a sympathy card when Isabelle died, tasteful if impersonal, so maybe she'd catch him off guard yet again.

What fools they'd be to think they understood his motives. He hardly understood them himself. All Millard knew for certain was that he did not want to die dependent or diminished like so many of his threadbare colleagues—like Hal Storch—*like Isabelle!*—and that everyone had to go someday, eventually—and, dammit, that he had fallen madly in love with the woman he intended to kill.

2

F alling in love at seventy-five had not been the game plan. During those final six months of Isabelle's illness—after the chemo failed and the radiation turned palliative, as her flesh evaporated daily into the ether—he resisted any talk of a future without her, but his wife, ever practical, refused to drop the subject. "I've made a list," she'd announced. "It's in the red notebook under the telephone. What to do on day one, what to do on day two, etc. All *you* have to do is follow the directions. . . ." On another afternoon, propped atop cushions in the hospice dayroom, she'd said, "I hope you find love again. Seventy-three is too young to be alone." She coughed viciously into her tissue, squeezed his hand. "Don't let me be an impediment. But the one thing I do ask is that we're buried together. For Maia's sake." *And seventy-one is too young to die,* he'd wanted to respond. But then she was gone—how helpless she'd looked without breath, how unlike Isabelle—and soon he was laboring his way through the red notebook, everything laid out step-by-step like instructions for assembling an exercise bike. *Day 1 – Task 15: Water the plants in the parlor, so they don't join me in the grave. Do not water the aloe more than twice a month—you will drown it. Day 5 – Task 2: Let Maia choose any clothing she'd like to keep and donate the rest to Goodwill. NOT the Salvation Army. They are not interchangeable!* Until day thirty-one arrived and with it the final page of Isabelle's mandates. *Day 31: Thank you, Millard Salter, for bringing me such joy and love—for making me the luckiest woman alive. Now don't squander any more time or energy mourning me. And please, please, don't drown the aloe.* Her scent, sublime, ineffable, yet elusively suggestive of buckwheat honey and macadamia nuts, still cleaved to the fragile pages.

Even prior to Isabelle's illness—before those last days of muted agony, the torment plain on her sunken face despite the reassurances of the Calvary nurses—he'd known, deep down, that humanity had gotten the enterprise of dying all fouled up. Or, at least, Western allopathic medicine had gotten it wrong; he couldn't speak to Lapps and Bantus. If years of consulting for his neurology colleagues on cases of Alzheimer's and glioblastoma had taught him that lesson, then the deaths of his parents, his spinster aunts, his beloved older brother, all corporeally ravaged and emotionally ragged, had solidified his convictions. Isabelle's decline was not so much the motive for his foray into illicit dying as her absence liberated him to act. What was the worst they could do to him at seventy-three? Send him to the electric chair? Still, another fourteen months elapsed between the last of Isabelle's directives and his phone call to Compassionate Endings. And that was how, less than six weeks later, he'd found himself in love.

They'd been sitting at her kitchen table. Already, Delilah had lost power in her lower limbs, and the furniture had been adjusted to allow for passage of her motorized scooter. Scars from dislocated table legs gouged the hardwood. French newspapers lay stacked like death warrants on a Le Corbusier chair. Above the toaster hung a painting of a clock, all Mondrian-style blocks, forever frozen at half past eleven. Framed posters from Delilah's productions covered the other walls: *The Subject Was Roses*; *Come Back, Little Sheba*; Uta Hagen in *There Shall Be No Night.*

From the record player in the adjoining room rose the doleful strains of Birgit Nilsson as a yearning and tortured Salomé. How different from his own kitchen—Isabelle's kitchen—with its discolored linoleum and refrigerator magnets ("Have You Taken Your Blood Pressure Pill Today?") and vintage *National Geographics*, piled high on the same iron Stylaire stool with the foldout steps that had once graced his aunts' pantry. For nearly ten minutes, they had been wrangling over who would pay for the lethal dose of helium.

"For God's sake, you're impossible." Delilah sighed, smiling. "Why should *you* pay for *my* death? I swear, it makes a person want to keep living out of spite."

They'd developed an easy rapport since he'd shown up on her doorstep, so to speak, a complete stranger wielding an arsenal of empathy and do-it-yourself suicide instructions. And he'd been up front from the outset, telling her that he had never guided anyone before. *Well, I've never been guided before*, she'd answered, *so we'll sink in the same boat.*

Delilah had a gift for badinage, a contrast to Isabelle's plainspoken earnestness, yet less edgy and caustic than Carol's dry wit.

"Can I say something totally inappropriate?" asked Millard.

"If I say no, will that stop you?"

"Honestly, yes," said Millard.

"No, it won't," replied Delilah. More sober now. "You'll just find another way to say it. At a different time. Might as well spit it out and get it over with."

She waited. Patient? Coy? Opposite Millard, the ersatz clock stood permanently frozen along its tangent to midnight. He didn't even know how to begin. Or whether he should. The notion that he'd fallen in love after six weeks seemed implausible—outlandish. It wasn't as though he doled out his affections carelessly. He'd only said "I love you" to three other women in his entire life—and he'd walked down the aisle with two of them; he still wore Isabelle's engagement ring on a chain around his neck. There had been a time, of course, before Isabelle, before Carol, when his eyes trawled for sex, when every woman between seventeen and forty had the power to raise his prick to full staff. Or, at least, *almost* every woman. But lusting was not the same as sincerely desiring—and if he'd ever had a genuine opportunity to play lothario, which he hadn't, to cut in artlessly on the dance floor at Roseland or to pick girls willy-nilly off the beach at Coney Island, he'd have taken no pleasure in his conquests. His affair with Isabelle had been a fluke. An aberration. To his surprise, as much as he missed her, he hadn't been particularly lonely since her passing. When Art Rosenstein in pediatrics had offered to fix him up with his widowed sister-in-law—once a stage actress of some repute—he'd demurred. So why did he suddenly feel flustered, like a fourteen-year-old in the back of a picture house?

"You don't consider this a doctor-patient relationship, do you?" he hazarded.

Delilah's eyes honed, ruts deepening in her brow. "Why would I?"

"Because I am a doctor, after all. And I'm afraid I'm about to commit what in psychiatry we might term a boundary violation."

He paused, affording her ample opportunity to stop him. He'd never felt especially bashful around women—at least, not since adolescence; psychiatry had drummed the shyness out of him. If he didn't turn heads on the street, he'd kept trim and held on to his hair. But at sixty-two, Delilah, who eschewed all makeup and lathered her face every morning in rutabaga extract, looked closer to fifty. Young enough to pass for his daughter. What a fool he'd be to disrupt her final months with unrequited sentiments. What a narcissistic fool. Yet she was right: He *would* find another way to share his secret, however noble his intentions.

"I think I'm falling in love with you."

She laughed—a brief, warm laugh, as though he'd told a joke she already knew. She appeared more amused than displeased.

"Not a good idea," said Delilah.

"Not a good idea *why*? Because you can't love me? Or because you're dying?"

"Not a good idea because we each have a role to play. Like in classical Japanese drama. Noh. Kabuki. I am the dying woman. You are my gentleman guide."

"I'm sorry," Millard said quickly. "I shouldn't have."

She surveyed his face. He must have looked particularly hangdog, because she said, "My goodness. You really *are* falling in love with me."

"It was a selfish thing to say. Please don't be upset."

"I'm not upset, just surprised. Flattered, really. . . ."

Millard stood up. "Maybe I should go. . . ."

"Don't be ludicrous," replied Delilah. "Oh, Millard. You're a very romantic man—romantic in the artistic sense. Like Byron or Keats. Did anybody ever tell you that?"

"Carol called me a pipe-dreamer. Does that count?"

To Carol, who'd been the first female executive at Bell Labs, everything that couldn't be demonstrated with a scientific formula was a pipe dream. This included acupuncture, Reiki, yoga, even psychotherapy. *You headshrinkers and your psychoanalysis*, she'd once said to Millard's former chairman, a celebrated Jungian. *Overpriced astrology, if you ask me. A person might as well sit inside an orgone box all day.* How on earth had such a bonfire of gusto and disdain—for his first wife had been an incorrigible cynic, not merely a vigilant skeptic—produced a son who fostered orphaned bunnies and couldn't be bothered to wake up before noon?

Isabelle had been a better match for him: less ambitious, more forgiving. And Millard had realized, maybe too late, that he required a lot of forbearance.

"You know you won't get a dime out of me when I'm gone," said Delilah. "Half to my niece and half to the Theater Guild. It's entirely settled."

"Please don't think—"

"I'm joking, for heaven's sake. Jesus Christ. You *are* smitten. Poor boy," she said, almost as though he weren't present. "What are we going to do with you?"

"Let's just drop the matter," said Millard. "Please. It was a stupid thing to say."

"Okay, but I do want to offer one last word on the subject."

"Yes?"

Delilah's eyes met his again—and he looked away. "One of the aspects of theater I've always loved most is its room for experimentation, for breaking rules," she said. "What I'm saying is, sometimes you know something will be a bad idea, but you try it anyway."

Millard let his gaze meet hers. "Does that mean . . . ?"

"Yes," replied Delilah. "Why not? Just don't get mad if I die on you."

NOW FOUR MONTHS had passed and she'd be dead in under twelve hours. Millard surveyed himself in the Louis XIV mirror opposite the elevators, re-skewing his necktie in puerile rebellion against Elsa, and after affording his neighbor a solid thirty seconds to dissolve into pedestrian traffic, he exchanged good mornings with the Armenian doorman and pushed through the revolving doors into the early morning din, en route to the IRT. Only it wasn't the IRT any longer: No more IRT, BMT, Third Avenue El. Now the subways were all numbered sequentially for the benefit of tourists and nitwits. Referring to the IRT dated you—like calling the MetLife Building the Pan Am Building or pronouncing the second syllable of "Loew's" in Loew's Paradise Theatre. Another piece of his city gone the way of Schrafft's, and S. Klein on the Square, and Harmony Bar & Restaurant. He recalled one glorious evening of his adolescence—he must have been thirteen or fourteen—when his father took the family to Lüchow's to celebrate something (a birthday? an anniversary? Papa was always splurging!), and they sat two tables away from Eddie Cantor and Jimmy Durante. And today, you could ask every student in the entire medical school who Jimmy Durante was, and you'd get blank stares. What better sign that the time had come to throw in the towel? Good night, Mrs. Calabash—as Durante would say—wherever you've gone.

So he ambled along 86th Street toward Lexington. A teenager from the Korean deli was hosing down the sidewalk; delivery bikes wove between lanes. Already the July heat steamed off the asphalt, percolating, menacing, but Millard barely noticed. He was momentarily living in an era of gentlemen's bars and hat-check girls, of Automats, of milkmen and icemen and piano hoisters. When was the last time he'd seen anyone hoist a piano? Hal Storch had told him a story—with Hal you couldn't be sure if it were true, but it made its point nonetheless—about how he'd visited his son and new daughter-in-law in Santa Fe, and when she'd mentioned how much she loved New York City, Hal had grumbled that the city hadn't been worth a piss since they'd torn down Penn Station. "They tore it down?" the girl allegedly exclaimed. "Why, we were there just last year!" Millard might have been the only kid on the entire Grand Concourse who hadn't given a damn whether Mickey Mantle or Willie Mays were the better center fielder, but now that they'd razed the Polo

Grounds for public housing, he felt bereft, cheated. Opposite the subway entrance, he purchased a bouquet of freesia and delphinium.

"What's the occasion?" asked the florist.

An obese, olive-skinned man of fifty in a silk shirt with a Nehru collar. Afghan? Iranian? His short forearms rested on his enormous torso, a cardiac tinderbox, but he beamed with the confidence of an Adonis. Millard recalled when the man had been younger, but not thinner.

"Birthday celebration. Taking the missus to Lüchow's." A mischievous impulse seized Millard and he added, "We're meeting up with my old friend, Jimmy Durante."

The florist tied off his bouquet, beefing it with gypsophila. "Jimmy Durante, the comedian?" he asked without turning. "I thought he was dead."

"Different Jimmy Durante," Millard said quickly.

He accepted the flowers and waited for the florist to tally his bill. The man scribbled on an onion-skin order pad with a pencil stub. "I used to love Jimmy Durante," said the florist. "All those old-timers. Henny Youngman. Joey Bishop. You don't know funny until you've heard Alan King dubbed into Bengali."

Millard suppressed his urge to ask the natural question: How had a Bengali florist taken an interest in Borscht Belt comedy? Not today. And if not today, never. But that was unavoidable. Maturity meant accepting the infinite expanse of existence, that there were many things one would simply never know or do. A few weeks earlier, he'd sat down after supper and started to catalogue them—a bucket list in reverse: how to play mahjongg, paint, juggle, read Attic Greek; wine; gems; caves; string theory. He'd never be able to quote Shakespeare or the Bible at any great length—not for want of trying. He'd never swim with penguins in the Galapagos Islands or feed baby lemurs in Madagascar, never know whether another Clinton or Bush was to be elected president, never publish his paper (yet unwritten) reinterpreting Winnicott's theory of false selfhood. As July 15 approached, all of this seemed less essential. What mattered at the moment was an arbitrary date on the calendar: He'd initially suggested the day to Delilah as a joke—"I've always found birthdays morbid anyway"—and somehow that joke had transformed itself into a binding commitment. And now, riding the subway to 68th Street, he was going to fulfill his part of the bargain. *What a strange creature I am*, he reflected. *Nearly two million dollars in investments saved up and still too cheap to take a taxi.*

On the IRT—the so-called number 6 train—Millard thought about Hal Storch. Ever the Freudian analyst, Hal had kept his progressive heart failure from his patients to the end. When he finally succumbed—six months after Isabelle's death, just as Millard was regaining his sea legs—the task fell to Millard to inform them. Three hundred fifteen phone calls. *Are you Alice Albertson? My name is Dr. Millard Salter. I'm a colleague of Hal Storch's. . . . Are you Luis Arcaya? Are you Thomas Ardenhammer?* One woman refused to believe him—warned that she'd report him to the 19th Precinct; another had threatened to jump from her balcony. *Why on earth would I make something like this up?* he'd asked the doubtful woman. If Isabelle's death had fortified his belief in assisted suicide—"aid in dying," as the Compassionate Endings folks insisted upon calling it—then seeing Hal Storch propped on four pillows, gasping himself blue, confirmed for Millard that he wanted no part in a drawn-out death of his own. Quit while the going is good. That was the winning ticket, his father used to say. Fortunately, as a hospital-based consultation psychiatrist, he didn't have to worry about terminating care with any long-term patients.

Delilah's doorman, a burly Montenegrin, greeted him by

name. If the Compassionate Endings folks had heard this ex-change, they'd have choked on their own helium; at a minimum, his handler, a Hopkins-trained pathologist, would have sus-pended his assignment. (Millard still found the jargon that his sponsors used—handler, asset, cell—unsettling, as though these diehards had read *Darkness at Noon* one time too many.) At first, he'd strived to maintain some semblance of cover, sharing only his first name with Delilah, and avoiding visits that overlapped with her neurologist's house calls, yet by week three, he'd listed himself as the emergency contact on her Do Not Resuscitate forms and recommended a pulmonologist in Tel Aviv to her niece. Once he'd decided on his own suicide, the whole Compas-sionate Endings protocol went to the wind: What was the point of maintaining anonymity if you'd be dead within months—or, now, by morning?

"How's Miss P?" asked the doorman.

"Dandy," replied Millard.

He tried to give the fellow the benefit of the doubt—but how was Delilah supposed to be when she hardly had the strength to raise her forearms? With each passing day, Millard found his sympathy for these inquiries—curiosity, masked as empathy—ebbing. Okay, maybe that was too harsh: The door-man seemed a compassionate enough sort, and a far improve-ment over the weekday doorman in Millard's co-op, bull-browed Barsamian, who had a knack for conveying tacitly, during every interaction, that his time would be better spent elsewhere. But did this fellow really want him to describe how frequently Delilah missed the bedpan?

"Please send her my best," said the Montenegrin. "Obviously, if she needs anything . . ."

"I'll let her know," promised Millard.

He was relieved to find himself alone in the elevator. One

by one, he unlocked each of Delilah's deadbolts and entered the
apartment. By prior arrangement, she'd cancelled her private
nurse for the day—some tale about how an apocryphal cousin,
visiting from Philadelphia, would be looking after her. A lethal
stillness hung in the warm air of the foyer. On the kitchen table,
he noticed Delilah's "library of self-extermination": Derek
Humphry's *Final Exit*; George Mair's *How to Die with Dignity*; a
collection of bittersweet essays titled *How to Succeed in Suicide
Without Really Trying*. Also a paperback volume of Edna St. Vin-
cent Millay's poetry. Atop the counter beside the toaster, like a
handy kitchen appliance, stood the helium canister. She had
paid for it in the end: $37.50. Death's price tag. Just like the
Hindenburg, he'd quipped—and Delilah had reminded him in
her sandpaper voice that the Hindenburg had run on *hydrogen*
fuel.

He called out her name, announcing his presence before re-
trieving a vase from the cabinet and arranging the bouquet. Then
he gave her a full two minutes to compose herself—following
the second hand on his watch—before advancing up the railroad
hallway into the sitting room. Delilah had once staged table
readings for emerging playwrights in this space, including one at
which a newly divorced Jason Robards signed an actress's bare
thigh with a fountain pen; now she lay at a seventy-degree angle
on a hospital bed, angelic in the early morning light. She'd slept
in her velour dressing gown with the cherry blossom print, a lover's gift from a Japanese set designer. (One of countless lovers—
dozens? scores?—of which he'd be the valedictorian. He'd
mustered the audacity to ask how many, but she'd just laughed
coquettishly and replied, "A lady never turns down quality.")
Oleander-scented candles flickered on the bedside table, masking
the nascent odor of human decay. Shadows rolled like ghost
ships along the plaster. With considerable effort, Delilah re-

mained able to self-transition from the therapeutic mattress to the motorized chair, but over the past week, she'd fallen twice. The queen-sized bed in the adjoining room, where they'd first made love, had long been surrendered to boxes of adult diapers and cases of puréed baby food. A second childhood lacking the only solace of the original: hope.

That first night together in bed—there had been nearly forty, all told—Delilah had already had difficulty unfastening her skirt. She'd shared a joke as a stalling tactic to cover her ineptitude. "So Wilbur is in a nursing home, but at the age of ninety-nine, he still has certain urges," she'd said with false cheer. While she spoke, she fumbled with the buttons. "One afternoon, chatting with ninety-eight-year-old Edna, he explains how much he misses the feel of a woman's hands on his member . . . and not having had sex in four decades, Edna readily agrees to cradle Little Wilbur. This goes on for several months, until one day Edna walks into the nursing home garden and discovers her roommate, Gertrude, clutching the old man's organ." By now, Delilah's face had flushed with frustration. "'You two-timer! How could you do this to me?' Edna demands. 'What does *she* have that I don't have?' Wilbur smiles sheepishly and answers, 'Parkinson's.'" As she delivered the punch line, Delilah's own hands dropped to her side, her fingers useless as hams. "Damn these buttons," she cried. "Damn, damn, damn."

Millard had the skirt unfastened in an instant. "Next time, you should get yourself a funny disease like Parkinson's," he'd said. "Something you can laugh about."

"Next time, I'm going to get something contagious," she'd rejoined, "so I can pass along a memento to my enemies before I go."

A desperation clung to their lovemaking, as though Delilah's impending demise added a teenage urgency to each caress. Also a candor. No room for promises, expectations. No question of whether they would formalize their arrangement. The idea of proposing to her had crossed his mind in the final weeks, but to what purpose? A marriage license would be a windfall for the probate lawyers, nothing more. (He couldn't even consult his college roommate, Art Hallam, who'd written his will pro bono, because Art, that son of a bitch, had gone rafting on the Colorado River and capsized.) Yet over the past few days, he'd taken to calling Delilah "the missus" when interacting with the strangers who frequented her apartment: delivery boys, rent-a-cleaners, a Filipino manicurist willing to make house calls. How long could he do this, he wondered, before he risked a common law union?

He set the bouquet beside the candles and settled onto the cusp of the mattress. Delilah reached for his arm and clasped his wrist.

"Fancy meeting you here," she said. Each word was a struggle, a minor miracle of tongue and voice box and palate. "I thought we said later. . . ."

"I came to check up on you."

"To rush me, more like it."

He kissed her forehead. Dry lips on dry flesh. He offered to assist her into the motorized chair, to serve her breakfast in bed. She shook her head. "Nothing, not now."

Delilah squeezed his wrist a second time, clutched for his hand. Moisture appeared at the corners of her eyes. "I keep thinking, I'm going to miss you," she said. "But I won't. I won't miss anybody. I'll be dead."

They'd had long discussions about the afterlife. Neither of them was optimistic, although Millard clung to some vague, inchoate notions of eternity.

"How will you spend your day?" he asked.

"Tennis. Croquet. Maybe a jog around the reservoir. You know," she said.

The humor kept them sane. A mature defense mechanism—but nevertheless a defense.

"Actually, I still have a handful of farewells to record. I was going to limit myself to a few close friends, but it has snowballed." Of late, unable to write, except in the jagged block letters of a kindergartener, she'd been taping farewell messages on miniature cassettes. "You'll mail them for me, won't you?"

"As you wish," he agreed.

That wasn't as easy as it sounded. If Delilah ended her life at seven PM, the local post office would already be closed—and he'd be dead as ice the next morning, before it reopened. Since the cassettes weighed too much to drop into a mailbox—thank the terrorists for that—his only feasible approach was to haul the packages to the central post office on 33rd Street, the one that would soon enough be a train station, where the staffed windows remained open until late. (So much for *neither rain nor snow nor heat nor gloom*: They'd delivered mail twice a day on the Grand Concourse when he'd grown up, the letter carrier blowing a tin whistle inside the stairwell, before the Postal Service became a glorified employment agency for loafers and ne'er-do-wells.) Yet Delilah's request reassured him in one respect: She clearly had no inkling that he intended to follow her into the unknown so rapidly. A younger, selfish Millard might have shared his plans, believing true devotion was about breaking down barriers. Now he understood that authentic love meant toppling barriers selectively, while buttressing others.

"Happy birthday," said Delilah. "I almost forgot."

"I'd rather wish you had. . . ."

Seventy-five seemed an absurd age. Almost implausible. There'd been a time, not too long ago, when sixty had qualified as a full lifetime. Estes Kefauver, his father's hero, had died at sixty—another name as alien to the medical students as hieroglyphics. Yet had Kefauver's aortic wall proven stronger, one could easily envision a world in which LBJ had plucked the Tennessean in the coonskin cap, rather than Hubert Humphrey, as his running mate in '64. (Not that the medical students had heard of Humphrey.) But Humphrey hadn't survived far into his golden years either. How old? Sixty-five? Sixty-six? And Millard's own father, a vigorous swimmer, had made it only to sixty-three. If you'd lived to seventy-five, like his great-uncle Lou, they'd have thrown you a party at the Concord. Millard still had a group portrait from that remote shindig propped on a shelf in his study—all of the Salters and Mishkins bedizened in their synagogue finest, tight-faced, dour, lined up like mourners at a funeral. And how depleted they all appeared! Mama, in her mid-forties, already a babushka, with dim, vacant eyes and a wattle of angry flesh beneath her chin; his aunts, a few years older, swathed sexless in spinsterhood; Cousin Max, a Fuller Brush man, only sixty, yet nipping at the heels of Methuselah. Before detox cleanses and organic moisturizers and CrossFit workouts, before Jane Fonda and grapefruit diets, mighty nature demanded her toll with impunity. Even his father, at fifty-two, once so hale and vigorous, looked as old as Millard did at seventy-five.

The trouble was that Millard didn't *feel* seventy-five. Maybe when he bent over to retrieve one of the grandkids' toys, or when carrying his fishing tackle out to the skiff, but not often. Some mornings, he honestly believed he might live another twenty years. Good years. Productive years. Of course, there lay the dastardly trap. Nobody really believes in quicksand until they can't extricate their feet.

"I was going to bake you a cake," said Delilah.

"Tomorrow," replied Millard. "Let me eat cake tomorrow."

A smile curled across her lips. How lucky he was, even now.

"You'd better go," said Delilah. "I'll see you at five."

"Are you sure you don't want anything?"

Again, she shooed him off. "Unless you see Cary Grant in the lobby."

He cupped her frail hand inside his for a moment, cradling it like a robin's egg; then he rose, galvanized, and retreated to the door. "I love you," said Millard.

"Enough with the sentimentality already. Geez. You'd think I was dying."

From the street below rose the dopplered wail of an ambulance or fire truck—somebody else's catastrophe. Light beamed through the curtains, radiant off waltzing dust.

"Don't start without me," said Millard.

"Then don't be late," Delilah rasped back. "You'll miss all the fun."

3

To the hospital—that unforgiving shrine of secular desperation! When he'd first come to St. Dymphna's, the megalith had towered over Carnegie Hill like an ocean liner flung ashore, its rounded stone façade impregnable as the great vessels of yore. Now the patchwork of extensions and annexes that connected the "Old Hospital" to the germinating laboratories and conference centers and specialty suites along its periphery recalled a Rube Goldberg contraption. The institution's mission had evolved too—all the talk of "service" and "duty" gone the way of Blakemore tubes, and of Harrington rods, and of the hospital's two dozen iron lungs, their carcasses now beached like sea mammals in the subcellar. Where his bosses had once been content to mend the local community, a respectable mix of wealthy Upper East Siders and the urban poor in the housing projects north of 96th Street, now the focus was on recruiting, publicizing, promoting. Patients had become clients, customers—as though the hospital were running a discount car wash or a branch bank. Millard had read somewhere that Cadillac-style benefits for retired auto workers had transformed General Motors into an enormous healthcare insurer that happened to produce cars; well, St. Dymphna's had become a colossal marketing firm that happened to treat sick people—or so it seemed, at least, each time he walked under the titanic banner reading, YOU GET BETTER BECAUSE WE ARE BETTER.

What-ever, as his daughter Maia was always saying. *We bring good things to life*, he thought. *See the USA in your Chevrolet. You can be sure . . . if it's Westinghouse.* They might as well hire Dinah Shore and Betty Furness to do the ads—although he was confident his current bosses wouldn't recognize their names. *Whatever. Not*—as Maia said—*our problem*. He ducked through the hospital garden, its transepts abloom in heliotrope, and took the back stairs past the chapel. The Gothic clock above the oratory already read 8:15: St. Dymphna's, a beast that roused with the dawn, growled and flailed in its madness.

Entering the hospital at that late hour, passing beneath the gargoyle-crested arch, DISPENSARY engraved in the sandstone, Millard always felt a tad sheepish, like a theatergoer slinking into his seat during the second act of a play. On the medical floors, the overnight residents had long since signed out their patients to the battle-ready interns. In the operating rooms, orthopedists were closing their second cases of the day. "Walking to work this morning," he joked when he taught the fourth-year medical students, as part of his recruitment pitch for psychiatry, "I ran into surgeons going out to lunch." As a consult psychiatrist, providing mental health services to the physically ill, Millard savored the best of both worlds—part of the lifeblood of the institution, yet still able to hit the snooze button on his clock radio with impunity. How Hal Storch had handled all those years as a classical analyst, exploring the perceived childhood slights of commodities brokers and sporadically filling Ativan prescriptions for overwrought housewives, mystified him. Of course, Hal's perch on Park Avenue had sheltered him from the relentless and obdurate injustices of human suffering.

The consult team convened at 8:30 in the patient lounge opposite the Eating Disorders Unit. A paper sign taped to the door read "Reserved 8:30 AM–9:30 AM"—but that didn't keep squatters (patients' relatives, canoodling nursing aides) from fighting Millard's crew for its territory. The vending machines hummed through their meetings, and occasionally a janitor or orderly on break sauntered in to buy a bag of chips. Over the years, the space had also become a repository for the portraits of less-distinguished former department chairmen: Norm Schumaker, who'd lost his license for sleeping with a patient; Clyde Terwilliger, escorted off the premises by security officers after allegations of embezzlement; dour, pipe-wielding David Atkinson, a man known for "letting heads roll first and then asking questions." All white, all about sixty with the same Harvard clip; all dead as Napoleon's undertaker. Over the years, Millard had called each of these men a friend—in the era before he realized that the boss, no matter how amiable, is *never* your friend. Back then, the consult team had met in the boardroom.

Millard's minions arrived, bedraggled and bleary, between 8:35 and 8:40: Stan Laguna, lapels stained, cuffs frayed, shoes scuffed—a first-rate clinical mind in the attire of a billing clerk; hypomanic, flamboyant Sameer Patel; Gabby Lu, his former fellow, lordotic with her third pregnancy. Not a single Harvard clip among them. And then there were the new residents, Greek, Liberian, a polychromatic stew of genius and timidity. Third-year med students too, in their pristine, truncated white coats, Snellen vision charts protruding from their overstuffed pockets, reflex hammers gleaming. (When he'd first arrived at St. Dymphna's, the *senior fellows* had worn short coats, a hierarchical sign of their medical immaturity.) Laguna handed Millard a cup of tepid coffee from the cart on 98th Street. One cream. Two sugars. His team was loyal, and gifted, if somewhat tatterdemalion. While they assembled, Lu passed around a cell-phone video of her son toddling his first steps.

"Good morning," said Millard. "Anything exciting happen over the weekend?"

"Define exciting," quipped Laguna.

The gaunt bulrush of a resident who'd covered the service on Saturday and Sunday—a Dutchman named Kip—produced his rumpled sign-out list. "Yes, Dr. Salter," he said. Stiff, deferential. "That patient on 9-East who we diagnosed with hysterical blindness. It turns out she's actually blind. Ophthalmology reassessed her. Anton's syndrome."

"Score one against our malpractice insurer," said Laguna.

"And Mr. Cappabucci has filed a formal complaint against us with the Office of Mental Health. He says he told you he felt suicidal and that you treated him like a joke and threw him out of the hospital. . . ."

Jack Cappabucci was a celebrated malingerer. Six hundred psychiatric admissions across the nation—in forty-two different states—and no mental illness. He'd feigned a schizophrenic break during his third week in the army to obtain disability benefits, which he'd been collecting since 1973; even the local VA hospital had banished him from its inpatient unit. The man owned a three-bedroom apartment on 79th Street and came to the ER during the weeks that he was able to rent it to tourists.

"Mr. Cappabucci *is* a joke," said Millard. "Tell me, after I threw him out of the hospital, did he kill himself?"

"No, Dr. Salter. He told OMH he would have, but he felt a moral obligation toward other suicidal patients to stay alive until his complaint was reviewed. . . ."

Impostors like Cappabucci had once been a rarity, but now the hospital seemed to swarm with men and women faking illness. Defendants avoiding court dates. Deadbeat parents hiding from child support payments. Dope fiends escaping drug deals gone wrong. A teeming multitude of refugees from responsibility—

from decency. Most on the bottom rungs of the socioeconomic ladder, but not all: Last month—and this was a first for Millard—a well-known television newscaster had feigned mania, hoping a brief stint in a mental ward might create an alibi for his extramarital affair. As the orange signs along interstate highways announced: *Your Tax Dollars at Work*. There was an old joke on the service that Republicans were former Democrats who'd worked in a psychiatric emergency room.

"Anything else?" asked Millard.

Kip shook his head and sat down.

"I have one," said Laguna, glancing up from his phone. "Fresh off the presses . . ."

"We've all been fired?" suggested Millard.

"Better. It turns out there's a baby lynx on the loose. A patient apparently brought an eight-month-old lynx cub with her to the dermatology clinic on Friday and it escaped. . . ."

"You for real?" demanded Patel.

"Urgent message from the president's office," continued Laguna. "If said lynx is spotted, please call security immediately."

"How about if it's *striped*?" asked Millard.

Not a single smile. Several of the foreign residents appeared befuddled.

"As I was saying," said Laguna, "whether the lynx is spotted *or striped*, you should not attempt to apprehend it on your own."

"At last! The missing lynx," said Millard.

Again, nobody laughed.

In his heyday, he had prided himself on his wordplay. Discussing a patient from Bangkok who'd returned to his native country so that his own brother, a surgeon, could perform his coronary bypass, Millard had drawn guffaws from the house staff with his off-the-cuff remark, "Ah, the Thais that bind." And while visiting Hal Storch at his summer "cottage" up in the Berkshires, when a plumbing van had blocked in the neighbor's gardening equipment, he'd delighted Storch's houseguests with "He wanted a snake, but not a mower-constrictor." Isabelle had adored his puns; she'd never understood why he couldn't publish them. A best seller, she'd predicted, so proud, if woefully naïve. Delilah enjoyed his wordplay too and even served up a few verbal jousts of her own. But these young doctors responded to his puns as though they were . . . a punishment.

Then there were the as-yet-unused puns, the arsenal of one-liners stockpiled like precision weapons—awaiting their moment of glory. If only someone, possibly his younger daughter, might describe a French novel as "monstrously cheesy," so that he could remark, "That's Gorgon-Zola." Yet that had never happened. And now, with the clock ticking, his pent-up repartee would be lost to humanity forever, like a non-extant Greek tragedy, like the final symphony of Sibelius. *Whatever happens*, he mused, *to a pun deferred?*

"That was a joke," Millard emphasized. He considered making a reference to Katharine Hepburn's pet leopard in *Bringing Up Baby*, yet figured this would also fall flat.

"Aren't they going to shut the place down until they find it?" demanded Lu. "I mean, isn't this thing a safety hazard?"

"I guess it's too small to be dangerous," said Patel. "Or they have no idea where it is. They can't shut down the entire city over a single lynx."

"According to the president's office, lynx cubs have been known to attack human beings when threatened," interjected Stan Laguna. "An eight-month-old cub can take down an adult white-tailed deer."

One of the junior residents—the pudgy Greek girl—raised her hand. "What is a lynx?" she asked.

"A big cat," explained Laguna.

"Big like this," inquired another foreign resident, spacing her hands as though miming a toaster and then broadening the gap between them. "Or like this?"

"Big like a leopard," said Laguna. "Big like a tiger."

"Not *that* big," objected Patel.

Soon all semblance of order deteriorated as both men searched for the sizes of various feral felines on their smartphones. "How do you like that?" observed Patel. "A bobcat is a variety of lynx. Who knew?"

"And now that this episode of *Mutual of Omaha's Wild Kingdom* has concluded," Millard interjected, "Dr. Laguna will assign the new consults." He stirred his coffee with the back of a plastic spoon. "And don't forget, I'm off this afternoon. Stan's the boss while I'm gone."

Stan would be the boss for good, very shortly. Or, at least, the acting boss; the final decision rested with the chairman. Millard could already picture his junior colleague presiding over their morning conclaves in dungarees and sandals, quizzing the residents on the previous afternoon's football plays, rehashing the plots of television dramas. But he'd be a benevolent leader, reflective and fair-minded, if a bit too laissez-faire for Millard's tastes.

"Famous last words," said Laguna. "As of this afternoon, I will be addressed as 'His Excellency' in all official interactions."

His Excellency Laguna proceeded to assign the day's cases. Delirium. Dementia. Altered mental states of unknown etiology. Also a heart transplant patient with bipolar disorder, a schizoaffective asthmatic, a woman with myasthenia gravis who feared she'd been betrothed to the devil. Every case claimed its analogue in a previous patient, an endless series of shattered souls trapped inside shattered bodies. Nothing new under the sun.

Millard enjoyed his job—especially the opportunity to provide succor, occasionally cure. Yet he would not miss it.

On the way out of the lounge, Millard surveyed the mismatched chairs, the recycling bins in variegated colors. Barring disaster, he would never see this room again. Stan Laguna followed him toward the elevator, an entourage of trainees trailing.

"An afternoon off, Mil?" asked Laguna. "You have a hot date?"

Millard hadn't taken a vacation day in two years—not since Isabelle's funeral. Before that, he'd consistently claimed one week in February and three in August. He could count on ten fingers—fewer—his other absences: Arnold's wedding, Sally's C-section, an incisor that broke off at the root. He had taken a full day when his father died, another for his brother's death, an afternoon to attend his mother's funeral. His aunts had both been interred on the weekends. He'd learned from experience that he more than paid for any time away in spades.

"A date with destiny," replied Millard.

"Destiny. Sexy name." Laguna slapped his shoulder. "I hope you get lucky."

4

Two glossy stickers graced Millard's office door. One, a gift from Hal Storch, read: "If Moses had been a committee, the Israelites would still be wandering in the desert." The other—from a former patient who designed irreverent bumper stickers—warned: "Life is unfair. Get over it." This latter message never drifted far from Millard's thoughts as he rounded in the hospital. Life *was* unfair—in countless ways, major and minuscule. One could dwell infinitely upon the grander injustices, the children born without limbs, the adolescents raped in refugee camps, the journalists roasted alive inside oil drums in Eritrea. But at least these victims had the solace of acknowledgment, even if only self-acknowledgment, that they'd been given a colossally raw deal. Yet so much suffering arose from the small wrongs, the petty inequities, as painful as splinters: the less attractive sister sitting home alone on prom night; that doting aunt and uncle who *would have* made such great parents; a beagle crushed by a taxi; a parakeet lost through an open window; his mother's black nanny, Dora, who *should have been* a college professor. Psychiatry was the art of helping people to cope with this unfairness—with the latent, unvoiced recognition that if only one had been born with different attributes, raised under different circumstances, loved more . . . Early in his career, Millard had toyed with the idea of writing a book, *Letters to a Young Psychiatrist*, modeled after Rilke's *Letters to a Young Poet*, which was to have expounded upon the nuanced cruelties of existence. Instead, he had deceived Carol and seduced Isabelle, doing his own part on behalf of injustice.

And in spite of everything, reflected Millard, *I've gotten a far better deal than most.*

Among those worse off than Millard were the three patients remaining under his care. (Over the course of the preceding month, he had pared down his list of cases, using the service director's prerogative to delegate; his coworkers hardly seemed to have noticed.) Regrettably, none of these three unfortunates could be foisted upon a junior colleague without drawing unwanted attention and causing unnecessary affront. One was the daughter of a retired ICU nurse—a longtime friend of Isabelle's—who'd lost a leg and a pregnancy in a traffic accident. Millard had also been corralled into looking after the psychiatric needs of a well-heeled St. Dymphna's donor, Lucius Jeffers, who'd developed precocious dementia in his fifties. They'd set aside a VIP suite for Jeffers, paid for out-of-pocket, where the one-time hedge fund executive alternatively ranted about the future of the Polish zloty and pinched the rumps of the phlebotomists. And Millard had also acquired the duty—part professional, part social—of visiting Rabbi Steinmetz, the recently minted St. Dymphna's chaplain, sequestered in an isolation unit after a bone marrow transplant. As he traversed the glass-enclosed atrium for his final meeting with the first of these victims, pausing briefly at a cork announcement board to read one of the myriad flyers warning passersby against the escaped lynx, Millard sensed an ominous presence—like a scythe-bearing demon—sidle up behind him. The shadow belonged to the all-too-corporeal form of Denny Dennmeyer, St. Dymphna's deputy finance director.

The glorified accountant, who might generously have been described as rotund, had earned the disparaging moniker of

"Quantity Control Officer" for his officious insistence on relent-less auditing. He'd been riding Millard's ass for months about a delinquent report regarding the consult service's staffing needs; no matter what he wrote, Millard sensed, the data would be used to lay off providers and to increase caseloads—so he had submit-ted nothing at all.

"Dr. Salter," declared Dennmeyer, "I've been looking every-where for you."

The administrator sported a seersucker suit and a bolo tie. He bellowed as though testing the acoustics inside a cathedral, nearly pinning Millard to the corkboard with his gut. His breath smelled mephitically of cinnamon.

Millard sucked in his own abdomen. "And now you've found me."

"None too soon, Dr. Salter. Don't you check your email . . . ?"

Dennmeyer had the habit of adding "Dr. Salter" to every phrase—probably something he'd learned in corporate training, or from a self-improvement manual. The tic made the fellow sound like an English butler gone haywire. "I'm too old for email," lied Millard, who had actually grown rather adept at computing in his seventies. And was quite proud of it. "You might have tried to reach me the old-fashioned way. . . ."

"In all fairness, Dr. Salter, I've been leaving messages on your voicemail for nearly a month," persisted Dennmeyer. "*And* I sent you a written memo."

"Voicemail? Who has time for voicemail?" said Millard. "Go low-tech, next time. Two paper cups and a string. Works like magic."

"Dr. Salter?"

"Or smoke signals," continued Millard—biting his inner lip to suppress a grin. "The Native Americans have been using them for thousands of years. . . ."

For a man with only half a day to live, Millard was surprised by his own good spirits. How free he felt, for the first time in ages, maybe ever, to voice his mind. Yet he did not have much time to waste on Dennmeyer, not even to mock him, if he intended to keep his noon lunch date with Lysander. Blood swelled into the accountant's neck, his cheeks, his simian forehead. The vein along his temple pulsed, limned with a fine bead of sweat. He appeared to sense that Millard was enjoying a joke at his expense.

"See here, my man," objected Dennmeyer, now visibly flustered. "I really do need that report. Every other division head in your department has submitted an annual assessment—some more thorough than others, I'll admit—but, at least, they've submitted *something.*" He rubbed his brow with his fingertips, regaining a modicum of composure. "This is important, Dr. Salter. How can we plan for the future unless we understand the present?"

The best laid plans of mice and men, reflected Millard, *and whatever species Dennmeyer belonged to, also* . . . "I'll make you a deal," he replied. "If I'm alive tomorrow, I'll have that report on your desk by five o'clock."

His pledge caught Dennmeyer by surprise. "That would be very helpful, Dr. Salter."

"Oh, I don't know how helpful it will be," said Millard. "But you have my word." He glanced at his watch for effect. "Now if you'll please excuse me, I have sick people to heal and dead people to raise and all that. . . ."

5

The victim of the motorcycle accident, Dolores, had been dispatched to radiology for a scan of her femur, so Millard crossed the seventh-floor walkway to the VIP unit. Along the way, he exchanged waves and hellos with half a dozen colleagues, including Saul Duransky and Art Rosenstein, the latter rolling his left foot in a traction boot; the charge nurse from the pulmonary care center, who'd been a nursing student during Millard's own internship, gave him a hug; one of the housekeepers from the Luxdorfer Pavilion, where he'd once had an office, greeted him by name. What a good feeling it was to be known someplace, to have been part of something in this way. Not that he considered himself irreplaceable—he wasn't foolish enough to believe that. *Everybody* was expendable. Presidents, kings. When the pope died, they found a new pope. Fools and narcissists forgot that at their peril, as, over the years, had several of Millard's bosses. So no, he wasn't irreplaceable, but he was well-liked, and he was grateful for it. Reflecting on his encounter with Dennmeyer, Millard found himself grinning, almost giddy.

In nearly five decades at St. Dymphna's, Millard had encountered his fair share of celebrity patients: politicians, performers, a retired five-star general. As a fourth-year resident, he'd sat up late one evening with a dying Tallulah Bankhead; during his first months on the faculty, he'd prescribed a sleeping aid for Charles Lindbergh after the aviator's appendectomy. Back then, the VIP unit had been located across Madison Avenue, on the top floor of the Hapsworth Annex, affording critically ill power brokers a 270-degree view of Manhattan. The titans of entertainment and industry had since been ousted from this perch by hospital executives, who'd appropriated the penthouse for office space, but the new VIP digs, overlooking Central Park, proved none too shabby. In the spacious entryway, furnished with damask wing-back chairs and a baby grand piano, a glass-encased waterfall tangoed under kaleidoscopic lights. At four o'clock every afternoon, white-gloved orderlies served high tea in the visitors' lounge. The most striking contrast between 7-West, as the unit was known, and the rest of the hospital, was its stunning silence. Yet the floor also harbored a secret, known only to senior clinicians: When compared with the treatment provided elsewhere in the hospital, the medical care itself was substandard. No amount of complimentary scented bathing gel or gourmet Equatoguinean chocolate compensated for the benefits of having medical students and junior residents and nursing trainees bustling through one's room, always on the lookout for an errant tube or a wrongly hung bag of electrolytes. Lives had been saved, many times over, by the fresh-eyed neophyte asking, in complete innocence, "Why are we giving *that* medicine to *this* patient?"

Millard encountered Lucius Jeffers as he had left him. The currency guru relaxed on the sofa, lanky limbs splayed like branches, watching the stock ticker scroll across his plasma TV. Mrs. Jeffers lay on her stomach atop the patient's bed, reading an airport novel, her stockinged feet a pair of scissor blades. She was a pleasant, soft-spoken woman in her forties. Not unattractive, but certainly not a former fashion model. They had a daughter at Vassar, Millard vaguely recalled—or possibly Bryn Mawr. *Name the Seven Sister schools*, he mused: now *that* was a good challenge for the medical students. At one time, he'd been a frequent visitor to several of these diminished institutions, including Barnard, when he'd dated a botany major, and Wellesley, Carol's alma mater, where he'd grown intimately familiar with the shadowy pull-off behind a nearby country club. Back in the days when you could get an Ivy League education at a women's college. Long time ago.

Over the years, Millard had discovered that the wives of the terminally ill—which Jeffers likely was, despite the absence of a formal diagnosis—fit into one of two factions. In a first group clustered the loyal victims: women who never left their husbands' bedsides, transforming overnight from homemakers or schoolteachers or retired librarians into devoted nursing assistants whose lives revolved around applesauce feedings and sponge baths. He could picture Isabelle as one of these votaries, stoic with forced cheer, singing him lullabies in his dementia. Carol also fit this mold—although one could more easily imagine her bullying house officers than reading bedtime stories. So did Mrs. Jeffers. At the opposite extreme were the fair-weather mates, often younger women on their second or third marriage, who dropped their moribund husbands off at the hospital like so much soiled bed linen and vanished into the ether. As one wife had said to Millard, when he finally reached her by phone, "I love my husband, Doctor, but I didn't sign up for this." Millard wondered whether, had circumstances proven different, Delilah would have camped out in his hospital room or fled into the night. He honestly didn't know.

"Look who's here," said Mrs. Jeffers. "It's Dr. Salter. The psychiatrist."

Jeffers looked up. He had a towel draped over one knee, as though at a sauna.

"Good morning, Lucius," Millard said. "Do you remember me?"

"Of course, he does," interjected Mrs. Jeffers. "Don't you, honey?"

Millard threw her a silencing look. He pulled up a chair alongside her husband.

"Do you remember who I am?" Millard asked again.

Jeffers nodded. "Sure. You're the fellow from that place." He grinned, tapping his thigh methodically. "I'm so glad you're here."

"What kind of building is this, Lucius?"

Millard's question educed a benighted shrug. "This . . . this is a . . . you know," said Jeffers. "Anyway, I'm glad you're here. I was just saying we should strike a stake in the Brazilian real. Latin America is where it's at. Not China. Not India. Have you been following the Paraguayan guarani and the Uruguayan . . . and the Uruguayan you know . . . ?"

Millard waited for a break in Jeffers's rambling.

"I have to ask you a few basic questions," he said. "I want you to tell me where we are. Is this a bank? A library? Or a hospital?"

Jeffers frowned, irked. Millard glanced at Mrs. Jeffers, his eyes warning her not to assist.

An uncomfortable pause followed, punctuated by the low murmur of the financial news rumbling from the television console. Then Jeffers pounded his fist on the cushions without warning and snapped, "A bank, dammit. Do you think I'm stupid?"

Confabulation was one of the symptoms of the financier's dementia. A costly battery of tests—MRIs, LPs, EEGs, PET and SPECT scans—had revealed no explanation for his sudden decline; next on the agenda would be a brain biopsy. Not that the results particularly mattered: Anything they discovered at this stage in the dismal game was probably irreversible.

"Nobody thinks you're stupid, Lucius," soothed Millard. "I have to ask *everyone* these questions. It's a formality."

Millard thanked Jeffers for his time; he was about to promise to visit again the following morning, but he checked himself—no need to deceive gratuitously. What he really wished to do was to return to the afflicted man's room after lunch, while Mrs. Jeffers was running an errand, and to serve him a lethal injection of potassium chloride. In his fantasy, Millard imagined wandering from ward to ward all afternoon, euthanizing the tortured, senile casks of flesh who lacked the power to terminate their own indignities. He doubted the authorities would catch him before he offed himself—not if he operated with stealth, choosing only the most severe cases. By the time the coroner unraveled the etiology of this daylong epidemic—the "Millard Salter Massacre"—he'd be playing shuffleboard and canasta on a cloud with his so-called victims, or toasting crisply in Hades. Needless to say, Millard knew that he would do no such thing, that after five decades saving lives—at least, to the degree a headshrinker could claim to save lives—he did not have inside him whatever *je ne sais quoi* was required to kill strangers, not even with impunity, not even if justice and morality linked arm in arm at his side. Helping Delilah die with a mite of self-respect was a deed that strained at the far reaches of his moral tether.

Mrs. Jeffers escorted him to the door. "Not his best day," she said, almost apologetic.

"He seems comfortable," replied Millard. "That's important."

They stood face-to-face in the dim vestibule. *The man you love is dying*, thought Millard, *and the woman I love is dying, yet we're each trapped in our separate hells.*

"Any news?" she asked.

"Not yet," said Millard. "We'll hope the biopsy shows something."

He offered her a few additional words of solace and ducked into the corridor, grateful to have escaped without confessing his own secret.

A young girl, unchaperoned, had commandeered the piano. The child was decked out in a white taffeta dress, overlain with tulle, as though truant from a first communion; an indigo bow in her butterscotch ponytail offset the pallor of her long, bare arms. What a pleasure, reflected Millard, to see someone—even a child—dressed up to make a sick call for a change. How recently, it seemed, that one had been expected to don a necktie, or at least a sweater and slacks, when traveling by airplane or dining out; now middle-aged men wore dungarees to the opera. He watched the child perform with admiration. Her fingers danced across the keys, filling the forecourt with a perfectly respectable, if uninspired, rendition of Liszt's second Hungarian Rhapsody. At the height of the *friska*—that moment where Liszt leads his listeners into the eye of the hurricane, as the key shifts from F-sharp minor to the cadenza—the music halted abruptly. The girl had caught sight of her parents regarding her from the far end of the plaza.

Millard nodded at the couple. With his rumpled white coat and his stethoscope draped over his shoulders, he looked avuncular, grandfatherly—not threatening. And what a crazy world he'd be leaving, where, without these accoutrements, a seventy-five-year-old widower, pausing to admire a child's piano performance, might be mistaken for a pervert.

The girl's mother clapped softly, urging the girl to continue, but the child refused and dashed across the atrium for a hug. For many, the great miracle of life was parenting—childbirth, the transformation of a helpless infant into an autonomous adult—but for Millard, who'd found fatherhood meaningful, but not particularly magical, the great marvel occurred earlier, in the pairing off of unsuspecting young men and women. Or, these days, men with men and women with women, which was just as improbable and miraculous. Parenting, after all, had a logical, al-

most inexorable drive: conception, pregnancy, labor, nursing—
and then cowboys and princesses, bar mitzvahs and communions
and sweet sixteens, college visits to Cambridge and New Haven.
But romance! One could be casual acquaintances for twenty
years, as he'd been with Isabelle, and then a single, brief conversation in an elevator—about Leontyne Price, of all people—
could lead you down a path of loaning cassette tapes and making
love in vacant call rooms. Or one could be casual acquaintances
for twenty years, and chat about Leontyne Price, and never experience some embryonic spark that sent one down the road to fu-
sion. Why Isabelle? Why Carol before her? And why Delilah
now? Why these women and not that leggy, fern-obsessed coed
from Barnard whom he'd dated before Carol, or Art Rosenstein's
widowed sister-in-law, who'd been nominated for a Tony Award
in the '70s? Or doe-eyed, coquettish Lettie Moshewitz, who'd
taken a mortar to his heart at age twelve? Yes, that mutuality was
the true miracle. Millard watched as the young girl buried her
head in her mother's skirt; her father stood by, momentarily su-
perfluous, exchanging a troubled glance with his wife. From the
sorrow on the man's face—he couldn't have been more than
thirty himself—Millard sensed that the sick call had not gone
well, that soon the junior musician would be wearing black
crêpe.

What an old man I've become, he scolded. *Lost in other people's business.*

He turned toward the elevator bay and nearly toppled the
young woman behind him.

"I'm sorry, Dr. Salter . . . ," she stammered. "I didn't want to
interrupt."

"I'm the one who should be sorry. Not looking where I'm
going. I am becoming one of those dotty old men, walking into
walls. . . ." He inched backward, keeping a suitable distance be-

tween himself and the busty brunette. "But you really do have to call me Millard. One of these days, you're going to be an attending yourself—and then it's going to be awkward to change, so we might as well start off on a first-name basis. . . ."

He had been urging the medical students to call him Millard for nearly forty-five years, and had gained absolutely no traction. Of course, Lauren Pastarnack—his eyes darted across her ID badge to confirm her name—would be deprived of the opportunity that he'd promised. By the time she graduated to the rank of attending physician, he would be nothing more than "that psychiatrist who hanged himself, the old guy," if he were lucky, or possibly his name would merely elicit blank stares. No matter. In any case, Millard felt fondly toward the young woman; she had rotated through his service the previous autumn, during her third year, and had conducted herself admirably. The girl had proven a tad naïve—a delusional patient had convinced her that he'd trained as a commercial airplane pilot—but, at her age, that was probably far better than being prematurely jaded and cynical.

"I'm not sure if you remember me," she began.

"Of course, I remember you. Lauren Pastarnack. You took care of that aviator. . . ."

Pastarnack blushed. Immediately, Millard regretted his remark.

"I'm just pulling your leg," he said quickly. "You did a fine job on our team."

Her face colored even further. "Thank you, Dr. Salter. I mean Millard." She shifted her weight from one foot to the other, her shapely, stockinged calves exposed below her skirt. Millard did not feel desire. Whatever lust he'd once had for women in their twenties had evaporated long ago. Yet he'd retained the self-consciousness that comes with fearing that others might still suspect him of desire, so he looked away. The butterscotch-haired prodigy and her parents sat ensconced at the far side of the atrium, conferring in hushed tones; both father and daughter appeared tearful. "I've been meaning to stop by your office," said Pastarnack.

"Have you now?"

"I was kind of wondering if you might feel comfortable writing me a letter of recommendation?" she asked. "I'm going to apply for a residency in psychiatry—and I think I did some of my best work on the consult service. . . ."

Now the girl looked away. What a crazy system, reflected Millard, that compelled a strikingly intelligent young woman—she'd graduated from Stanford, he recalled—to approach a fossilized fool like himself as a supplicant. He did not wish to disappoint her; at the same time, his day was already packed solid—and he wasn't sure he wanted to spend his final free moments attempting to fit letterhead into his printer. If only she had asked a week earlier. The logical thing—the path of least resistance—was to steer her to Stan Laguna for the letter. But the difference between his imprimatur and his junior colleague's might mean the difference between remaining at St. Dymphna's and ending up at a community hospital in Milwaukee.

"If you don't think you can . . ." stammered the girl.

"What are you doing right now?" asked Millard.

"Nothing. . . . Studying for boards, I guess. . . ."

"Walk with me. I'm on my way to see a patient."

They passed through the steel fire doors and climbed the stairs to the ninth story. Millard had a rule against taking the elevator for fewer than three flights up or four flights down while rounding, a principle he'd held to even after losing cartilage in his knee—although accruing the benefits of an additional five minutes of exercise seemed absurd under the circumstances. But if he didn't need the workout anymore, at least he was setting an example. And saving energy, which on a scorching summer day might prove his last service to the commonweal.

"How is your studying going?" he inquired.

"I guess I'll find out in three weeks. There's so much to learn."

And most of it thoroughly useless, thought Millard: the chromosomal positions of various gene loci, the patterns of trinucleotide repeat disorders, the symptoms of enzyme deficiency syndromes one would never encounter in practice. "I have a question for you," he said. "In the 1920s, there were two acceptable treatments for an acute myocardial infarction in New York City. Do you know what they were?"

"Aspirin?"

"Not in the 1920s. The belief back then was that aspirin *weakened* the heart. . . ."

They paused opposite the orthopedics unit. Pillars of sun beamed through the rectangular skylights, dappling the carpet. Millard could sense the gears of gray matter churning behind the girl's vast hazel eyes. "What cured everything a hundred years ago?"

"Chicken soup," guessed Pastarnack.

Millard grinned. At least she was thinking, and thinking outside the box. He wished Lysander had found himself a girlfriend like Lauren Pastarnack.

"Bed rest," said Millard. "At the exalted St. Dymphna's Hospital, they treated a heart attack with six months of bed rest."

The girl smiled up at him. He wondered if he were boring her.

"On the other side of Manhattan, a pioneering Hopkins-trained cardiologist, John Davin, adopted a different approach. This was at the height of Prohibition, and Dr. Davin's cure for heart disease was a daily stein of beer."

"Beer?"

"Indeed, beer. He did a land-office business, I'm sure, doling out prescriptions. Now I want you to use your extensive medical knowledge and tell me which worked better—bed rest or beer?"

"The answer has got to be beer," said Pastarnack. "Or you wouldn't be asking me. But I don't know why. . . . Is there a microbe in beer that dissolves blood clots?"

"*Is there* a microbe in beer that dissolves blood clots?" echoed Millard. "Do we still prescribe beer for heart disease? We may have sold our souls to Merck and Pfizer, but not to Budweiser. Not yet." He paused to let his wisdom, or at least his wit, settle in. "Beer, I'm afraid, has absolutely zero effect on clogged arteries. Dr. Davin's patients ended up no better off than before they took up drinking—at least, from a cardiologic standpoint."

"So bed rest *is* better?" Pastarnack asked.

"Heavens, no! Beer is neutral. Bed rest is fatal." Millard heard the pedantry in his voice—but at seventy-five, wasn't he entitled to wax a smidgeon pedantic? "Imagine all of those patients lying in bed for months at a time, without anticoagulation, without aspirin, clotting up their arteries, developing deep vein thromboses, when what the situation called for was a spirited walk around the block. . . . The exalted St. Dymphna's Hospital and its competitors killed tens of thousands of people. A man suffered a mild heart attack—and then took to bed, and died of a major coronary event or a stroke a few weeks later. Clark Gable. John Steinbeck. Bed rest nearly killed President Eisenhower. You have heard of President Eisenhower, haven't you?"

"He built the highways," chirped Pastarnack. "I still remember *something* from high school history."

"Yes," conceded Millard. "He built the highways."

But why should this girl know about Ike? What did he have to say about Calvin Coolidge or Grover Cleveland?

"You hear a lot about 'the days of the giants' in internal medicine," observed Millard. "Back in that golden age when residents worked ninety-six hour shifts and performed lumbar punctures on two different patients simultaneously." Even during his own training, there had been legacies of giants one could never venerate sufficiently or manage to slay—Halsted, Osler; men who towered over the profession like soldiers in the memories of war brides. "Claptrap. Romanticized bunk. I lived through the era of the giants, and I can tell you, as an eyewitness, that those so-called giants slaughtered lots of innocent people. I'd gladly throw in my lot with today's pygmies."

Millard stopped himself, mid-diatribe. "Pygmies" was the sort of slip that could land one in the doghouse with the associate dean. "The good news," he said, "is that there won't be any questions about the therapeutic qualities of beer on your exam."

"One fewer thing to study," said Pastarnack.

Now he was certain that he was boring her. She'd have worn the same smile while listening to him read the telephone directory like a senator conducting a filibuster; *anything* for a recommendation. He still recalled the humbling process of requesting his own letters half a century earlier—accompanying one self-absorbed clinician to the sauna, helping another carve gourds into bird feeders on his suburban patio. While he doubted this young woman would join him in the sauna or the steam room, he was confident that he could have her sculpting gourds with little effort.

"I have to look in on a patient—just for a moment," he said. "Will you come with me? Then we can talk about your letter." Assuming she'd agree, he added, "It's a case of what we used to call reactive depression. *Exogenous* depression. Poor woman was riding her motorcycle when a fire truck came through an intersection. She miscarried and lost her leg."

"That's got to be the saddest thing I've ever heard," said Pastarnack.

You dear, innocent child, thought Millard. *You don't know what's ahead of you.*

He said nothing of the asylum seekers he occasionally treated for free in St. Dymphna's torture clinic, nothing of his days on the AIDS ward during the 1980s. He could have told her about the homeless grandmother set afire by the marauding teens, about the Pakistani illustrator blinded with lye. He didn't even point out that, in his passé, admittedly chauvinistic opinion, women who were nine months pregnant had no business riding motorcycles.

"You'll hear sadder," he said, matter-of-fact.

They paused at the nursing station long enough for Millard to greet the clerk and scan the room assignments on the monitor. Patients had a knack for shifting locations during the overnight—like infantry strategically repositioned for battle. Every junior clinician had experienced the sinking terror, the sense of depth charges detonating inside one's abdomen, when one entered the room of a young, relatively healthy patient, for an early morning physical, to find the bed bare, the linens crisp and unsullied. More often than not, this tragedy resulted from staffing logistics, not death or disease, with the perpetrator of the atrocity carrying a clipboard rather than a scythe, and the victim merely relocated across a corridor or up a flight of stairs. Dolores, it turned out, had been so moved. An MRI of a femur lasted long enough to banish a person as far as an entirely different unit, so they were fortunate to find her only two doors down from the room she'd previously occupied. She looked uncomfortable, almost contorted, tilted slightly to her side and propped at a sixty-degree angle, a turquoise scarf wrapped around her scalp. In a nearby chair, portly as a walrus, basked her torpid minder.

The suicide minder's job was to sound an alarm if Dolores attempted to harm herself in the hospital, but she looked as though she might just as easily doze through the event. Their entrance was her cue to visit the restroom.

"Good morning, Miss Noguerra," said Millard.

Dolores gawped back at him indifferently, her affect as blunt as a pewter plate.

He leaned against the radiator and lowered his voice. "I've brought one of my students with me this morning," he said. "We wanted to see how you're doing."

"The same," said Dolores. Monotone. Her blankets had shifted over the edge of the bed, revealing her bandaged stump. An ugly scar crossed her remaining ankle. "May I?" asked Lauren Pastarnack—and with the delicate alacrity of a skilled nurse, she re-draped the covers. Dolores grimaced, but said nothing.

"Yesterday, you expressed that you were having some concerning thoughts," observed Millard. "About hurting yourself. Are you still feeling that way?"

The patient shook her head—a whispered gesture.

"Please take her away," said Dolores. "She breathes too loud."

For a moment, Millard thought she meant Pastarnack, but then he registered that she'd been referring to the suicide minder. "Are you sure you'll be safe without her?"

"She breathes too loud and her stomach growls," said Dolores. "I swear she's going to drive me over the edge. . . ."

Millard had little doubt that the minder *did* breathe too loudly. And over the years, he'd come to the realization that if someone was determined to kill herself, there wasn't much a physician—or anybody else, for that matter—could do about it. You might prevent a person from taking her life this morning, or this weekend, but not next month or next year. "How does this sound? Why don't we keep you under observation for one more day—to err on the side of caution?" he proposed. "And if you're still feeling safe tomorrow, we'll cancel the one-to-one. . . ."

Dolores closed her eyes, shutting him out. The truth was that he didn't really suspect she'd harm herself—and if she did, who could say that wasn't a reasonable decision for a thirty-one-year-old woman who'd lost a leg and a baby? Yet even on his final workday, Millard found himself unable to call off the minder prematurely. Maybe it was instinct, a habit so ingrained that it mimicked a reflex—like his late brother's aversion to crustaceans. They'd been raised kosher, and although both of them had drifted from organized Judaism, Lester had never been able to stomach a lobster or a shrimp cocktail. "How can I?" he'd once asked Millard. "It's the curse of upbringing. You might as well ask me to drink human blood." Millard, who'd grown to savor bay scallops and cheeseburgers, had suffered no such atavistic compunction.

"I'll have Dr. Laguna stop by tomorrow to check up on you," said Millard. "He's a very good doctor. I think you'll like him."

Dolores rolled farther onto her flank. Millard waited for the minder to return from the restroom before departing. The endomorphic woman did indeed gasp as she waddled—like a pregnant basset hound on a summer afternoon—but what could be done? You couldn't exactly instruct the woman to stop breathing. He was glad to return to the corridor, which smelled vaguely of antiseptic. Nearby, a stoop-shouldered fellow buffed the floors, humming Irving Berlin's "This Is the Army, Mr. Jones." Now there was a tune you didn't hear every day! Millard steered Pastarnack past a phalanx of meal carts fortified with discarded breakfast trays, grateful to leave the unit. He didn't say a word until they'd reached the ninth-floor courtyard, where a frangipani tree rose implausibly amid the wrought iron tables and benches. One of his self-imposed rules was that, whenever possible, he never discussed a patient while still on the unit, much as one didn't conduct a postmortem of the opera within a ten-block radius of the performance. Who could say that the mezzo-soprano's mousy sister from Des Moines wasn't ambling behind you in that ragged pea coat? No need to wound feelings unnecessarily.

"So what do you think?" asked Millard. "Should we let her kill herself?"

His provocation failed to fluster Pastarnack. "Absolutely not. She's visibly depressed. . . ."

"But her depression could be perfectly rational. Maybe you don't know the whole story. I didn't tell you that she was a professional marathon runner, did I? Or that her husband was killed in the accident. Or that she can't have any more kids. She's lost her career, her family—who wouldn't be depressed under the circumstances?"

Flames surged into Pastarnack's pale cheeks. "I'm not saying her depression isn't rational—or a valid response to her suffering—only that it's not *permanent*."

"How do you know?"

"I don't. Not for sure. But there are no guarantees for anything in medicine. We don't know for sure that bypass surgery or a Whipple procedure will succeed, yet we still perform them. Let her try an antidepressant. Or shock therapy."

"Shock therapy won't win her the Boston Marathon."

"There's always the Paralympics. Or she could be a leading advocate for the disabled. Would you have let Helen Keller kill herself?"

"And what if shock therapy fails? What if fifteen years go by and you're the head of the consult service and she's *still* sitting in that room?"

"We'll deal with that when it happens," rejoined Pastarnack. She spoke forcefully, free from her shell of deference. "I see what

you're driving at. And yes, maybe there is a place for rational suicide if you've been depressed for fifteen years and failed all
interventions—but that doesn't mean every sixteen-year-old girl
whose boyfriend breaks up with her should be allowed to over-
dose on Tylenol."

Now Dolores Noguerra wasn't exactly a rejected teenager. . . .

Pastarnack's intensity surprised him. He feared he'd touched
a live wire: Maybe she had a parent or sibling who'd succumbed
to despair. Yet he was delighted that she'd put up an argument—
even if he was no longer certain that she possessed the better
part of it.

"Okay, you win," he said. "We won't let her kill herself just
yet." Many of Millard's colleagues shared the girl's caution
when it came to so-called rational suicide. Outcomes after
trauma proved consistently hard to predict. Some people endured the Bataan Death March, or a failed escape from So-
bibór, or seven years as "guests" of Ho Chi Minh in the Hanoi
Hilton—and survived psychologically unscathed, able to em-
brace joy like Elie Wiesel and practice forgiveness like Nelson
Mandela. Others found themselves crippled for life by minor
setbacks—a nonviolent mugging, a fender-bender, a lost passport. His own mother had once taken to bed for weeks after
misplacing her evening gloves. "Let's at least give her natural re-
silience a chance to kick in."

He afforded Pastarnack a moment to savor her victory before
revealing his artifice. "For the record, Miss Noguerra wasn't a
marathon runner," he said. "She's a special ed teacher. With a devoted boyfriend, I might add, who has never been hit by a fire
truck—at least, as far as I know. And there's no reason to think
she can't have as many children as she'd like. . . ."

Now *that* flummoxed the girl. "So you made that all up?"

"I wanted to see how strongly you'd defend your case—and I

give you a lot of credit. If psychiatry doesn't work out, there's always law school."

At once, like a punctured Bobo doll, the cheer slackened from Pastarnack's face.

"That was a joke," said Millard. "So where were we? That's right, we were discussing your letter of recommendation. . . ."

"I can write the first draft myself, if that's helpful," offered the girl.

She hadn't meant to be impertinent, he knew. Many of his colleagues had embraced this shortcut. To Millard, the idea exemplified lunacy—like having criminal defendants serve as their own jurors. "That won't be necessary," he said. "But I do want to get a sense of your knowledge base if I'm going to write you a letter. Do you think you're up to answering a few more questions? Nothing about beer, I promise."

Pastarnack's entire body, without moving, seemed to uncoil like a spring. Answering questions was what she'd been trained to do all of her life. "Sure," she agreed.

What choice did she have? He wouldn't have held a refusal against her, at least consciously, but she had no way of knowing that.

"First question," said Millard, channeling his internal game-show host. "Can you name the Seven Sisters?"

A look of bewilderment took hold of the girl's delicate features. "I'm sorry, Dr. Salter. I'm not sure what you're asking. Do you mean from Walt Disney?"

Brilliant! She thought they were cartoon characters, maybe the brides of the Seven Dwarfs. He recalled there'd been a soppy musical, *Seven Brides for Seven Brothers* starring Howard Keel and Jane Powell, but he didn't think that was Disney—and anyway, if she knew nothing of Eisenhower, she probably also didn't watch obscure films from the '50s.

"Let's try again. I imagine you're familiar with all eight Ivy League schools," said Millard. He ticked them off on his fingers: "Harvard, Yale, Princeton, Brown, Columbia, Cornell, Dartmouth, and the University of Pennsylvania."

Pastarnack nodded, wary.

"My challenge for you is to name the Seven Sister schools—the Women's Ivies, if you will. I'll give you a hint to start. You might be tempted to guess Pembroke, because it was affiliated with Brown, but Pembroke was *not* a Seven Sister."

The young woman eyed him as though he'd walked off the moon. Clearly, Pembroke had not been on the tip of her tongue. "I really have no idea," she stammered.

"You were expecting a question about neurotransmitters, I suppose." He'd tried to sound sympathetic, but feared he had come across as smug. "Give it the old college try. . . . You must know some all-girls schools. . . ."

"I don't know. . . . Barnard?"

"Very good. That's one."

"And the one in Massachusetts. That Hillary Clinton went to. Mount Holyoke?"

"Kind of. Mount Holyoke is one of them, but Mrs. Clinton went to Wellesley, which is also a Seven Sister," replied Millard. "I'm feeling generous, so I'll give you credit for both. Four to go."

Lauren Pastarnack's lips pursed, but she shook her head.

"I'm sorry. I just don't know."

"Very well. Three out of seven isn't so dreadful. If you were a baseball player, you'd make the Hall of Fame. Ready for your next question?"

"I guess."

"What field did Jimmy Durante make major contributions to?"

Again, the girl's expression faltered. He recalled the first puppy he and Carol had adopted for Lysander, a dopey schnauzer, his eyes beset with perpetual dejection. Of course, the girl's gloom was entirely his own fault. Seconds passed, each moment like a boulder struggling to squeeze through the throat of an hourglass. "Do not squander time, Dr. Pastarnack," he warned. "It is the stuff from which life is made."

"If I had to choose, I'd say pharmacology."

"In a way," Millard said. "To the degree that pharmacology is a form of stand-up comedy."

He glanced at his wristwatch. What compulsion kept him tormenting this gifted young woman, when he ought to be consoling Rabbi Steinmetz, was impossible to articulate. "A final question, Dr. Pastarnack?"

Now the girl merely looked at him with incredulity.

"Who composed the song 'This Is the Army, Mr. Jones'?"

Millard realized that a bystander might interpret this quiz as a manifestation of sadism, but he suddenly understood that his motives were actually masochistic: He was reminding himself how obsolete he'd become, how irrelevant his knowledge was to a woman in the prime of life. Yet his victim couldn't be aware of that. Anguish stewed in the girl's limpid eyes and Millard's face flushed with shame.

"These questions aren't fair," said Pastarnack—timorously, as much an appeal as a statement. "Honestly, I *was* expecting questions about neurotransmitters. Or, at least, medicine. . . ."

So she'd called his bluff. Kudos to the kid. "Of course, they're not fair," he agreed. "I was waiting to see how long it would take you to say something. . . ."

"Oh."

"If you see something that doesn't make sense to you in the hospital, there's a good chance it doesn't make sense to anyone else either—only they're all afraid to express anything. You could save somebody's life by saying, 'This isn't fair' or 'That's unreasonable.'"

"Wow. I thought you were being serious. . . ."

Millard beamed, pleased with himself. This was likely to be the last lesson he ever taught, even unwittingly, so he was delighted that it had gone so well. But writing the girl a recommendation, no matter how talented she might be, would require time, time that he didn't possess. And yet, the notion of her talents being squandered at a community hospital in Milwaukee, or wherever, genuinely pained him. Not that there was anything wrong with Milwaukee—if you were looking to open a brewery or locate a television sitcom.

"Now about that letter of yours," he said. "I'll make you a deal. I'm going to be out of town for a while, but if you send me the link to upload your recommendation today, I'll do it before I leave. . . ."

She actually clapped her hands together at first—like seal flippers—then clasped them in front of her as though he'd answered a prayer.

"Thank you, Dr. Salter—Millard—Millard Salter," she spluttered.

"But make sure you get the link to me by five o'clock."

"I'll do it right now," she promised.

"And in case you're wondering, Irving Berlin composed 'This Is the Army, Mr. Jones.'"

"I won't forget that."

As though she had any notion who Irving Berlin might be.

"Now I have patients to see," he added, "and you have lynxes to avoid."

She looked at him puzzled again, eyebrows raised in doubt, so he pointed to the flyer on a nearby pillar, styled like a wanted poster out of the Wild West in carnival font with sepia lettering: ESCAPED LYNX CUB. "You're *not* joking," she said, surprised.

"Occasionally, I do say something serious," he replied. "For variety. Now please go send me that link before I forget who you are. . . ."

The girl thanked him again and vanished into the elevator. He strolled in the opposite direction, toward the bone marrow unit, where Rabbi Steinmetz lay imprisoned in an immunological bubble. Steinmetz would likely be his final patient (*ever!*), and at the rate the clergyman's fever had progressed, he might prove Steinmetz's final doctor. Lost in his reverie, Millard suddenly realized that he was humming—"This Is the Army, Mr. Jones"—and he checked himself abruptly.

He retrieved disposable gloves and a mask from a cart beside the rabbi's door. Inside, he found Ezra Steinmetz seated at the window, alone, gazing down at the traffic below. The young chaplain—he was closer in age to Maia than to Lysander—wore a cozy royal purple robe with a shawl collar; the *Post*'s sports pages lay scattered across the tangled sheets. On the bedside table, the checkers board from their Friday morning match stood intact, men and kings standing in scattered ranks as though arrested by a neutron bomb. Steinmetz flashed Millard a smile, but his visage quickly retreated back to a look of fatalistic despair.

"How are you?" asked Millard.

"Honestly, scared scriptless, as they say. I think I've run out of words."

"You don't have to talk."

Millard had brought along the checkers board the previous week; in his experience, tangible challenges like checkers or chess provided a soothing alternative to reflection. Half of his job, he'd once said to Isabelle, entailed throwing sets of backgammon.

"I don't mind talking," said Steinmetz. "I just don't think there are words to express how I feel. Reality is kicking in. I'm going to die."

"Are the doctors saying that?" asked Millard. "Or are *you* saying that?"

"The doctors are saying that I've got a good chance of pulling through. They're oncologists—they *always* say that. They'll be saying that at my funeral. . . . 'If only we give him one more round of chemo. . . .'" Steinmetz smiled at his own macabre humor, but his lips quickly flatlined. "I try to sound optimistic, for the sake of Janice and the girls, but I can read the writing on the wall. My goose is cooked."

"You'll outlive me yet," said Millard.

"No, *I won't.*" The rabbi rose from his chair with considerable effort and shuffled to the bed. He poured a few sips of club soda from a miniature bottle into a plastic cup and swallowed, his Adam's apple stark against his skeletal throat. Only once the rabbi had settled onto the bed, frail as a relic on a concrete slab, did Millard realize that he'd done this act selflessly, to vacate a seat for his guest.

"There's nothing special about dying," said Steinmetz. "It's one of those few universals. Even dying at thirty isn't *so* unusual. I keep thinking of those lines from Ecclesiastes: *A living dog is better than a dead lion, for the living know that they will perish, but the dead know nothing. . . . Nevermore will they have a share in anything done under the sun. . . .*" The rabbi wiped the crook of his eye, rapidly, as though hoping not to be seen. "I thought I'd be at peace—and I'm not. I'm scared, Doc. I didn't expect to be scared, but I'm terrified."

"Of anything specific?" asked Millard.

Steinmetz shook his head. "That's just it. I can't even articulate what I'm afraid of. Not of pain—that's well-controlled . . .

and even if it weren't, pain is merely pain. And Janice and the girls will be provided for. Her father's quite well off, you know." The rabbi adjusted his pillows beneath his corroded spine. "The closest that I can get to what I'm afraid of is some nebulous uncertainty—not the unknown, not the afterlife, not the *olam ha-ba*, if there even is one—just an aching feeling of insecurity. Does that make any sense?"

"As much sense as anything."

"In the Book of Job, we are told, *So man lies down, and rises not: till the heavens be no more, he shall not awake, nor be raised out of his sleep.* . . . . What happens after that, of course, has kept sages far wiser than myself awake at night for many centuries. . . ."

Millard listened as the rabbi quoted various Biblical passages. The only one he recognized came from the 146th Psalm: "*Do not put your trust in princes, in human beings, who cannot save. When their spirit departs, they return to the earth; on that very day their plans come to nothing.* . . ." What puzzled Millard wasn't Steinmetz's fear—that made perfect sense. What unsettled him was his own *lack* of trepidation. He *had* somehow arrived at an inner peace. Maybe not the serenity of swamis and mystics, but a matter-of-fact acceptance of what was to come. If he feared anything, it was the physical act of asphyxiation—he intended to souse himself with Courvoisier and Valium before he stepped into the bathroom—but not the great nameless maw beyond. Death wasn't an evil, not at his age. It was a neutral. Like Dr. Davin's beer. Unnecessary suffering—now there lay the true iniquity.

"What's most amazing," said the rabbi—and Millard realized with guilt, like a scribe at a medieval deathbed, that he'd lost a crucial portion of Steinmetz's final testimony—"is that people think I'll be cheered by their own bad news. Well-wishers actually say things like, 'If it makes you feel any better, my sister-in-law also has myeloma.' Now how could that possibly, under any conceivable circumstances, make me feel better?"

Steinmetz readjusted his pillows, but his ongoing discomfort was obvious. "What I really want—I probably shouldn't be saying this to a psychiatrist—is to get it over with. Not that I'm planning anything, but I wouldn't mind if someone lit a fire under God's ass." The rabbi balled up a sheaf of newspaper and lobbed it toward the wastepaper basket; it fell several yards short of the rim. "I don't really mean that. But there are moments when I find myself thinking, either let me live or let me die, but don't keep toying with me. Don't keep toying with my family." The rabbi added, "When I'm alone, I use a much stronger word than toying."

Millard glanced out the window. On the avenue, the morning sun blistered the grime coating the tops of ambulances and delivery trucks. Children cavorted in the schoolyard opposite: Tag? Kick the can? Some novel amusement? One could not tell from this height. How recently, it seemed, his brother, Lester, had been stickball king of 177th Street.

"You're not listening," said Steinmetz. "You have that same polite, glazed look I sometimes fall into when a sick person starts rambling."

"I'm sorry. I got lost in my own head. . . ."

"Who could blame you?" asked the rabbi. "Don't worry. I'm not offended. It was helpful to talk things out. . . ."

Before Millard had an opportunity to apologize further, the nursing assistant arrived to check Steinmetz's vital signs. "Saved by the thermometer," said the rabbi.

"I don't want you to think . . ."

"Think what? That you're also human? That you have worries of your own?" He extended an emaciated hand and shook Millard's with surprising vigor.

"If I'm still around tomorrow," said the rabbi, "you'll make it up to me by letting me beat the pants off you at checkers."

Millard understood that any further expression of contrition at the moment would do more harm than good. Disheartened with self-reproach, he retreated into the corridor. His watch read ten o'clock. Already, he'd fallen behind schedule.

A midmorning lull had settled over St. Dymphna's. Interns and residents, pre-rounding complete, sipped coffee in the atrium and waited for their attendings. Visiting hours remained a gleam on the day's horizon. An overhead page announced a Code 1000—a cardiac arrest—in a distant corner of the hospital, but the fluorescently lit walkway beneath Madison Avenue remained as still as the nave of an abandoned cathedral. Alas, even here some fastidious retainer had pinned up warnings about the missing lynx cub. Clearly, the hospital's risk management and legal departments—the twin powers behind the throne—were taking no chances, although Millard didn't see how warning people of the escaped lynx absolved anyone of responsibility. Once you saw the signs, after all, you'd already reached the zone of danger. Shutting down the entire facility until the animal was recaptured might shield the institution to some degree, but he had no doubt that the bean counters and actuaries had already weighed the odds of calamity against the costs of precaution and found them wanting. So here he was, on the day of his death, vigilant for a feral feline.

That's when a crazy thought tickled his mind. There was no lynx. Most likely, the whole enterprise would prove a social psychology experiment of some sort, an assessment of how people in public settings responded to low-grade threats. Ingenious—if true! Of course, he'd never know for sure, but even if he'd lived to see a panel of investigators announce their results, even then one couldn't truly be certain. After all, maybe they had concocted the study as a cover to hide their negligence in permitting a dangerous cat to enter a medical clinic. Who could say? He was reminded of Oedipus's warning: *Count no man happy until he is dead*. While he mused on the purpose of the lynx experiment, his feet carried him toward his office, navigating the pipe-lined passageways of the hospital underbelly, where crossbeams and open ducts might conceal packs of truant panthers and ocelots. Here whirred the institution's most essential—and least glamorous—departments: dining services, housekeeping, maintenance. Only now housekeeping was known as "environmental amenities" and maintenance had been rebranded "plant operations"—a challenge for a geezer who still thought of flight attendants as stewardesses. Opposite Millard's office, a workman in paint-mottled coveralls was in the process of taping a pristine drop cloth along the tile while his colleague lounged against a nearby trestle ladder. Millard's secretary, Miss Nickelsworth, had stepped away from her desk—a note read "Will return in 15 min"—and, as a stickler for protocol, she'd secured his door during her absence. Millard had the key in the lock when Hecuba Yilmaz rounded the corner like a damp breeze.

"Precisely whom I was looking for," Yilmaz bellowed in her Turkish accent, pointing the end of her severed index finger at him. Coarse hairs protruding from the mole atop the bridge of the woman's fleshy nose, glistening like barbs. The embossed fleur-de-lis print of her ill-fitting blouse recalled nineteenth-century upholstery. "I have been searching for you."

"Who hasn't?"

Yilmaz frowned as though deciding whether his remark was insulting.

"I don't have time for you today, Hecuba."

Millard had never personally had a run-in with this egocentric creature, but that likely made him a minority of one. Stan

Laguna, who despised the young woman, alternately called her "The Royal Embellisher" (because she claimed direct descent from King Priam of Troy) and "The Beauty Queen of Sycamore Hill," (not in tribute to her appearance, which resembled a well-fed aardvark's, but with ironic reference to the location of the second-rate satellite hospital—a St. Dymphna's affiliate on Sycamore Hill Boulevard in Queens—where she ran a methadone clinic). Her much older husband, the outside hospital's chief operating officer, was a former insurance company litigator who bore a striking resemblance to vintage character actor Karl Malden, and had been a chum of the dean's during his Andover years. That had led Laguna to remark, too loud, at last year's Christmas party, "Apparently screwing Mr. Snout gives her license to screw the rest of us." And once, when a colleague observed of the peculiar couple that "every pot has its lid," Stan had pointed out that the correct quotation from Balzac (*and when had Stan Laguna ever been the sort to read Balzac?*) read: "There is no pot, *however ugly*, that does not one day find a cover."

"We can talk tomorrow," Millard pledged. "I'm free all afternoon."

He didn't want to unlock his office door until the woman departed.

She scrutinized him, as intense as the Grand Inquisitor. "You *are* going to be here tomorrow, are you not? You are not planning a vacation."

"No," he assured her. "I am not planning a vacation."

That didn't seem enough to pacify her.

"All I need is five minutes. *Five minutes.*" She held up her hand, four-and-a-half knotty fingers splayed, as though the concept might be alien to him. "You cannot possibly be so busy that you cannot spare *five minutes* for an old friend, can you?"

"I can't spare you even four-and-a-half minutes, Hecuba. Not today."

"But you must," she insisted, oblivious to his malice. "To tell you the truth, I have heard a rumor that you are stepping down."

He turned to face her, his back against his office door.

"Who told you that?"

"I'd rather not say," said Hecuba. "But if it's true, I feel you *owe* it to me to tell me. I don't think it's any secret that I'm interested in the position—when you're ready to step down—and I'm hoping we can arrange a seamless transition."

"A seamless transition?" echoed Millard.

"That's all I'm requesting."

Did this woman really believe he owed her *anything*? Phenomenal! If he owed her something, it was, as Jackie Gleason would have said, a good sock in the kisser. How could a forty-something assistant professor believe herself in line for his job? No sane person would appoint Hecuba Yilmaz dog catcher, let alone head of her own division, but he'd served up similar predictions many times before, only to be proven wrong. Anything was possible in academia, especially with the right bedfellows.

"I do not want there to be any conflict between myself and Stanley," she said. Yilmaz had the habit of calling people by their "full" names—which often involved butchering these names for her own pleasure, almost sadistically, as though the distortions gave her power over her victims like the spells of a Shakespearean witch. Stan Laguna's given name was actually Stanislaw. "People will commend you for a smooth transition, Millard. I am looking out for your legacy."

Yilmaz touched him on the elbow—a benign gesture that, bestowed by another party, might have come across as endearing, but originating from Hecuba, the act made him want to wrest free his arm. Or change his clothes.

"Thanks for your concern, but rumors of my retirement are greatly exaggerated," he said. "Especially anonymous ones. I'm far more likely to die than to retire." He looked pointedly at his wristwatch: nearly twenty past ten. "If I plan on expiring unexpectedly, would you like me to give you advance notice?"

"I am sorry," answered Yilmaz, "but it is irresponsible to leave these things up in the air."

"I'm sure you're right," he agreed. "I am a grossly irresponsible person."

He'd given up on courtesy; now he was merely striving to remain civil. Already, a fantasy was leaching into his psyche, a desire to tell this hideous woman exactly what he thought of her.

"Come back tomorrow, Hecuba. . . ."

"You'll be here? You're not going to phone in sick, are you?"

"Even if I'm dying of cholera or yellow fever, I won't call in sick."

He unlocked his office door.

"Five minutes? Is that really so much to ask?"

"At the moment, I'm afraid it is," he said—and he shut the door behind him.

You're an unbearable narcissist and nobody likes you, he thought, but he resisted his compulsion to reopen the door and give voice to his contempt. Because even if he told her how unpleasant he found her, she wouldn't believe him. That was the amazing thing about disturbed personalities like Hecuba's: everybody else suffered, but she plowed forward without insight, sowing exasperation and fury in cheerful oblivion.

6

Millard had arranged to meet Lysander at a restaurant in Morningside Heights, on the roof of a one-time luxury hotel just north of Columbia University. He repeatedly assured himself that the choice of location was largely incidental—selected because his own father had favored the Overlook for business lunches—but as the rendezvous hour approached, day by day, he could not shake his other, quiescent motive: Carol, his first wife, lived in one of the park-front high-rises around the corner. Millard had never, obviously, visited her apartment. He wasn't even certain which of the several upscale towers she inhabited. But as his final breaths grew closer, he found himself drawn to her mesmerically, like a male mantis inching fatally toward a mate's open jaws. His plan, nonsensical as it sounded, was to stand opposite her complex, across from the cast-iron gate with its hostile finials, from eleven o'clock until noon, allowing fate to determine whether he encountered her on the sidewalk. He recognized the absurdity of this providential approach—especially for a man who'd exiled the Tooth Fairy from his home and had once written to his state assemblyman urging a ban on commercial fortune tellers—but that insight didn't prevent him from taking the IRT (emblazoned with its bright red numerals) up to 116th Street. He arrived at Carol's address with five minutes to spare, although his only appointment was with himself.

Twenty-three years had elapsed since he had laid eyes upon

Carol, twenty-seven since he'd last spoken to her. But he kept tabs on her life, intermittently, at a distance. During the first decade following their split, he'd read the wedding announcements in the *Times* every Sunday, hoping to encounter her name; how much less self-reproach he'd have felt if she'd also found a match. Marriage—heterosexual marriage, at least—he'd come to realize, too late, was a tortuous cat-and-mouse game of implicit contracts between the sexes: You exhausted a woman's youth and beauty, then kept her company during middle age, eschewing fresher, more alluring mates, until the tables turned once again and she looked after you in your decline. Unless, of course, you breached that contract as Millard had done—absconding with Carol's halcyon years and then shifting his affections to Isabelle, ten years her junior, ultimately cheating destiny once again by offing himself before he grew dependent upon others. Regrettably, Carol's name never did appear in the Lifestyle section. He'd gladly have fixed her up, if she'd have let him—but he understood she'd have sooner disemboweled herself with a *tachi* than accepted such humiliation. As the daughter of an alcoholic bookie who drank on credit, his first wife had cared deeply about pride, appearances. On open school night, she insisted the teachers address her as Dr. Sucram. Never, God forbid, as Mrs. Salter. (*I didn't spend seven years studying signal processing to be Mrs. Anything!*) Precisely the sort of woman to suffer the most from his treachery. More recently, as Millard's plans solidified, he'd taken to scanning for her name in the obituaries, afraid that her demise would forestall his own. Of all the contingencies that might have foiled his ambitions, he'd decided, only two commanded any weight: a miraculous recovery by Delilah, which was implausible, or Carol's sudden death. He didn't want his older children, especially Lysander, to mourn both parents in short order. And if that sounded calculated—even cold—he wouldn't deny it; losing Isabelle and Hal in succession, two final blows along a brutal gauntlet, had ossified whatever remained of his capacity for grief.

The last time he'd seen his first wife had been at Arnold's marriage. That had been only three years after they'd finalized the divorce. In hindsight, he realized, bringing Isabelle with him to the wedding had been a grave error in judgment. Carol refused to acknowledge his existence. Standing only inches from him in the shadow of the billowing *chuppah*—his son's cheerfully committed in-laws beaming at the opposite end of the raised platform—his ex-wife wore a tense, unyielding expression that was neither smile nor frown, just pure pain. His mind revved blindly, searching for some word or phrase to palliate her wrath, but you couldn't undo high treason with a remark about the balmy morning or the beauty of the Missouri Botanical Garden. (He recalled, bitterly, the hackneyed joke: But other than *that*, Mrs. Lincoln, how did you enjoy the play?) During the closing processional, his elbow inadvertently brushed the trumpet sleeve of her gown, and a glacial chill goose-stepped up his arm into the pit of his neck, as though the blood had congealed solid in his arteries. Five years later, when Sally married her naval architect, he'd stayed clear. So that had been a small portion of his penance: shelling out $60,000 for a lavish affair where he dared not show his face. Of course, it wasn't true penance, because absolution demands remorse. While Millard deeply regretted *how* he'd betrayed Carol, and especially the eighteen months of deception he'd perpetrated, which had culminated in Maia's birth, all under the self-serving delusion that he was protecting his wife and children, he did not regret Isabelle—not one kiss, not one stolen caress, not one precious moment of her company. That was asking too much.

Millard seated himself on a bench opposite Carol's complex.

Someone had abandoned a partially consumed sandwich on the adjoining bench; flies circled the wax paper and a company of red ants carried off grains of what looked like roast beef and pastrami. A homeless young woman and her dog, a well-tended beagle, dozed on a slab of cardboard under a nearby linden. From the park below rose the shouts of toddlers scampering through sprinklers. Pedestrians emerged from the ivy-coated walkways on either side of the speared gate—an elderly couple holding hands, a bare-chested jogger with a mynah bird atop his shoulder—but not Carol. Lurking at her door in his necktie and sweater on the warmest day of the summer, his sport jacket draped over his forearm, an uneasy self-consciousness overcame Millard. He'd hoped to appear inconspicuous, just another old man out for a harmless bask, but he couldn't shake the feeling that he looked like a stalker—a deranged ex-lover come to spy on his former spouse. Rationally, of course, he understood his fears to be groundless: He'd sat on countless park benches on summer mornings, clad in identical clothes, and not once had such a fear crossed his mind. Deep down, he realized that had he been seated on the very same bench, engaged in the very same behavior, but for a different purpose—let's say, waiting to pick up his granddaughters from ballet—he'd have felt perfectly at ease. Context, alas, proved defining. Murder, as they say, will out. And prowling too. Strangely enough, waiting for Carol also had a regressive effect on his psyche—he momentarily felt like her husband once again, beset with all of the fears and anxieties that had cleaved them apart.

A particular experience with Isabelle came to mind: They'd attended her fiftieth high school reunion at the Hotel Pennsylvania. Millard had been there once before—with his father, in 1964, to cheer Robert Kennedy during his run for the Senate. In his memory, the gold-lacquered balustrades had glistened, as though polished hourly, while the ceilings in the grand ballroom had towered twenty yards. One could easily picture Glenn Miller on the bandstand or the Boswell Sisters warbling "I Found a Million Dollar Baby" beneath the cut-glass chandeliers. In contrast, the hotel they actually entered that evening had a shabby, poorly tended aura of evaporated swank. Plastic plants poked from oversized brass tureens in the lobby. "I don't think Glenn Miller would be caught dead in this place," he whispered to Isabelle—knowing that she would jab his side, her cue that she wanted him to behave himself. He tried his darnedest. He rocked his hips to Martha and the Vandellas, slow-danced with his wife to Dean Martin crooning "Everybody Loves Somebody," listened with clamped tongue to her childhood girlfriend, Linda Blauer, extoll the virtues of Ayurvedic medicine. He even took his turn at the karaoke mic, belting out "Under the Boardwalk" in the wrong key. Isabelle, who looked truly radiant in her strapless evening gown, appeared to be enjoying herself, so Millard was dumbfounded when, in the cab on the ride home, she burst into tears.

"I know this is crazy, dear," she explained, "but I'm *still* not popular. I'm sixty-eight years old and those girls—women—*still* made me feel like a gangly, unwanted teenager." She'd even cursed several of these sexagenarian matrons by name. "I'm sorry," she apologized. "I don't know what's come over me. . . . One too many Mai Tais, I'm afraid. . . ."

Millard had helped Isabelle laugh off the episode with an onslaught of kisses. Now, regressing to his former married self, he understood what his late wife had experienced. Even the act of standing impotent opposite Carol's development, rather than ringing her bell, aroused feelings of inadequacy that he hadn't stomached in decades. He could imagine his former spouse storming onto the sidewalk, fists balled, ranting at him for his cowardice. "Spineless as ever," she'd declare. "You're going to take the easy way out and you don't even have the courage to face your own ex-wife before you do it. Do you really expect to build up the pluck to loop a belt around your neck?" And she'd have him dead to rights: He still dreaded her displeasure.

The homeless young woman stirred on her makeshift blanket. All that was required were a few words from him and the disheveled girl could be napping on his sofa, freshly soaked in his brass-fitted bath and wrapped in Isabelle's favorite magenta robe, the one he'd withheld from Goodwill, despite the instructions in the red notebook—whose terrycloth he still pressed to his nostrils in moments of yearning. He might, on a whim, leave his entire estate to this unfortunate creature. Arnold and Sally certainly didn't need the money, while Maia, who'd nearly completed her chemistry PhD, already had six-figure job offers from industry. So the only person who'd really suffer was Lysander—and who could say that a surprise disinheritance wasn't precisely the kick-in-the-pants the boy required. Anyway, his mother would always help him in a pinch, so he was unlikely to end up starving or street homeless. How easily a few kind words to this dozing stranger could reload the dice. Yet some primeval, clannish instinct kept Millard from acting. Instead—as though to protect his estate from the pull of her misery, he launched himself off the park bench and made a beeline for the elevated security post that guarded Carol's sanctuary.

The stout, acne-scarred guard slid open a pane in the booth.

"I was just wondering . . ." said Millard.

His words caught somewhere about his Adam's apple. Inside the guard booth, on the radio, two voices argued in Spanish. Water trickled from the head of a nearby hydrant. Millard reached for the side of the security post, catching his balance on the metal rail.

"You okay?" asked the guard.

Millard had planned to ask whether Dr. Sucram was home, but that sounded shady, he realized, possibly even illicit, unless he planned to visit, so he had little choice. "I'm here to see Dr. Sucram," he announced. "I've forgotten the apartment number."

"East tower or west?"

Millard shook his head. "It's been a while. . . ."

The guard did not appear persuaded. He opened a three-ring binder and ran his thumb down a list of residents until he found Carol.

"And your name?"

"Lysander," Millard lied quickly. "Lysander Salter."

What a farfetched moniker: Lysander. He'd wanted a distinctive, indelible name—Carol had already gotten her way with Arnold and Sally—and calling the boy after a Spartan *navarch* seemed, at the time, both dignified and ambitious. Maybe also a slap in the face to his wife, who'd sought something "simple and all-American." In hindsight, of course, the name proved a farce, as improbable as a city-state run by two kings, and Hal Storch— never one to hold his tongue—had pointed out that the original Lysander had been an assassin and a pederast. Yet the most substantial irony was that Millard's son, named after the greatest admiral of the ancient world, had never learned how to swim. According to Jewish tradition—as related by Rabbi Steinmetz— this fact alone confirmed Millard an abject failure as a parent in the eyes of God, for Talmudic law required that a father pass along only three skills to his sons: a knowledge of Torah, a trade, and a steady Australian crawl. *Or, at least, enough dog-paddling know-how to keep his head above water*, explained Steinmetz. *There's no consensus among the commentaries on precisely what is meant by swimming.* Steinmetz, of course, hadn't used the words "abject failure"; that was all Millard's self-scourging. What the rabbi had actually said, when Millard had sought his wisdom on the subject of parenting, was that different men marched to different drumbeats. *Is he killing anybody? Is he worshiping idols? No. Then let him find his way.* Easy enough to say when your son wasn't the one whose drumbeat wandered onto an ice floe.

The guard dialed Carol's number. He looked as though he might yawn when he announced Millard's false name, but betrayed no surprise when instructed to send him up. "East tower. Apartment 15-C. Follow that path on the right to the second set of doors and take any elevator."

"That's right. 15-C," said Millard. "On the tip of my tongue."

The guard gave him a curious look—a look that said, *I'm on to you, Mister*, but he slid the pane shut without comment.

Millard advanced into the courtyard. Judiciously manicured stands of hydrangea and viburnum guarded the brickwork—but the atmosphere was overly lush, almost oppressive, like the interior of a hothouse. Squirrels, gray and black, gamboled raucously on the adjacent lawn, where signs warned pedestrians off the grass. A trio of luxury sedans lazed nearby, two wheels banked indifferently atop the curb. Nothing prevented Millard from darting back through the entryway, past the security booth to freedom—nothing except his own will, somehow warped and corrupted by Carol's proximity. He did not have the mettle—the impudence—to turn back. Rather, he sensed that, all along, his psyche had secretly intended this visit, that each step closer to Carol's lair was a manifestation of what Hal Storch called a "fit of the unconscious." What could he do? Opposite the second set of doors, a solitary mockingbird chirruped from the depths of a rhododendron. He crossed into the air-conditioned vestibule and glided up to floor fifteen.

The door to 15-C stood slightly ajar. He pressed the bell.

"Come in," cried Carol—more command than invitation.

He dared not cross her threshold under false pretenses. He thumbed the bell again.

"It's open! I'll be with you in a minute."

Millard waited what felt like an hour and rang a third time.

"All right, all right," called his ex-wife, her voice laden with pique. "I left the door open for a reason," she said, her words growing closer. "Really, Lysander, I don't—"

And then they were facing each other in the doorway.

How old Carol looked—how old, and yet, still beautiful, her skin stonewashed and her hennaed hair bound in a no-nonsense bun.

"I should phone the police," she said. "This is trespassing by deception."

That sounded like one of those ersatz offenses from television crime dramas.

"There's no such thing."

"Well, there should be."

A new notion unsettled Millard: she might not be alone.

"If you'd like me to go . . ." he offered.

Carol shook her head. "No, you don't need to go," she said.

She stepped out of the doorway, effectively inviting him inside.

Her apartment was spare, almost austere, furnished as though ready to let. A plinth coffee table. A wall-mounted television. Jonquils in a countertop vase. Carol's color scheme ran a narrow gauntlet from ivory to obsidian. She'd insisted on moving out after his infidelity, although he'd offered her the apartment. *From you*, she'd said, *I want nothing.*

"Let me look at you," he said.

She sported a chambray blouse and a knee-length burgundy skirt. While he appraised her—as though admiring a fine work of art—she blushed ever so slightly.

"When you're finished ogling," she said, retreating toward the window, "would you mind telling me to what I owe this honor?"

"I'm having lunch with your son at the Overlook," he said. "I was in the neighborhood. . . ."

"You were in the neighborhood and the urge seized you to barge in on your ex-wife?"

Now Millard felt self-conscious. "I guess you might say that."

She drew open the drapes, bathing the white upholstery in white light.

"Heavens, Millard. Please stop looking at me like that."

"Like what?"

But he knew precisely what she meant.

"Like I'm about to perform a striptease. That's like what," she snapped. "I'm just a woman of a certain age, as they say, and when someone leers at a person at my age, it's not flattering. Quite honestly, it's suspicious."

"I'm sorry. It's just . . . well, I forgot how beautiful you were."

Carol snickered. "You're being ridiculous. . . . I'm just a discarded old lady. You want a cocktail? Now that you're here. . . ."

"Sure. Why not? I'd love a cocktail."

Millard couldn't remember the last time he'd touched anything other than wine. And he would be returning to the hospital later—but it wasn't as though he were a neurosurgeon. What would they do if he had a nip of vermouth on his breath? Give him the heave-ho? Suddenly, he sensed that Carol was staring at him, expectant. "What kind?" she prodded.

He'd nearly forgotten that cocktails came in varieties. Like women.

"Oh. How about a Rob Roy? Or is that too much to ask?"

"I can make you a Manhattan. This isn't a nightclub."

Carol vanished into the efficiency kitchen and returned several moments later with a pair of collins glasses. "A Rob Roy. Seriously?" she mused as she handed him his drink. She settled herself opposite him on the sofa, her legs crossed.

How improbable, it seemed, that in a long-gone age he'd possessed the audacity to propose to this brilliant woman—at once so lovely and so austere. He remembered strolling with her as they examined the mounted butterflies with the exotic names: the chocolate albatross, the tawny rajah, the common Mormon. And right beneath the common Mormon, he'd been seized with the insane notion that he might build a life with this byzantine beauty, only twenty-two years old and already publishing doctoral-level work in array processing—whatever that was. How bold he'd been, and how naïve. Yet he'd certainly gotten what he bargained for. What was that old advertising slogan? "It does exactly what it says on the tin." Well, Carol Sucram had proven as brilliant and austere and implacable on the last day of their marriage as she had on the first. Only after intercourse, as she lay on her back, eyes shut, lips slightly parted in a faint smile, did he ever sense her vulnerability. Usually, like now, her front appeared impregnable.

"Do you really feel old and discarded?" he asked.

"Good God, Millard. What kind of question is that? Are you a fool . . . ?"

"It's just . . . Well, I'd like to think you could forgive me."

Carol rose from the sofa and paced. "Amazing. Just amazing. You still think the universe revolves around your likes and dislikes, don't you?"

"I didn't mean—"

"Of course, you didn't. You never did. But you started this, so

I'm going to finish it." She set her glass down on the cusp of a bookshelf. "Do you remember Howard Logan?"

"Vaguely."

"Widower with a salt-and-pepper beard. His daughter played field hockey with Sally."

"Wait. Tennis, right? He's the guy you played mixed doubles with."

"God, you're a chump sometimes," said Carol. "Howard wasn't my tennis partner. Howard was my lover."

Carol stood with her back toward him, the knobs of her shoulders fluttering with her diaphragm. He couldn't process this information—not now, not with her standing only feet away. It was the sort of revelation he'd want to sleep on, to consider fresh on the morrow—only in this instance, there would be no morrow. She turned toward him again; her faced had hardened, its texture like that of a clam shell.

"I don't understand," said Millard. "But why? If you also wanted out . . ."

"Who ever said I wanted out?" Carol lowered her voice. "I don't resent you for the cheating," she said. "That could be normal—healthy—in a marriage, for all I know. Within certain limits. What I resent you for is the humiliation. For God's sake, Millard, why do you have to do everything in public?"

"I didn't think . . ."

"Everything always had to be dramatic with you. All or none. I'm surprised you don't set yourself on fire in front of an embassy like one of those Buddhist monks. . . ."

Maybe, feared Millard, she had a point. He had a thousand questions to ask: When had her affair started? When had it concluded? How many of his trivial deceptions—a late night at the hospital, a day conference in New Jersey—had actually facilitated his own betrayal? How much guilt had he shouldered for naught? He dared not inquire. An image rose before his eyes of the ouroboros, the serpent devouring his own tail.

"I haven't seen Howard Logan in twenty years. Last I heard he'd moved to Nevada and was involved in commercial real estate," she said. "And they're all yours. All three of them."

That was so quintessentially Carol. Laying out the facts. Going straight for the jugular.

He sipped from his cocktail, fearful of what else his ex-wife might divulge.

"Now that we have that out of the way," she said, "why are you really here?"

One had to credit any woman who could degrade you from a contrite philanderer to a cuckolded dolt over midday cocktails—and then change the subject.

"I'm worried about Lysander," said Millard, grateful for the familiar ground. "He's lost."

Carol laughed. "You're just realizing that? He's been lost for years."

"I guess I wasn't paying enough attention. We won't live forever. . . ."

"Nor will he," replied Carol. "You know Stanley and Livingstone, right? Well, Livingstone didn't consider himself lost, even if Stanley chose to find him."

"So what are you saying? That we give up?"

Millard sensed he was fighting a battle that had long been decided—like a colonial minister advising Mad King George not to let his colonies slip away. If Carol, who fed on a currency of status and credentials, had chalked off Lysander as a capital loss, who was he to insist that the boy might yet rise to his promise? He cupped his fist in his palm.

"Not give up. But maybe we need to lower our expectations," said Carol. "You're the one who wanted to name him after the great Spartan lawgiver. . . ."

"That was Lycurgus," said Millard. "Lysander is named after an admiral."

A smirk flickered across Carol's lips. "Do you always have to be right about everything?"

The reality was that they'd *both* been that way. Stiff-necked; pigheaded. In the era before Internet searches, they'd argued for hours—without respite or irony—over whether the Great Wall of China could be seen by the Apollo astronauts and if the actresses Jean and Maureen Stapleton were sisters. For two straight days, they'd spoken only when essential, divided by the riddle of which hand Australians used to hold their forks while dining. (A phone call to the consulate had ultimately vindicated Carol.) Neither of them had been willing to let anything slide, so life degenerated into constant scorekeeping, an endless quarrel over trivia—often literally—with both of them tabulating mental chit sheets. During their marriage, Carol might even have insisted that Lysander had been a lawgiver. How frivolous it all seemed at a distance of thirty years. . . .

"I'm sorry," apologized Millard. He glanced at his watch. Nearly noon. "I should go."

She retrieved the glass from his hand. "I'm glad you stopped by," she said. "Truly I am. I'd like to do this again . . . if you would. Maybe have lunch?"

"Sure," agreed Millard. "I'd like that too."

"How about tomorrow? Japanese?"

That was when he sensed that she might seek more than an armistice. He had mentioned nothing of Delilah—so how could she know? After all, he had spent forty-five minutes leering at her as though she were the reincarnation of Betty Grable.

"Call me tomorrow," he said. "Okay?"

"Very well. I'll ring you up at ten," said Carol, pleased. To his surprise, she added, "I already have the number."

"I'm so glad I had a chance to see you," said Millard. "Really, I am."

Yet as the elevator descended into the blistering heat of the courtyard, he wasn't even sure that this was true.

7

L ysander showed up at the restaurant with his dogs.

As Millard entered the majestic lobby, its walls lined with Tiffany mosaics and ringed with ornate Gothic friezes, he heard the commotion before he saw it—and immediately he recognized that, one way or another, his younger son would be at the center of the uproar. This didn't especially surprise him. He was accustomed to Lysander's role in spawning mayhem, however unwittingly: bringing a crippled raccoon that he found in a drainage ditch, and that later proved rabid, to his brother's engagement party; stopping his rental car at an intersection to help an elderly woman change a tire, but forgetting to engage his parking brake. Yet if this latest trouble wasn't unexpected, it was nonetheless disappointing. Millard had been looking forward to a quiet tête-à-tête over squab pie and Westphalian ham. He recalled the rare occasions when his own father had invited him to the Overlook—once, before the birth of Arnold, for a homily on parenting, and on another occasion to discuss revisions to his will—and he regretted already the lost comfort of the oak-backed chairs and the reassuring strains of the full-time harpist. Yet one glimpse of Lysander—lumbering, prematurely stoop-shouldered, a horseshoe barbell glinting from his septum like a medieval torture device, and his chin-length hair already sprinkled with frost, as though he'd forgotten to shake out the snow—told Millard they would have little choice but to dine elsewhere, that the Overlook was no place for an overgrown teenager.

Lysander stood beneath the rotunda, at the base of the marble stairs, remonstrating with a tungsten-faced bellman. Or, rather, the bellman appeared to be doing the remonstrating while Millard's son listened, slack-jawed, his collie mutts yapping playfully at his knees. An elderly porter in livery stood behind the bellman, arms akimbo, further barring Lysander's path.

Onion and Puddle, thought Millard. Those were the names of the dogs. Leave it to his boy to find the least canine names in the history of cynology.

"It's all right, Edgar," called Millard—glad that he recollected the bellman's name, and that he'd tipped him generously at his last visit. "That's my son. Lysander."

Edgar's eyebrows raised slightly, his only concession to surprise. "Good afternoon, Dr. Salter," he said. "I did not realize the gentleman was your guest."

"It's hard to fathom, isn't it?" said Millard.

Lysander did not appear offended. Nor did he look the slightest bit fazed by the chaos he'd engendered; quite the contrary, he seemed amused. *Don't you realize this is the last time we will see each other?* Millard thought. *That you're spoiling our final lunch?* The poor boy had no inkling, obviously. He assumed they'd continue lunching forever. Hadn't Millard taken his own father for granted in the same way?

"I was explaining to the gentleman that with the exception of service dogs, we do not permit animals in the dining room," said the bellman. He had a crescent scar across one cheek, as though he'd shaved drunk with a cutlass. "I am afraid that exceptions cannot be made."

"I totally get it," interjected Lysander. "But since we're already here, I was hoping you—or someone else—could look after them for an hour or so. While we eat." He turned to Millard and asked, "We won't be more than an hour, will we?"

"That's simply not possible, sir," said Edgar.

"It would be a huge favor," Lysander persisted. "They're extremely well-behaved. . . ."

Rarely, reflected Millard, have two men stood in such contrast: Lysander in slack, ragged cargo shorts that made one think—mistakenly—that he'd lost considerable weight, and the caparisoned bellman who spoke with an affected lockjaw reminiscent of William F. Buckley or George Plimpton. "Forgive me, sir," said Edgar, addressing Millard. "But my responsibilities here are not consistent with tending to house pets." His tone hinted at grave professional duties, like protecting the president from assassination or maintaining the eternal flame of Vesta.

"Of course they're not," Millard apologized. "I'm sorry about this. We'll be lunching elsewhere today, I'm afraid—but let me give you something for your troubles."

He fished a crisp fifty from his billfold and tucked it into Edgar's palm over the bellman's half-hearted protestations. "And something for you as well," said Millard, slipping another bill into the hand of the red-capped porter. A man with two million dollars in the bank and eight hours to live can afford to be magnanimous. "Now if you'll excuse us. . . ."

Lysander led the dogs into the street and Millard followed. The heat hit them like a wrecking ball as they departed the vigilantly controlled atmosphere of the lobby.

"Glad we're not eating *there*," said Lysander, scratching his groin. He'd sweated through the underarms of his T-shirt and a comic book protruded from his shorts pocket. "I don't mean to sound judgmental, but that dude had a stick up his ass." He squatted down and rubbed the tousled heads of the collies. "Isn't that right, Onion? Good girl. Aren't we glad we're not eating in that stuffy old prison?"

"He was just doing his job," said Millard. He didn't want to bicker—not today. "Anyway, I'm very glad to see you. I feel like it has been ages."

Lysander shrugged.

"I didn't realize you were bringing the dogs," said Millard. "Foolish of me. Let's find an outdoor café and have some lunch." He scanned the block: a stationery shop, a supplement retailer hawking vitamins and quackery, a half-constructed Columbia University dorm—nothing remotely resembling a bistro with sidewalk seating. "Do you know a good place around here? Or should we wander until we find something?"

Lysander shrugged again. "Can we walk in the park for a bit? Puddle is getting restless."

"Isn't it rather hot for a walk?"

"Only because you're dressed like an Eskimo."

Millard had good reasons for his sweater and slacks—not just formality, but the brutal air-conditioning system that cooled his basement office like a butcher's locker. Yet he strenuously wished to avoid an argument—at least, an extraneous one—so they strolled into the park, descending the steps that separated the upscale heights from the miasma of Harlem below.

This was not, to paraphrase the expression, his father's Morningside Park anymore. When Millard had visited his brother at business school in the 1950s, a sign had warned Columbia students: *It is not safe to enter at any time of the day or night*. Even in the 1980s, when he'd visited colleges with Arnold, the narrow, tortuous lanes of greenery had been a magnet for crack dealers and unemployed young men wielding tire irons. Three decades later, following the steep path along the lichen-clad retaining wall, they encountered only a West Indian nanny chaperoning three young children and a group of Scandinavian tourists. One of the dogs scooped up a discarded chicken bone, prompting a stern rebuke from his master. You had to give Lysander credit: He cared for those mutts as though they were royalty. *If only the boy could muster such passion for something more productive.*

"Well?" asked Millard. "How are things going?"

"The same," said Lysander.

"Something must be different. What do you do with your time?"

They crossed under an arbor and onto a sloping lawn. On the other side of a stubby hedge, men in their sixties and seventies played league bocce.

"What does *anyone* do with his time?" asked Lysander.

Sometimes Millard wondered if this gumminess wasn't the norm for father-son conversations, if his own ease with his father hadn't been the exception. Or maybe Lysander was more forthcoming with others—that it was his own fault that he couldn't draw anything from the boy beyond a few terse syllables.

"I haven't seen you in a month. *Something* must be new."

"I did come up with a great idea for an invention," said Lysander.

"That's *something*," said Millard, fishing. "We'll make another Edison of you yet."

Lysander didn't acknowledge his prediction.

"My idea is for a car that can't speed. You place sensors on the headlights that read traffic signs and then reduce the fuel delivered to the engine accordingly."

Not an earth-shattering idea, thought Millard—but not hopeless. Hadn't some 3M clerk banked millions of dollars off Post-it Notes? In any case, it was far better than Lysander's last attempt at innovation: a self-opening umbrella for dogs.

"That sounds promising," he said. "What will you do with it?"

"Nothing," said Lysander. "It's just an idea. . . ."

Arnold would already have secured the patent and drawn up a blueprint for monetizing this proposal. Maia might have developed a working model. But Lysander, not surprisingly, was perfectly satisfied to let the notion float to the heavens like stardust. Millard swallowed the urge to prod him—that was a different battle for another day. Although, now, there would not be another day. More important, at the moment, was engaging the boy in a broader discussion of his future. Yet how to do this left Millard at a loss.

In hindsight, he sensed something had been off in his relationship with his younger son since the boy's earliest years. How else to explain the smog that enveloped his memories of Lysander's upbringing—so different from the concrete moments of discovery and joy that his other children vividly evoked. With Arnold, he'd brushed up his knowledge of philately and numismatics: Jenny Inverts, buffalo nickels, mercury dimes. They'd driven five hours one Sunday to the Smithsonian, and another five hours back, to glimpse a special display of a rare Swedish stamp called the "Treskilling" Yellow. Maia had wanted to know the differences between "New World fruit" and "Old World fruit," between African and South American monkeys, between stalactites and stalagmites. She'd grappled with beastly llamas and priestly lamas, tocsins that warned and toxins that afforded no warning. He'd mapped the three parts of Gaul for her on a paper napkin in an Indian restaurant, revealed the cycle of clocks springing forward and falling back with the seasons, recited irregular plurals at her bedside while she recovered from a bout of pneumonia. *Why aides-de-camp and coups d'état*, she'd asked at age nine, *but tête-à-têtes?* He had no idea. And Sally, whose intelligence ran more visual than verbal, had been able to sketch the inaugural gowns of every First Lady by her twelfth birthday. But Lysander? Millard had a vague memory of the boy catching a water snake in a net, another of his training a pet chinchilla to rear on its hind legs for food. What could one say to a boy whose greatest feat, in forty-three years, had been teaching a crepuscular rodent to stick out his ass?

They exited the park at 110th Street and meandered into Harlem, pausing periodically for the dogs to paw at a tree root or sniff a passing mongrel. Construction workers on lunch break, greased, shirtless, lounged against a timber parapet. Taxis crawled toward a service station, honking their hunger and frustration. To their southeast, the glass façade of the Hapsworth Annex loomed with futuristic macho, reflecting clouds. From his penthouse office suite, St. Dymphna's president, Harvey Bloodfinch, a former navy sharpshooter turned healthcare economist, could likely have spotted them with his binoculars—or put a bullet between Millard's eyes. But to Harvey Bloodfinch, clinicians like Millard were slightly less significant than barnacles. He'd demonstrated this countless times, turning down requests for expanded retirement options, and enhanced security on locked wards, and staff discounts for overnight parking. Millard's death, if Bloodfinch even noted the event, would merely mean inconvenience: an irksome moment for the hospital's optics, maybe a sympathetic email dispatched to the psychiatry faculty. How different from Millard's first day on service, in 1968, when the hospital's chief medical officer, a chain-smoking Brahmin, had invited him to lunch.

They drifted along the northern border of the park, weaving their way through bicycle traffic. Lysander paused near the Warriors' Gate to let the dogs relieve themselves. Millard couldn't find the right words to broach the subject of the boy's future, so they rambled in silence, past the women's detention center and the gargantuan statue of Duke Ellington. He found himself missing Delilah—wondering if he shouldn't have spent these evaporating hours with her instead. She'd be dictating her final letters now, verbal missives packed with wry humor and disarming sincerity and snippets of Alexander Pope. (She'd probably have arranged to send him one too, he realized, not knowing that he wouldn't be present to receive it.) Or maybe she'd turned on the record player with the voice-activated remote, as she'd done the previous afternoon when he'd surprised her, to hear von Karajan conduct *The Merry Widow*. How different it was to sit in silence with Delilah, where nothing needed to be verbalized, than to walk in silence alongside his layabout son, when so much still had to be said. He wondered what the boy was thinking. Was the boy thinking anything at all? Maybe the inside of his son's brain looked no different from the floor of his apartment, strewn with tooth-pocked dog toys and wrappers from vegan cheeseburgers. The hush between them didn't seem to faze the young man at all.

On the corner of 103rd Street—they had approached within a few blocks of the hospital—a homeless derelict wearing a leg brace called out to them for coins. He had a youthful face and crystalline gray eyes, giving him a gaminesque appeal that might prove charming, or evidence of criminal intent. He looked vaguely familiar to Millard—but after years covering the psychiatric emergency room on intermittent weekends, most undomiciled young men acquired an aura of familiarity.

"Yo, brother," he called out, from his perch on the sidewalk. "Help a vet in need."

Millard wished to keep walking, but his son paused—almost as a reflex—and fished a five-dollar bill from his pocket. "Here you go," he said.

The gesture infuriated Millard. Not that he had any particular objection to aiding the downtrodden—although he believed systematic assistance, such as a donation to City Harvest or a local soup kitchen, to be far more sensible. Even if this fellow weren't a veteran, a claim which he sincerely doubted—even if the man planned to exchange the bill for crack or crystal meth or PCP—that was forgivable in Millard's book. He'd long ago gotten past the need to blame desperate souls for their addictions or their petty deceits. If well-intentioned but clueless medical students wanted to yield their hard-earned pocket change to panhandlers, why did he care? But in this case, none of Lysander's pocket change was hard-earned. Not by Lysander, at least. Every dime the boy spent came directly out of Millard's wallet, out of the inheritances of his siblings. And the notion of his son giving away money that wasn't truly his—at least, not in the sense of earned income, of blood, sweat, and tears—defied Millard's most fundamental sense of justice. The only real difference between Lysander and the recipient of his largesse was that Lysander had a well-off father. Millard's anger mounted as he watched the homeless guy slide the bill into the pocket of his camouflage pants.

"It's good to meet a fellow vet," he volunteered. "What branch did you serve in?"

"Marines," the man replied. "Afghanistan and Iraq."

"I was in the navy," said Millard. "Korea."

None of this was true, of course. Millard had been thirteen years old, resisting his bar mitzvah lessons, when the armistice was signed at Panmunjom. Later, a bone spur in his heel and a friend of his uncle's on the draft board had kept him far from Vietnam. "Just out of curiosity," he asked the vet, "what's your E-grade?"

E-grades, and O-grades for officers, were the universal ranks that transcended branches of the service for matters of ceremony and pay—so that no confusion existed between the precedence of an army captain (O-3) and a naval captain (O-6). Every enlisted man knew his E-grade. Hal Storch, who had flailed for two years in the merchant marine before med school, had educated Millard on the nuances of the E-and-O hierarchy. He found these ranks proved invaluable in establishing that someone had *not* served his or her country.

The vet looked up, puzzled. "I got an honorable discharge, if that's what you mean."

"I'm sure you did," said Millard.

He turned quickly and tramped away. Taking out his frustration on the bogus vet had distracted him momentarily, but hadn't placated him.

"Jesus. What was that about?" asked Lysander. "I didn't know you were in the navy."

Millard took a deep breath and chose his words carefully. He sensed they'd reached the brink of the wrong fight. Instead of saying, *That's five dollars that could be spent on your nieces' college fund*, he merely replied, untruthfully, "I was probing him. If he'd been a real veteran, I'd have given something too."

He looked at his watch. Approaching twelve thirty. Roughly one-sixteenth of his remaining hours wasted on this fruitless trek across Manhattan. "We should be able to find a restaurant along Madison," he announced, cutting down a side street. "There's a new pan-Asian place on Ninety-Fourth, if you're up for it. . . ."

Lysander assented with his feet and, soon enough, they had commandeered an outdoor table at Bamboo Landing. Not surprisingly, with the mercury well over ninety, they were the *only* customers seated along the sidewalk. Inside, the place teemed with the retinue of tertiary care centers: conclaves of patients' relatives, rumple-coated post-docs, residents wolfing in packs. Patrons eyed them warily through the green-tinted glass—as one might a disturbed stranger on an aircraft or an elevator. Who dined outdoors in such heat? They'd be fortunate if they didn't collapse of dehydration or sunstroke. Although the menu covered a vast swath of Eastern geography from Thailand to Japan, the waitstaff was overwhelmingly female, blond, and well-endowed in the bust. Their server, who sported blue liner over brown eyes and a visible panty-line under her skirt, appeared less than thrilled with their choice of seating. She handed them their menus as though distributing live grenades.

"Miss, can I have a bowl of water?" asked Lysander.

"Just water?"

"For the dogs."

Puddle and Onion loafed on the pavement, panting; Lysander had hooked the leashes over the edge of the makeshift metal rail.

"Health department won't let us do that," said the waitress. "You can buy a disposable bowl across the street at the Superette. I'll be glad to fill it with water for you."

Millard detected a hint of satisfaction, even spite, in the girl's words. *If you're going to make me schlep you food outside in this unbearable weather*, she seemed to be saying, *then no dog bowls for you.*

"If you'll excuse me a second," said Lysander, rising.

"Can you wait until we order?" asked Millard. "I only have a little while. . . ."

Lysander glanced at the dogs and slid back into his chair. Millard feared he'd sounded testy, as though he viewed his time with his son as lacking value. "I hear the noodles are excellent," he said, striving to take the edge off his previous remark.

"They're probably boiled in chicken broth," said Lysander. "I may just order a Coke."

So get your lousy Coke, thought Millard. *Why does everything with you have to be so goddamn difficult?* He wanted to say "Your brother would eat a used Jeep if it were the only item on the menu," but he held his pique and surveyed the specials. He felt an obligation to choose wisely, this final meal, like a death row inmate or an early Christian martyr. Most probably, he'd have a snack at Delilah's that evening, maybe a can of soup or half a grapefruit, but he didn't want to kill himself on a full stomach. So he splurged now: Singapore rice noodles, Thai-style lamb curry, sweet-and-sour breast of duck. From the Japanese fare he added a platter of sashimi, a side of pumpkin tempura, and taro potato stew. "I'll take home the extra," he assured the waitress. "For lunch tomorrow." Lysander ordered a cup of brown rice to accompany his soda.

Once they found themselves alone again, Millard wanted to broach the subject of Lysander's future before the boy wandered off to purchase his disposable bowl. He felt sorry for the thirsty dogs, but a man had to have priorities. How could one weigh a brief moment of canine discomfort against his son's prospects for long-term stability? He rested his cheeks on his palms, searching for the right mode of entry, and looked up only when he sensed the buxom torso of the waitress shielding his face, however ephemerally, from the sun. Instead, he discovered that the shadow over their table belonged to Elsa Duransky.

"Elsa," he exclaimed. "Twice in one day."

She'd stopped on the sidewalk, opposite the railing. His neighbor had her husband in tow: Millard's colleague hunched over an orthopedic walker—the sort that used tennis balls for slider feet. Eyebrows as thick as kudzu sprouted above his bulbous nose; his hearing aids hummed to their own tune, possibly "Chattanooga Choo Choo." Millard rose long enough to shake the endocrinologist's hand. Saul's blink lacked recognition. It was hard to imagine that this man's laboratory had once transformed

the field of hormone synthesis or that he'd treated the likes of
Nelson Rockefeller and Adlai Stevenson.

Elsa picked lint off Millard's shoulder. "Did you hear there's
a lynx on the loose?"

"I hadn't heard," he said.

"Well, there is. I'm surprised you don't know. There are flyers everywhere."

"I'm not very observant."

"You'll have to be—with a lynx on the loose," said Elsa. "Anyway, when I told Saul, he thought I'd said a baby *minx*, not a
lynx. Didn't you, dear?"

Saul rested his forearms on the walker. "What's that?"

"I was telling Millard what you said about the lynx," said
Elsa, in a half-shout that carried like a foghorn. "Tell them what
you said."

"Really, doll. I don't think they're interested."

Elsa turned back to their table. "What he said was, 'I already
have the only little minx I need right here.' Isn't that just darling?"

Lysander cleared his throat. "I should go buy that bowl."

"It's so good to see you again," said Elsa, directing her re-
marks toward Millard's son. "And your dogs are just adorable."

She stooped forward and ran her manicured fingers through
Puddle's nape.

"They're getting thirsty," said Lysander. "I should get them
some water."

Elsa nuzzled the other dog. She lowered her voice to a braying whisper and asked, "Which one is Hitler?"

Lysander flashed a look that hovered between surprise and
self-doubt. "What?"

"Which one is Hitler?" Elsa asked again, her voice louder.
"And which is Mussolini?"

Millard sensed he ought to intervene. But what could he possibly say?

"This is some kind of joke, isn't it?" said Lysander.

"It's *irony*," interjected Millard. "I thought your generation was into irony. If gays can say queer, and blacks call each other nigger, what's wrong with Jews naming their dogs after fascists?"

Saul, who'd appeared to have absorbed only one or two choice words, looked bewildered—as though mistrusting his own ears. Millard relished this dash of irreverence. Let the associate dean stuff that in his tobacco-free pipe.

Lysander made an effort to puzzle out the matter. "Okay," he agreed. "I can play along."

Elsa paid them no heed. "This one here looks a bit more German, don't you, Little Adolf?"

"His grandfather was a German shepherd at a POW camp," replied Lysander, grinning—and, for an instant, Millard could see himself in the boy. "Pure Aryan blood."

Saul's eyes drifted from Lysander to the collies to his wife. "What's going on?" he asked.

"Lysander was telling me about his dogs," said Elsa, bellowing into her husband's ear. "One of them is named Hitler and the other is named Mussolini. It's *ironic*."

"I don't think I heard you, doll. It sounded like you said Mussolini."

"Hitler," repeated Elsa, loud enough to alarm passersby, "and Mussolini."

The waitress arrived at that moment with Lysander's drink and the first of Millard's entrées. "Will your friends be joining us?" she asked.

"Oh, no. We must be on our way," said Elsa. "Good to see you again, Millard. Lysander. Too-da-loo." She waved farewell with her fingertips, while wrapping her other hand around her husband's elbow. A moment later, Millard found himself alone with his son.

"Now I'm really going to go," said Lysander.

"Hold on a second," objected Millard. "I have something I want to discuss. . . ."

"Please, Dad. I'll be back before you know it."

Millard tore a page out of Elsa's book and plunged forward. "I was talking to your mother this morning," he said.

"Okay."

"Doesn't that surprise you?"

Lysander remained impassive. "Not really."

"It should. Your mother and I haven't spoken in twenty-seven years."

The boy's attention drifted to the dogs, then across the street toward the Superette.

"I'm glad you're speaking again," he said. "If you two both are, that is. . . ."

Millard could have put his fist through the tabletop. He finally understood the frustration that had prompted Khrushchev's shoe-pounding tantrum at the United Nations. "We were speaking about *you*. About your future. What do you have to say to that?"

"Not much. I guess it depends what you said."

Lysander glanced at the restaurant doors, then held his water glass over the side of the railing and let Onion lap at the contents. Next he seized Millard's glass, without asking, and dribbled the contents onto Puddle's tongue. "That should tide them over," he said. A trio of female medical students watched through the plate glass; one of them was Lauren Pastarnack. Millard elected to let the episode pass.

"I want to speak to you openly, father to son," he said. "Your mother and I aren't going to live forever, and quite frankly, we're afraid that you're off-track. . . ."

In college, his son had owned a T-shirt that read *Not all those who wander are lost.* When your son was a sophomore at Wesleyan, a slogan like that was clever.

The waitress arrived with the second and third of Millard's entrées. Also a cup of brown rice. Lysander requested another glass of water. "Let me try it a different way," said Millard. "What do you plan to do with the rest of your life?"

That was the million-dollar question, wasn't it? Everything else was secondary—water under the bridge, so to speak. Even at this age, if the boy made good, all of his past blunders would be forgiven. Nobody described Harry S. Truman as a former second-rate haberdasher, did they? With a few years of effort, the boy could yet find himself in the same place as Lauren Pastarnack.

"*Candidly*, Dad," replied Lysander. "I haven't decided yet."

So there they stood: at an impasse. Even at this late juncture, he could cut the boy off, of course, write him out of his will—but that would just increase his son's disappointment, not his productivity. Besides, withholding his inheritance from the boy would serve no practical purpose, because Carol could be counted upon to make up a good portion of the difference. She expected less of Lysander, so she avoided Millard's aggravation. It was enough, as the saying went, to make you want to kill yourself.

"Am I allowed to leave yet?" asked Lysander.

"In a minute," said Millard—but he wasn't sure how to proceed.

A blustery greeting sliced through his thoughts like a handsaw. Denny Dennmeyer. The deputy finance director carried a stack of manila envelopes under one arm.

"Just dashing across the street to mail a few items, Dr. Salter," he said—as though his every moment outside the hospital had to be accounted for. "Why wait for the clerk to send them out tomorrow when I can drop them off today?"

"Sure. Why wait?" agreed Millard.

He considered introducing his son to the junior administrator, but didn't.

"How's that report coming, Dr. Salter? Any progress . . ."

"You have my word." *And it's the only damn word you'll ever get out of me*, he mused. "As long as I'm still breathing tomorrow morning, it will be on your desk. . . ."

"Good enough for me," said Dennmeyer. "We're counting on you, Dr. Salter. There's this widely held belief that the future is unpredictable, but this is only true to a very limited degree. Much of the future is *highly* predictable. Let's say I walk across the street to mail these envelopes. I know the post office will be where it was yesterday, that the government will accept my currency, that the mail carrier will make an effort to deliver my letters. All predictable. But in order to anticipate the future, what is required is data regarding the present. . . . And so far, in your division, I'm afraid that such data has been sorely lacking."

"I swear you'll have it," replied Millard. "On my life."

"Oh, no need to swear. I have full faith you'll do your duty." Dennmeyer chuckled at an unvoiced joke. His bolo tie glistened a blinding turquoise. "Everyone gets their report in *eventually*. The system guarantees that. Sometimes, it just takes an added push."

"You have a lot of confidence in your system," observed Millard.

"All of it well-founded, Dr. Salter," he said. "Enjoy your lunch."

The financial officer ducked into the street, jaywalking. Lysander pushed his empty rice bowl toward the center of the table. "Say, do you smell something?"

Millard sniffed. It was hard to tell.

He glanced across the avenue, to where Dennmeyer was about to enter the post office, when a gust of sizzling air tore over the asphalt, followed by the clatter of pelting debris. Pedestrians dove for cover behind mesh garbage cans, gutted phone booths. A pregnant nurse, whom Millard recognized from the TBI unit, took cover behind their table. Denny Dennmeyer staggered toward them from the remnants of the post office, an ugly laceration slashed across his forehead. On the avenue, a box truck had toppled upon its side, crushing a bicycle rack. Screams rose like flames from the disintegrated storefront of the Superette.

Shock waves from the explosion had shattered the window beside Lauren Pastarnack and sent Millard's duck breast soaring into its dangling shards. Millard checked to make certain his own body remained in some degree of working order, then looked up to find his son, seated calmly, hands toying with his napkin ring. The dogs, equally unfazed, lounged like seals on a beach.

"I knew I smelled something," said Lysander.

PART 2

MIDDAY TO NIGHTFALL

8

Miss Nickelsworth studied Millard through her pince-nez, simultaneously sympathetic and displeased, as though he were a songbird dragged in by her cat.

Millard's secretary—technically his "executive associate"— had claimed various titles from "senior clerk" to "administrative director" in the offices of six department chairmen, including the ill-fated Norm Schumaker and Clyde Terwilliger, during her first thirty years at St. Dymphna's, until joyless David Atkinson had traded her in for a gloomy young Welshman who typed one hundred ten words per minute. During those three decades, she'd defended the corner office on the twelfth floor of the Hapsworth Annex like a Praetorian guard shielding her emperor, but her reward had been a perch deep in the entrails of the "Old Hospital," where the consultation psychiatry division shared a suite with the department of medical records and the deaf-mute Korean who processed death certificates. She arrived at her desk every winter morning in the same oatmeal-hued duster coat with the faux fur collar that she'd worn on her first day at St. Dymphna's, when Dwight Eisenhower was concluding his final weeks in the Oval Office, at a time when a hospital-wide ban on frontal lobotomies for intractable cases remained three years away, and the site of the Luxdorfer Pavilion, then opposite the main hospital complex, had housed a live poultry market frequented by Jewish refugees from Eastern Europe. Her bubble-cut coiffure remained unchanged as well, although her natural auburn locks had turned a synthetic henna. Above her left breast she displayed one of five brooches, among these a tin parrot and a rhinestone octopus, which she rotated systematically in tune with the days of the week.

"Your daughter Maia phoned," said Miss Nickelsworth. "Consider yourself reminded that you're meeting her at seven thirty at Grand Central. Under the clock."

That was news to Millard. Highly unwelcome news. "Tonight? Are you sure?"

"I'm just the messenger," said Miss Nickelsworth.

Millard retained absolutely no memory of making plans with his daughter. Could he really have agreed to such an appointment? On this of all days? Clearly, *she'd* mangled the dates *on her end*, although that was so out of character for his youngest, who'd coordinated a schedule of sixty-two credits—allegedly a university record—during her junior year at Yale. More likely, he reconsidered, this was self-sabotage. He could hear Hal Storch ascribing this flub to his subconscious, a sign of a latent "life instinct" wrangling with his manifest desire to die. Storch relished tales of patients undermined by such psychodynamic snares: the adulterous husband who billed his mistress's abortion to a joint credit card; a band of armed robbers who realized, too late, that they'd planned their heist for a bank holiday. To Millard, all of this psychobabble was utter bunkum: No purported field of science other than Freudian analysis operated without the benefit of systematic study and double-blind testing. For years, he'd shared a good-natured disagreement with his friend regarding the merits of exploring the unconscious, taking jabs at Storch's relentless interpretation of dreams and parapraxes, while Storch derided headshrinkers who downplayed talk therapy as shills for the pharmaceutical industry. But how could he explain an en-

gagement with Maia of which he possessed absolutely no recollection? Hal Storch, undoubtedly, would have laughed like a
madman until he choked on his cigar.

"Also, there's a woman in your office," said Miss Nickelsworth, eyes narrowing like an opium fiend's. "Not a patient. Says
she's an old friend of yours." Her look exclaimed, at two hundred
decibels: *You naughty old codger, you!* An instant passed in which
Millard imagined that Delilah had achieved a miraculous recovery and had come to surprise him with the good news—but he
understood this was just wishful fantasy. "I couldn't let her wait
out here in the corridor with them painting like that. All that
lead would be the death of her."

Millard inhaled through his nose, but his nostrils detected
nothing beyond the usual St. Dymphna's must. Miss Nickelsworth, who was only four years older than Millard, still dwelt in
a universe where paint contained toxic minerals, and soda cans
were manufactured with tin, and the mercury harvested from
thermometers made safe, entertaining toys for children. She was
his chronological contemporary, but psychologically belonged to
his aunts' generation: In fact, after they'd passed away, Millard
had discovered a hoard of lead-based Dutch Boy paint in his
aunts' cupboard, alongside a leather case of stale, cork-tipped
cigarettes and a Royal Dansk cookie tin filled with the complimentary playing cards from defunct airlines.

"But you're immune, Miss N.?" asked Millard.

"I'm paid to take risks," replied Miss Nickelsworth—without
a trace of irony. "You'll forgive me for saying this, but you look
like you've survived the Dust Bowl."

"It's nothing. Only a minor explosion on Ninety-Fourth
Street. . . ."

He'd attempted to spruce himself up in the washroom, but
some damage couldn't be remedied: an ember-sized hole had per-

forated his sweater and the left shoulder of his jacket wore a badge of soot like an epaulet. Not that it mattered: Soon all of his clothing, and even what little remained of Isabelle's, would belong to indigent strangers. At least the wounds had been confined to his attire. Denny Dennmeyer had required nine stitches above his eyebrow. Two people, a Superette manager and a second-story tenant, reportedly died at the scene. Lysander and his dogs had emerged entirely unscathed.

"You should really be more careful," urged Miss Nickelsworth.

"Don't worry," he said. "I'm paid to have an immunity."

He left Miss Nickelsworth to her anxieties and steeled himself for whatever unwelcome surprise awaited him inside his office. Yet the woman seated opposite his desk, casually perusing the personal calendar atop his desk blotter, appeared relatively harmless: a soft-curved creature on borrowed time with features like lumpen clay. She sported cat-eye sunglasses, a gauze kerchief, and a drab checkered wrap that recalled Greta Garbo in decline. At first, Millard took her for a patient, or a patient's relative, but when she looked up, there was no mistaking her static right eye and saddle nose: Virginia Margold! He hadn't seen her since his fortieth Hager Heights reunion, although she called religiously on his birthday—like a mechanical toy gone berserk.

"Salty Salter!" she cried. "As I live and breathe. You don't mind my dropping in like this. I was in the neighborhood . . . and I realized it was your big day . . . so I figured, why not . . . ?" It took him a moment to realize that she'd meant his *birth*day, not the opposite.

"Well, actually—"

"I can only stay a few minutes," said Margold, holding up a palm to silence him. "You heard the news, I'm sure. Whit Kendall passed on. . . ."

Millard had a vague recollection of Whit Kendall as someone very unlike himself—the sort of overconfident fellow who rode crew at Princeton and swiveled in a partner's chair at a white-shoe law firm. But maybe he was merely holding Whit's uber-WASP name against him.

"I'm in town for the funeral," she continued. "Or I was in Connecticut, rather, but from Spokane it's practically the same. . . ."

"So you came all the way down from Connecticut?" asked Millard.

"Not far. Darien. Less than an hour by train."

Millard glanced at the clock on the bookshelf behind his guest. Already 1:15. He had to phone Maia to cancel their supposed plans before she went out for the afternoon.

"You've caught me at an awkward moment," he ventured.

"Don't worry. I can't stay long," repeated Margold, who looked as settled as an encampment of squatters. "But I do have a few things I want to show you. You don't mind, do you? It's not every day I get to reminisce with Salty Salter."

She reached into a paper shopping bag, the sort that usually contained groceries or a pipe bomb, and produced a shoebox. Across the top, in blue marker on masking tape, was lettered: M. SALTER. Millard wondered if his classmate possessed a similar receptacle for each of their Hager Heights comrades, a cohort that must have once numbered close to three hundred. Even thinned out by heart disease, and cancer, and a newsworthy murder-suicide in the 1980s, the survivors likely still merited a good two hundred such containers. Poor Virginia and her mementos. She'd married late, probably to the first male who actually took her seriously as a woman. A nearsighted Moroccan archaeologist, affable if not talkative. Millard had shared an hors d'oeuvre table with the leather-skinned chap at a reunion. As surprised as he'd been to learn that Virginia had married at fifty, he'd been even more shocked to hear that the husband had left her, a decade later, to shack up with an Andean tribeswoman he'd met on a dig. "It makes sense," Isabelle had observed. "At least, *she* won't drag him to any high school reunions." Later, after lovemaking, she teased, "Maybe that's what you need next, Mil. An Inca." But as much as he and Isabelle had once mocked Virginia Margold and her ubiquitous scrapbooks, he now felt genuinely sorry for her.

"Take a look at this, Salty," said Margold. "September 12, 1954."

She'd spread out a handful of photocopied articles from the *Hager Herald* on his blotter. One quoted a fourteen-year-old Millard, who'd just moved to suburban Westchester County from the Bronx, on starting at a new school; another catalogued his victories in an eleventh-grade Latin competition. "And here's a piece you wrote for the school paper: 'Millard Salter Reviews *In the Court of Public Opinion* by Alger Hiss.'" Alger Hiss! Now there was another name to run past Lauren Pastarnack. How passionately, in his review, Millard had pleaded for the official's innocence. Alas, history had cast a far harsher light on the folk heroes of his liberal Jewish childhood—not just Hiss, but Harry Dexter White and Julius Rosenberg, who really had passed secrets to the Soviets. Now even the Soviets were gone.

"It's amazing what you can find on the Internet, isn't it?" observed Margold.

"I suppose," said Millard. "If you're looking."

"Oh, I'm *always* looking," chirped Margold. "I was talking with Whit's widow—the *third* Mrs. Kendall—I'm not sure you've met her—and she was telling me how she went online and found clippings in the *Daily Pennsylvanian* archive from Whit's old shell races."

"Close," muttered Millard. "So close."

"What's that?"

"Nothing. I was just thinking how close we all used to be. You and me and Whit . . ."

A bit of dissembling never killed anyone. In his mind's eye, he had no trouble imagining himself and Margold and Whit Kendall sauntering arm in arm through the hushed streets of Hager Heights, or taking a sunfish out on Long Island Sound, or even skinny-dipping illicitly after hours at the municipal swimming pool. None of this had happened, of course. But Whit was dead, and he'd soon be dead, and then Margold could spin any yarns she wished with absolute impunity. So why not speed her fantasies along if that made her happy? History did not necessarily belong to the winners; it belonged to the last witness off life support.

Margold sighed. "Do you remember that time I came to your house?"

Was this woman serious? These days, he hardly remembered where he'd left his bifocals. Last year, he'd mistakenly given the Armenian doorman two checks for Christmas. How was he supposed to recall a trivial event that might—*or might not*—have occurred while he was a teenager?

"It's been a long time," he said.

"Not *so* long," rejoined Margold. "But I do have a memory for these things. It must have been our junior year, because I was going door-to-door, raising funds for the marching band. For our annual spring trip to the national competition—that year was Saratoga Springs, I think. . . . Or maybe Nantucket. And I remember it must have been late October, or November, because you and your dad were on your way to the garage to have the snow tires mounted on his DeSoto."

Millard wasn't sure whether to pity his classmate or to envy her. She seemed genuinely content living on the fumes of an unpopular adolescence. He'd entirely forgotten his family's DeSoto, or even the days before all-weather tires. Everything was "year-round" now: patio furniture, electoral campaigns, windows. He recalled—with some fondness—the annual autumn ritual of installing the storm windows in the upstairs bedrooms at his parents' place. And digging up tulip bulbs each October, for storage under mulch in the basement, before Burpee began stocking varieties that could endure a New York winter. To Lauren Pastarnack's generation, mounting storm windows or winterizing tulips was as alien as shoveling coal—which his aunts had actually done by hand, well into the 1960s, before they finally splurged on a boiler.

"It was a Firedome, right?" added Margold. "A hard-top sedan with turquoise trim."

Unbelievable, thought Millard. *Just unbelievable.*

"You looked so handsome that afternoon. And quite the rebel too with those white buckskin shoes." Margold laughed—a nervous twitter. "You don't mind hearing that from an old lady, do you?"

"Did I really wear white buckskin shoes?"

"Indeed you did. And a boar's tusk necklace. And a beaded belt too. . . ."

Millard shook his head. "Impossible."

"Very well. Have it your way," conceded Margold. "But there's no denying how handsome you were. If you'd tried to kiss me, I swear I would have swooned."

Millard's neck muscles tensed up. He didn't understand how the notion of his kissing Virginia had entered the conversation, but that struck him as a sound place to stop. "I'm glad you dropped by," he said with an air of finality. "Thank you for the birthday wishes."

Margold looked flustered. Possibly tearful. "I do have a few more things I wanted to show you," she said as she rummaged inside the shoebox. "Here we are. . . ."

She produced a yellowed extract from *The New York Times*: MISS SUCRAM TO MARRY M. K. SALTER. What struck him most was how beautiful Carol looked with her sharp cheekbones and schoolgirl bangs; what had a woman like her seen in a drip like him? Needless to say, when he'd remarried, he hadn't sent an announcement to the papers.

"Two hundred eighty-three graduates in our class," she reported. "Two hundred ninety-seven marriages. At least, those are the ones I'm aware of. . . ."

How tempting to wed Delilah in secret—even now—to muddle Margold's numbers.

"All but thirty-two married at least once," she continued. "But that includes openly gay classmates like Tom Truett and 'Goldy' Bernard. . . . Also the ones who died young. Did you realize Harriet Klein was only twenty-four when she overdosed?" Margold's lips tightened to emphasize the gravity of this realization. "Of course, Gina Tucker is now on her sixth hubby—she's actually Gina Tucker Sanford Delahanty Weisberg Krauss St. James Polk now—say that five times fast!—so these things even out, I suppose. In the aggregate. Sometimes I think there should be a law against changing your name more than once, or at least once a decade. Same with countries. I bought my great-niece a globe for Christmas a few years ago, and half the nations don't exist anymore. South this and east that and whatnot. Did you know there's an actual country named Djibouti?" Margold shifted her head, focusing on Millard with her good eye. "We had a wine and cheese reception at our community college last month and somehow I ended up asking a visiting professor of African Studies if he'd ever been to Rhodesia. My great-uncle had been stationed there before the war. You'd have thought I'd ordered the man to pluck the eyes from horses."

Had it really come to this? Discussing Rhodesia with Virginia Margold.

"It must take a lot of effort to keep track of all those marriages."

"I suppose," said Margold. "By the way, I'm sorry about Isabelle."

Now Millard just wanted the woman to leave. "I am too," he said.

"That was a rough year for wives. Cal Edwards and Jimmy Van Dale lost theirs on the same day. August 16. Tammy Van Dale was much younger too—not even sixty."

"Life can be unfair," said Millard. The clock on the bookshelf read 1:25. Overhead, an orderly was jangling a stretcher or a meal cart along the tile, producing a familiar earthquake on the ceiling. Virginia Margold thumbed through her clippings, organized in divided rows like coupons.

Millard stood up. "I wish we had more time. . . ."

"Do you really?" replied Margold, taking his words entirely at face value. "Because I meant what I said about you being so handsome. I confess I even had a little crush on you. . . ."

"Nothing like puppy crushes," said Millard, striving to sound indifferent. He walked to the door and opened it. The painters had returned from their lunch break and the corridor smelled of volatile chemicals. A fine dust of plaster—or chrysotile asbestos—hung in the air. It didn't matter: Not even asbestos was a danger to him anymore.

"The truth is, Salty," continued Margold, "I *still* have a little crush on you. . . ."

She held her thumb and index finger together, miming the size of her affection.

Millard had seen this coming, yet like a pedestrian who spots the headlights of an oncoming vehicle, identifying the threat was not the same as circumventing it. And he had stood in Virginia Margold's shoes before, albeit not since high school, when he'd been rebuffed by a varsity tennis player named Stella Vann— Stella Vann, who accounted for two of those marriages, one to a conservative congressman from Virginia and the second to a retired female horse trainer who'd taken three colts to the Preakness. He'd run into her at the fortieth reunion—but he'd found middle-aged Stella pleasant, and a tad insipid, rather than alluring. So he did not want to sound unkind to Virginia. At the same time, Margold was the last suitor he wished to encourage.

"Don't be silly," said Millard. "Trust me. You don't have a crush *on me*. You have a crush on some handsome kid who wore white buckskin shoes and a beaded belt."

Margold appeared unfazed. "Goodness, Salty, you *do* sound like a psychiatrist." She smiled, a glassful of hope. "I swear you could still make me swoon."

"Which is why they pay me the big money," he said. "But as much as I enjoy chatting with you, I really do have patients to see. . . . I'm sorry. . . ."

Millard stood at the open door, an awkward usher, as Virginia Margold gathered her belongings with a deliberate sluggishness—like a malingerer leaving the hospital after exposure. One by one, she tucked her treasured clippings into various envelopes and pouches, finally shutting the shoebox so firmly, and with such resignation, that the cardboard seemed to release a faint groan. Millard could have showered and shaved in the interval required for the woman to fasten the safety pin on her wrap. In the time she took to shuffle to the door, clutching her bag to her chest as though cradling an infant, he might have walked halfway to Boston. This, he thought, is how eternity must feel. For an instant, as she approached, Millard feared his visitor might peck him on the cheek, but she merely paused and asked, "Can I stop by again tomorrow? Maybe for lunch? My flight's not until the evening. . . ."

Goodness, how the tables had turned. Hal Storch claimed that any man over seventy with his own natural teeth and a motor vehicle could choose his women like rabbits at a state fair, but even without a car—Millard had given up his license after Isabelle's death, tethered as he was to Manhattan—he suddenly found himself an Adonis among elderly hens. Not that Virginia Margold was exactly a catch. But Carol certainly was, and the notion that his ex-wife still wanted him—that she might take him back, after all that he'd done—seemed as unjust as it did astonishing. And hadn't that fern-obsessed coed he'd dated before Carol phoned him after her second divorce—from the same man—to ask if he were single? What was that wisecrack of Storch's: "At seventy, all the women you lusted after in high school will finally want to date you. And at ninety, they'll think they did." Unexpectedly, Millard felt a sudden tenderness for Virginia, whose only romantic prospects had evaporated in the Andes.

"Why don't you call me tomorrow? In the morning," he offered. "We'll see how much I get done this afternoon."

The expression on Margold's loose-fitting face could only be compared with those of office girls hugging sailors on V-J Day— or possibly the joy his granddaughters had displayed when he'd brought them a life-sized grizzly from FAO Schwarz.

"Tomorrow it is," she agreed.

And then she *did* plant her damp, moribund lips on his cheek. He had to wait until she was safely past the trestle ladder and around the bend before brushing his sleeve across his skin. Miss Nickelsworth, who had obviously witnessed the entire exchange, kept her eyes glued to the penguin-shaped tape dispenser on her desk, and said nothing. But what did he really care if his prim secretary remembered him as a Casanova? At least, he was alone now! Gloriously alone. Not that he even wanted to be alone—just away from the Virginia Margolds and Denny Dennmeyers and Hecuba Yilmazes who encroached upon his sanity. His strongest desire was to phone Delilah—or to show up at her apartment, unannounced, armed with another bouquet—but he'd promised to leave her in peace until five o'clock. The more time he spent with her at this late juncture, after all, the more time he'd still yearn for—and they'd both suffer. So better a quick, loving farewell at the end of the workday. Besides, Delilah also had her own loose ends to tidy up. "We're starting a tradition," she'd jested. "Like not seeing the bride before the wedding."

Millard shut the door of his office, turning to face the tower of journals that would never be read and the stacks of reprint requests that would go unanswered. He'd already taken home any effects of sentimental value: his autographed copy of Erikson's *Young Man Luther*, photographs of himself posing with Carl Rogers and B. F. Skinner, a thank-you card he'd once received from Abraham Maslow in return for a reprint; also an amethyst geode he'd been given by his very first patient as a paperweight. Whatever remained in his office, he suspected, would be carted away with belongings left behind by unidentified patients and the used plasticware from the hospital's cafeteria. So be it. Yet deprived of these treasures, and his pincushion cacti, which he'd donated to a local nursery, the office felt bare as a padded cell, its deficiencies—sagging plaster, uncovered heating vents, a patch of mold above the baseboards—all the more discouraging. A jagged floor-to-ceiling crack cleaved the far wall like a seismic threat.

His failure with Lysander hung heavily upon him. Not even

an explosion, and the ten-alarm blaze that followed, managed to shake his son from his sloth. He'd considered telling the boy, point-blank, that he was wasting his life, but he hadn't marshalled the courage. It was one thing for his receptionist to remember him as a letch, quite another to stamp his son with a permanent badge of disapproval. When they'd hugged, it was like embracing a convict facing the gallows. Adding another blow to his drubbing, Lysander hadn't even remembered his birthday.

Millard returned to his desk, loosened his tie, and kicked his feet up on a makeshift hassock fashioned from milk crates. The notion of phoning Carol tempted him for a moment. She'd already fought this battle, after all. But he sensed any discussion of Lysander—*of his failure with Lysander*—would bring him to tears, and his first wife, for all her many gifts, hardly offered a shoulder to cry upon. And if he didn't want Lysander to remember him as a critic, he certainly didn't want Carol recalling him as a sniveler.

Instead, he dialed Maia's apartment.

His youngest daughter still did not carry a mobile phone. She'd read a study on the incidence of glioblastomas in Finland, which reported a four percent increase in gray matter pathology among "intense, chronic cellular phone users," and concluded that even casual use would give her a brain tumor. *It's a silent epidemic*, she'd chastised. *Wait until we've had cell phones for as long as we've smoked cigarettes*. No meta-analyses to the contrary could persuade her. So much for four years' tuition at Yale and a PhD in the hard sciences.

You have reached . . . replied the voicemail.

Millard still recalled the days of answering services, of renting your home phone from Ma Bell at fifteen dollars a month. He'd never forget how he'd mocked Hal Storch for shelling out $400 to have a fifteen-pound PhoneMate Deluxe answering machine built into the wall of his study. Now Maia was the only person he knew under sixty who couldn't be reached while on the toilet.

Maia's voice was followed by a mechanical warning: *This mailbox is full.*

He dialed again. *You have reached . . .*

As Einstein said, insanity was doing the same thing over and over again and expecting different results—but that didn't stop people from trying. He'd known a guy from college who'd been dumped by the same woman five times, and, more somberly, a couple who'd had three consecutive babies afflicted with Tay-Sachs disease. Again: *This mailbox is full.*

The last thing Millard wanted to do was leave his daughter waiting for him in a public railroad station, but he simply couldn't meet her at seven thirty. Or ever. He'd already telephoned her the night before and subtly conveyed his love. And not once, as he reflected, did she mention a word about meeting him the next day.

You have reached . . .

He hung up for the third time.

Millard flipped on the radio and logged into his email. The explosion dominated the news at the top of the hour. *Terrorism cannot be ruled out*, reported a "bureau chief" with a Polish name and a nasal voice. *But my sources tell me that an intentionally detached gas line in the cellar appears the likely cause.* Millard's attention drifted. He had innumerable messages reminding him to complete his annual training in patient confidentiality, which he'd already done, and blood-borne pathogens, which he never handled. The word *suicide* riveted him back to the broadcast. *That information is preliminary and unofficial*, declared the reporter. *But my sources affirm that the tenant had attempted to kill herself multiple times in the past. The unidentified woman has been taken to St. Dymphna's Hospital, but is expected to survive.* Millard flipped away from the station with irritation. That was why the public needed suicide training courses rather than suicide prevention. People who were set on killing themselves were going to do it—one way or another. But keeping them from massacring innocent other parties in the process—from driving station wagons onto railroad tracks or putting first responders at risk—was another matter entirely.

The link for Lauren Pastarnack's recommendation appeared on his computer screen. He genuinely liked the girl—a lot—even if she existed in a world where Bing Crosby and the Beatles belonged to the same generation. In all fairness, she hadn't been the most impressive student ever to rotate through their service. She didn't conduct any clinical research, as he recalled. And her facility with paperwork had proven adequate, at best. But since this was his final recommendation ever, what did he have to lose? Who gave a rat's patootie about his long-term credibility? For one day in her career, he decided, Lauren Pastarnack would be the Linus Pauling of residency applicants. He wrote:

Dear Committee on Admissions:
I have written over five thousand letters of recommendation in my nearly fifty years as a clinical psychiatrist.

That wasn't exactly true—not by a magnitude—but who could disprove it?

I have written good letters and great letters, but no letter as enthusiastic as this one, because Lauren Pastarnack is the most talented medical student ever to rotate through our service, and probably any psychiatric service in this country, in those five decades. Her range of knowledge is expansive—when you interview her, I urge you to ask her to name the Sister Seven schools or to identify the composer of "This Is the Army, Mr. Jones." Whether you ask her about neurotransmitters or comedian Jimmy Durante, she will know the answer. Because she is brilliant and personable, and if I sent one of my own relatives to a psychiatrist, I would want it to be someone just like Ms. Pastarnack—only, I suppose, someone already in possession of a medical degree. Judging by her paper record alone, one might let her slip away, allow her to end up training at a community hospital in Milwaukee. But that would be a tragedy, as she is destined to become the Linus Pauling of psychiatry residents, the Jonas Salk of psychiatry residents, the Alexander Fleming of psychiatry residents. She combines the genius of Marie Curie with the compassion of Albert Schweitzer with the diligence and drive of a thousand Manhattan Projects. In short, she is the best of the best. Sincerely & etc. . . .

There you go. Now he'd made up for all of his badgering.

Millard slid the recommendation out of the printer and tucked it into an envelope. The process had left him a bit giddy, pseudo-manic. *While I'm at it,* he decided, *I might as well leave Denny Dennmeyer something to remember me by.* So he typed:

MEMO ON STAFFING NEEDS: CONSULT-LIAISON PSYCHIATRY SERVICE

To Whom It May Concern:

The history of Western civilization is a narrative of brave, off-kilter people moving westward—first across the steppes of East Asia to Greece and Rome, then following Claudius and William the Bastard into Old Albion. From there came Emma Lazarus's waves of teeming refuse, first the uptight Puritans with their bawdy secrets, the Irish barmaids in search of potatoes, and, in their wake, the swarthy Italians and Slavs and Greeks and Jews who peddled from pushcarts, and set pins at manual bowling alleys, and ran numbers rackets along Stanton Street.

He paused for a moment, almost tearful, thinking of his own grandfather—Meyer Wolff, for whom he was named—arriving in steerage at the age of eleven, alone, and making his way in the cigar business.

Far from a representative sample, these west-bound migrants were the outcasts, the troublemakers, the young men and women mad with a desire to see a world beyond Pinsk and Patras and Palermo. And then those immigrants and their offspring plowed farther westward—in Conestoga wagons, and in jalopies along Steinbeck's Route 66—

Millard realized he was taking a few historical liberties here, but he doubted Dennmeyer could place the two world wars in chronological order.

—and in jets bound for the paradise of television dreams and twenty-four-hour sun and Buddhist biker gangs and drive-thru tattoo parlors and top-heavy bleach blondes in bikinis. As these lunatics progressed westward, they brought with them to California headshrinkers of all varieties, Lacanian analysts and Rorschach devotees, partisans of Melanie Klein and self-styled gurus, pill pushers and LSD pushers and holistic repatterners— all committed to rejuvenating the psyche. But along the way to paradise in the Hollywood Hills, the migrants too crazy to continue fell by the wayside, many of them right here in New York City. And since most psychiatric disorders are highly genetic, these crazy migrants sired and bore crazy children . . . but all of the psychiatrists had gone off to California for the higher reimbursement rates and the year-round sunbathing. As a result, I fear we have an overabundance of deranged people here in the Big Apple, yet a desperate shortage of providers fit to treat them.

Millard realized he was playing somewhat fast and loose with his definition of "crazy," as only a small fraction of people whom one might describe in this way genuinely suffered from a mental illness, like schizophrenia or bipolar disorder, that might yield to treatment. Many others were merely kooky, folks you might not want to sit next to on a Greyhound bus or invite home for Thanksgiving, but who also didn't meet DSM criteria or belong in a padded cell. He thought of his father's cousin, Irving, who'd run a letterhead organization that lobbied Congress to ban television advertisements depicting werewolves—because these ads fostered a negative opinion of real wolves in the public consciousness. Crazy, sure. But not mentally ill. Or his neighbor's daughter who insisted—with intense sincerity—that she was "a dragon trapped in human form." The planet teemed with balmy buggers denying the moon landing, chasing the Loch Ness Monster, protesting fluoridated water in tinfoil hats. Nothing that medication or psychotherapy might cure.

In practice, many of our patients here on the consult service are so sick that they require not one psychiatrist to treat them, but often two or three. And a few psychologists and social workers wouldn't hurt. So if one estimates that about half of New Yorkers are truly crazy, and each of these lunatics needs, on average, 2.5 headshrinkers to care for them, then our city could use approximately six million psychiatrists. As St. Dymphna's Health Network accounts for approximately 20% of all patients seen in the five boroughs, our current staffing demand is for 500,000 board certified psychiatrists by year's end—with a suitable number of psychologists, nurse practitioners, and social workers to support them. I realize this assessment may appear somewhat on the high end—even excessive—but I remind you of the promise draped across the central pavilion: You Get Better Because We Are Better. What are a few hundred thousand extra providers when the public's health is at stake?

MK SALTER, MD

He gave Lauren Pastarnack's recommendation to Miss Nickelsworth to mail and dropped off the report at Dennmeyer's office on the way to the cemetery.

9

Hailing a taxi outside the hospital was an easy endeavor, especially if you were Caucasian, and able-bodied, and appeared capable of doling out a fifteen percent tip. Persuading a New York City cabbie to carry you to suburban New Jersey, even at twice the meter beyond the city limits, was another matter entirely. Millard stepped to the curb and surveyed his options: a veritable yellow armada of Dodge Caravans and Nissan Pathfinders and Toyota Highlanders, all equally nondescript and interchangeable, greeted him from the avenue, punctuated intermittently by an apple-green "boro taxi" headed uptown toward the thankless Bronx. What the occasion really called for—after all, it *was* possibly his final cab ride ever—was an old-style Checker cab, a broad-bumpered Packard or Marathon with its phosphorescent "on radio call" sign protruding like a stylish tuft. That was the automobile of his prime, the muscular, unflappable sedan that had carried him and Carol to myriad cocktail parties and graduation banquets and premieres at Lincoln Center. He'd ridden home from Art Hallam's engagement bash on the jump seat of such a vehicle, pleasantly drunk, while that frond-fixated coed from Barnard, Judy Bell, squirmed in his lap; not until the following morning—or, rather, when he awoke, bloodshot, early the next afternoon—did he realize that she'd leaked urine onto his gabardine slacks. And once, on a frigid winter evening, he'd flagged down a cab at a stoplight outside

Carnegie Hall . . . or thought he had: When he'd pulled open the rear door, there were Mary Martin and Janet Gaynor, long past their primes, nuzzled like teenagers in the backseat. "His service light's broken," he'd said to Carol, shutting the taxi door quickly, without mentioning what he'd witnessed—treating these fading stars to the same discretion that he'd have afforded a psychiatric patient. And who today remembered *A Star Is Born*? Or had seen *Peter Pan* on Broadway? Or gave a damn if starlets and pop singers made out with each other on television or the National Mall? The prospect of a Checker cab recalled for Millard whatever innocence he'd once had and so insensibly lost—of Carroll O'Connor and Jean Stapleton warbling of a time when "girls were girls and men were men"—but he'd read somewhere, probably in the *Times*, that only three of these heirloom conveyances remained cruising the asphalt among the more than eleven thousand medallion taxis trawling the five boroughs, so he'd likely have died of natural causes before he found one. With an irrational twinge of regret, Millard flagged down the first passing cab.

The trick was to ask about the destination *after* entering the vehicle. He'd learned this technique from Carol, who, if denied a trip to Queens or Riverdale, merely folded her hands across her purse and said, matter-of-fact, "*Oh, but you will.*" Once, needing a lift to her cousin's baby shower in Astoria during a stormy April rush hour, she'd kept the aggravated driver waiting for nearly twenty minutes before he finally yielded. When the fellow, red-nosed under a wool scally cap, had appealed to Millard's sensibilities, he'd replied, "It's above my pay grade." He'd later tried the same "cab-napping" approach with Isabelle, but she'd refused to play along. *The city is full of taxicabs*, she'd said. *Why give anyone a hard time?* But Isabelle was dead and Millard needed transportation to Montclair, New Jersey, the "Jewish burial capital of the

Western Hemisphere," so he *was* willing to impose some minor inconvenience on a hack.

"Where to?" asked the driver.

To Millard's surprise, the voice was female. It belonged to a wispy young creature with highlighted hair and braided hoop earrings, passably good-looking too, with black eyeliner ringing her large brown eyes—in short, everything seventy-five years of experience had taught him *not* to expect in a cabbie. He didn't have any objection to a woman driving a cab, of course. (He re-called a flight to Miami, back in the golden era of Pan Am and TWA, when the couple seated in front of him, upon hearing a decidedly feminine welcome from the cockpit, had insisted upon deplaning.) But female cabbies were still novel to his dated sen-sibilities, like male flight attendants and African American rabbis, and he suddenly felt regret for dragging this girl miles into a neighboring state. It didn't help that she looked to be younger than Maia.

"Montclair, New Jersey," said Millard. "Mount Hebron Cem-etery."

"That's twice the meter over the bridge," replied the girl. Her accent was far more Scarsdale or Chappaqua than Brooklynese, bereft of the "fuggedaboutit" and "whaddayawant" of the lionized cabbies of yore. "You're going both ways, right?"

That question—obvious as it was—hadn't yet dawned upon Millard. "Round-trip, I guess, if you're willing to wait thirty min-utes."

"You pay. I wait," said the girl. She plugged the destination into her GPS. "I'm not driving anybody one way to a cemetery. I don't need that hanging over my conscience."

"Excuse me?"

"Think about it. Why would anyone want a one-way fare to a graveyard?"

The girl adjusted the rearview mirror—he could see her perfect orthodonture—and they eased into traffic. She proved ginger with both the accelerator and the horn. Turning onto 98th Street, she nearly clipped a parked ambulance.

"I don't know," said Millard. "Maybe they were meeting friends with a car."

The driver eyed him through the mirror. "That's a good one. *Meeting friends with a car.*" She pounded the horn with her clenched fist and sliced across three lanes. "A one-way fare to a graveyard is like a one-way airline ticket. You don't plan on coming back alive."

Millard ran his index finger between his collar and his neck, and tried to sound incredulous. "You don't mean suicide, do you?"

"You said it," said the driver. "Not me."

"Heavens. Do I really look like I might kill myself?"

He half-feared her answer. Maybe he was wearing his destiny on his sleeve, or giving off a scent of premature demise in his perspiration—the sort of "death sweat" that allowed well-trained cats to ferret out doomed residents in nursing homes.

"That's a trick question," said the girl. "Like: Have you stopped beating your wife yet? My philosophy is that we all live near the edge—and it just takes a little push to send us over."

"Now that's a cheerful outlook for a young lady."

She flicked her hair. "It is what it is."

"And may I ask where you developed such an uplifting view of the world?"

"Art school," replied the girl. "I'm a grad student at NYU."

"And a cabbie," said Millard.

They shared the same alma mater, which made him feel closer to her—*irrationally*, because so did thousands of other people, strangers he passed on the street without notice. Besides, his NYU wasn't her NYU, any more than his New York was

Peter Stuyvesant's or Jimmy Walker's. The assortment of stickers plastered to the dashboard confirmed this. One read: "Men Have Feelings Too, But Who Cares?" A second asked, "With So Many Boys, Why Test on Animals?" A postcard of Rosie the Riveter, biceps flexed, guarded the glove box—as out of place beside this cute suburban kid as she might have been sipping cognac at the Yale Club. Yet there were also decals for radio stations, and bubble gum, and a photo of three schoolgirls—the driver flanked by a pair of older sisters with nearly identical cleft chins—posing behind a muddle of overfed guinea pigs in a wire cage.

"*And a cabbie,*" echoed the girl. "Better than being a toll collector or a sex worker. Conceptual art doesn't go very far with the bills. Not yet."

Her casual mention of prostitution silenced Millard. He'd reached the age where the sexuality of young women either made men lustful or nervy, and he'd unequivocally entered the second camp, perennially panicked that busty nursing assistants and almond-eyed checkout clerks might mistake routine kindness for romantic pursuit. In his day, cash-strapped coeds had paid their way as tutors and babysitters. Or maybe working the summer as a receptionist in the dental office of a well-off *lantsman*.

"I'm Konrad, by the way. With a K," said the girl. "But you should call me Konnie."

"Konrad with a K? Like Adenauer?"

The notion that the musty German chancellor and this ethereal young art student might even share the same planet struck him as somewhat implausible.

"Who?" she asked. "I'm named for my great-uncle."

Millard considered telling her who Adenauer was, but checked himself. How could one understand the statesman in a vacuum—without a working knowledge of the Potsdam Conference and the Marshall Plan and the origins of NATO? What was required wasn't a brief mention of the *Wirtschaftswunder* or *Hei-matrecht*, or some contextualization for the Petersberg Agreement, but rather a broad survey of postwar European history, well beyond the scope of a cab ride. "Your great-uncle?" he asked.

"My parents had been planning on a boy. The obstetrician fucked up reading the ultrasound, but they'd already chosen a name—and even told my great-aunt."

The cab snaked its way along an elevated stretch of the Henry Hudson Parkway, leaving a chorus of irate and befuddled drivers in its wake. Beyond the guardrail, the embankment dropped steeply down to the river.

"A girl named Konrad," said Millard. "Like a boy named Sue."

"Hey, you're a weird one, aren't you?" observed the girl. Her knowledge of Johnny Cash was clearly limited. "And yes, a girl named Konrad. It's ironic, too, because my folks don't want me driving a cab. Not a job for a girl. According to my dad, I could get raped and murdered."

You could, thought Millard—but he didn't say this. The expression "raped and murdered" made him think first not of sexual violence, but of CNN anchor Bernard Shaw asking presidential candidate Mike Dukakis, *If Kitty Dukakis were raped and murdered, would you support the death penalty?* And how much he had cared—loopy as it now seemed in hindsight—whether Bush or Dukakis were elected president, although today it mattered to him, and possibly the world, about as much as the face-off between Warren Harding and James Middleton Cox. And then, on the subject of rape and murder, and of women named Connie, his thoughts drifted to crooner Connie Francis being victimized in a Long Island motel room. He vaguely recalled that Francis died recently . . . but it just as easily might have been Patti Page or Doris Day or even Rosemary Clooney. In any event, someone this girl named Konrad had never heard of.

"I *like* driving a cab," said Konnie. The girl's eyes met his in the mirror—curious, almost taunting. "I meet lots of interesting people. Some even stranger than you."

She had not asked for his name, he realized, and he had not offered it.

"Celebrities too, especially downtown. Guess who I picked up last week. I couldn't even believe they were really in my cab. . . ."

Or maybe Peggy Lee had died recently, he thought. Did it matter? Five decades beyond their heyday—and his—these fallen divas all seemed interchangeable. He knew it couldn't be Eydie Gormé who'd died, because she'd passed away the same week as Isabelle.

"Seriously, mister," said Konnie. "*Guess*."

"I have no idea. Connie Francis and Kitty Dukakis?"

The girl rolled her eyes. "*Famous* people," she said. "Try again."

He glanced out the window. They were halfway across the bridge. To the south, Lower Manhattan wilted under the midday sun—the Woolworth Building peeking through the caverns, and beyond that the gulf where the towers had stood. They crossed the state line and the girl pushed a button on the face of the meter to record the double rate.

"Come on. *Guess*."

She sounded peeved—like a child denied a toy. It was hard to imagine Rosie the Riveter pleading with him to play a guessing game.

"Mary Martin and Janet Gaynor?"

"What is wrong with you? Don't you know any *celebrities*?"

"All the celebrities I know are dead," said Millard. "Give me a hint."

"Fine. They're stand-up comedians."

"Got it," said Millard. "Jimmy Durante and Eddie Cantor."

Konnie with a K scrunched her nose with displeasure. "Z-Cube and Snogg," she announced. "Right here in *my* cab. Isn't that awesome?!"

"On the tip of my tongue," agreed Millard. "Z-Cube and Snogg."

"I even took a selfie with them," said his chauffeur.

"Lucky you," said Millard. He wasn't certain if Z-Cube and Snogg were male, or female, or possibly non-human. The idea crossed his mind that they might be ventriloquist and dummy like Edgar Bergen and Charlie McCarthy. Or animals with a trainer in tow. Now he knew how Lauren Pastarnack had felt when he'd grilled her on the Seven Sisters and Tin Pan Alley. And it served him right.

"You *have* heard of Z-Cube and Snogg, *haven't you?*"

"I've seen them on TV," he lied. "Once or twice."

"See. Even *you've* heard of Z-Cube and Snogg," she squealed. He tried not to take her remark as a slight. "They were working on their routine—the one about the Confederate flag at the pope's birthday party—you know that one, right?"

"I've heard of it," said Millard.

He hadn't.

"So at first they were practicing lines, going back and forth and—I don't know if I should be telling you this. . . ."

She paused. To his surprise, Millard was curious to learn the punch line of her story, even if it involved celebrities of unknown gender and species. "Who am I going to tell?" he asked. "Who would believe me?"

That seemed to assuage her. "So they were going back and forth with the lines—and then they started making out. Right in the back of my cab!"

"Amazing," said Millard. "Z-Cube and Snogg?"

He wondered if she understood that he was making fun of her.

They'd reached the New Jersey side of the bridge; Konnie cut short her story to navigate a constellation of ramps and merges. Not too long ago, at least by geological standards, all of this had been farmland. His mother's brother—the one who'd survived WWI—had managed an orchard out here on Route 46. During the '20s, affluent "automobilists" skippering Pierce-Arrows and Duesenbergs dropped in to pick their own berries. Later, after the market crashed, families in Hoover carts came scavenging for windfall apples. Millard's own parents had visited once, shortly after their wedding, taking the Dyckman Street Ferry to Englewood; they'd returned two days later with a year's supply of preserved quinces. Now, luxury condominiums dappled the Palisades and the fruit trees had given way to office parks.

Konnie failed to yield at the merge and came feet—possibly inches—from ramming a tanker truck. Millard braced himself against the back of her seat. "Do you know what the most amazing thing is about Z-Cube and Snogg?" she asked.

"Their names?" ventured Millard.

"They don't exist."

"What do you mean? I thought you gave them a ride."

"I lied," said the girl. "It's part of my master's thesis. I make up stories about things that don't exist—stand-up comedians, sports teams, best-selling books—and then I get men like you on tape pretending that you're familiar with them."

"They really don't exist?" asked Millard—incredulous that two people he'd never even heard of until minutes before were a sham.

"Celebrities don't ride in cabs these days. They take limousines," said Konnie. "Sorry."

"And you recorded me? Without my permission?"

"It's part of the project." She pointed at a Lilliputian microphone affixed to the rim of the overhead light. "Now do me a favor and sign a waiver so I can use your voice. There should be a clipboard with forms in one of the seat pockets."

Sure enough, Millard found a boilerplate waiver behind the passenger's seat. According to the document, her project was called: "Why Men 'Know' More: Gender Differences in False Assertions of Familiarity." Now he got it. Sort of like Gloria Steinem meets *Candid Camera*.

"So women don't pretend to know things they don't?"

"That's the hypothesis," said Konnie—without a hint of self-consciousness for exposing him. "I'll tell you for sure in eleven months."

No, you won't, thought Millard. *Thank heavens for that.*

"What I *can* tell you is that I've done about fifty of these recordings so far, and I've had men pretend they've heard of nonexistent planets and states—and one guy even bragged he'd had a great-grandfather who'd fought under Colonel Sanders and General Mills during the Civil War." The girl briefly ground the tires along the rumble strip, possibly for effect. "So far, not one woman has taken the bait."

"And what if I won't sign the waiver?" Millard asked.

Konnie turned for an instant—while sailing at seventy miles per hour in moderate traffic—and flashed him a look that warned, *Don't fuck with me, old man*. "What if I leave you at your wife's grave and go home?"

"How did you know I was visiting my wife?"

The girl sighed. "People your age don't visit their parents. And if you'd lost a child, you'd have already told me—said something like, 'You remind me of my dead daughter' or 'My son would be almost your age if he hadn't drowned."

"And what about a close friend?"

"Who visits the graves of close friends?! Jesus Christ. Once you kick it, you're down to your immediate relatives. Everyone else jumps ship. Don't take this the wrong way, mister, but you'd think you'd have realized this by now. . . ."

"Know-it-all."

She *did* know a lot for a girl roughly one-quarter his age, for someone born during—Millard did a rough calculation in his head—the first Bush administration. She knew a lot, yet she also knew nothing: What did she understand about watching the woman whose bed you'd shared for two decades melt away as quickly as snow on a spring afternoon? Or what it meant to see your own adult son, hearty and broad-shouldered, yet fit for ab-solutely nothing? Or of making a mistake that cost a fellow human being his life? Millard had done that: Shortly after his in-ternship, he'd cleared a patient for discharge from the psych ward—a professor of Old Church Slavonic, a brawny, goateed refugee from Dubček's Prague Spring—who took a cab straight from St. Dymphna's doorstep to the Triborough Bridge for a le-thal plunge into the Hell Gate's current. Fortunately, that had been during an era when physicians didn't testify against one an-other, and when patients sued their doctors only rarely, usually out of malice. (It helped that the Czech's closest relative was a stepsister in Vancouver.) What could his driver, clever as she might be, know of survivor's guilt, of having been entrusted with another's life and failed? You had to live through certain cata-clysms to appreciate their horror. If youth, as they claimed, was wasted on the young, then the wisdom of experience was squan-dered on the old.

Yet the girl had a point: Would anyone ever visit *him* at Mount Hebron? Maia would, at least at first, especially since Isa-belle's final demand—possibly her sole true demand, ever—was that they be interred side by side. Sally and Arnold might appear with their families, *once*, for the unveiling. As a courtesy. But that was that. After all, when was the last time anyone other than he or his daughter had visited Isabelle? Millard affixed his name—both printed and signed—to the waiver with his fountain pen and passed it over the divider.

"Thanks, Mr. Millard Salter," said Konnie, reading from the form. "Is that your real name?"

"Yes, it is, as a matter of fact," he said. "Why shouldn't it be?"

He didn't mention that his grandfather had plucked the name from a gentile's apothecary shop, Salter's Drugs on Rivington Street—that back in the Ukraine, in a bare-earth shtetl where his ancestors had circumcised and worshiped and mourned for generations, a village that was now an industrial suburb of Lviv, the Salters had been Zarakowskis. That was just what you did in those days—nobody walked around with their Ashkenazi names on their sleeves like the Maccabees. Eddie Cantor had been Edward Iskowitz. "Uncle Miltie" was born Mendel Berlinger. So what?

"I don't know. It just *sounds* made up." She yawned—as though indicting his conversation skills. "Do you mind if I listen to some music?"

That was chutzpah for you—deriding his name and then changing the subject.

She flipped on the radio without waiting for his answer. The vehicle filled with a rhythmic pulse, deep and cacophonic, with no discernable melody. Millard had read that the FBI blasted similar sounds through loudspeakers to flush out hostage takers.

"This is music?" he asked.

"Hogtie and the Pentacoastal Five, man," said Konnie. "Aren't they awesome?"

"Awesome," echoed Millard.

The meter read $55.00; they were still a good three miles

from Mount Hebron. And then a small miracle transpired: the hostile vibrations trailed away for the news at the top of the hour.

Two are now confirmed dead and sixteen injured, led the anchor, *on the Upper East Side of Manhattan in a blast that our sources confirm was a suicide attempt gone awry. A thirty-five-year-old woman has been taken to St. Dymphna's for third-degree burns, and is now listed in critical but stable condition. She is likely to face criminal charges. . . . In other news, animal control officers continue to search for an escaped lynx cub—*

Konnie turned down the volume. "Idiot," she said. "If I'm going to kill myself, I'm going to make sure I do it right."

"Maybe it's harder than you think."

"How hard can it be? I'd down a couple of shots of hard liquor and then I'd take this baby up to about ninety miles per hour and go straight over the Palisades."

"Not everybody drives a car."

"Whatever. There's like a billion skyscrapers in New York City. Bridges too. How difficult can it be to find one to jump off?" As though to emphasize the ease of suicide, the girl accelerated through a yellow light into an illegal left turn. "I know you'll say I'm crazy, but I think the government should offer suicide lessons—so that people who really want to die don't end up doing things that jeopardize the lives of others."

Millard had long propounded this heresy in private—but he wasn't particularly interested in engaging. The girl's *'whatever'* had reminded him of his misunderstanding with Maia.

"Excuse me," he said. "I have to call my daughter."

Once again, no luck: *You have reached the voicemail of Maia Salter. . . .*

If he couldn't reach Maia, or leave a message, he'd have no choice but to leave her waiting: another setback on a day that seemed haunted by misfortune—a day on which he'd encountered Elsa Duransky, Hecuba Yilmaz, Virginia Margold, and Denny Dennmeyer. Meeting any one of these unfortunate creatures was enough to dampen his spirits; all four in one morning was like appearing on the satanic version of *This Is Your Life*. On top of all that, his tête-à-tête with Lysander had accomplished nothing. Nada. *Gornisht*, as his mother used to say—the only Yiddish she ever used—while holding up empty hands to the dog. As long as the boy didn't view his lifestyle as problematic— and why should he with Millard footing his bills?—any effort to offer solutions was as futile as hosing water onto a volcano. Not that Millard didn't have answers. He did: concrete, step-by-step plans to get his son back on course. All Lysander had to do was ask. Or merely open himself up to the possibility of advice. But the boy was a slick wall of indifference. How could one realistically expect that a catastrophe four decades in the making might be remedied over a sashimi lunch? He had been a self-deluding fool to hope it. Still . . .

The cab jolted to a halt, nearly launching Millard's skull into the divider.

"Here we are," announced the girl. "Home sweet home."

They'd pulled up before the wrought iron gates of Mount Hebron. A metal chain secured the entryway, but a nearby postern in the brickwork allowed for the passage of pedestrians. Beyond that rolled the phalanxes of headstones—a few limestone markers dating from the 1890s, families of marble and granite fixtures of more recent vintage, and then the sharp curve around a mausoleum with a gambrel roof to the original Salter plot. He'd first hiked that hill at the age of eleven, following his Grandma Minnie's cortege. Then came his grandfather's sister, Esther, squat as a potbelly stove, and then Meyer Wolff himself, done in at seventy by his own cigars. Each trek to Mount Hebron bracketed an era in Millard's life—and now this would be his last visit, or rather his penultimate, as he still had one final journey ahead of him. How strange to be among the dead during the heat of July, he thought. Somehow, it seemed, his kin had always succumbed during the bitterest of winters, the branches above bare and without pity.

"You'll wait for me?" he asked. "I won't be long. . . ."

"Take as long as you want," said Konnie. "It's your dime."

"Thirty minutes. Tops."

"No rush," she said. "And I am sorry about your wife. Really."

Her sympathy caught Millard off guard. "Me too."

He passed through the postern and followed the slate path. A shirtless laborer mowed the slopes of a nearby ridge; the scent of fresh-cut grass tickled his nostrils. Ahead of him, enough graves to populate all the synagogues of Europe. The scene always recalled his grade-school assemblies on Armistice Day, when anointed students recited those haunting lines of John McCrae's: *In Flanders fields the poppies blow / between the crosses, row on row* . . . Ironic, too, because there wasn't even a single cross at Mount Hebron, which had started off as a German-Jewish resting place, in the era of burial societies and tontines, only later to expand to accept tribesmen of all customs and factions. (You could even be buried here with a tattoo, he'd learned—Maia, bless her soul, had actually called to check before inking a ringed Saturn on her ankle.) A *Who's Who* of obscure Jewish performers were interred at the site: vaudeville comedians Willie and Eugene Howard; Myron Cohen, that second-rate staple of *The Ed Sullivan Show*; Buster Kimmel, once hailed the "Victor Borge of the accordion." But Mount Hebron also contained its fair share of physicians and accountants, bookkeepers and card sharks, nobodies and no-goodniks—as well as a large number of ordinary working stiffs. *As long as you don't have a foreskin or a heartbeat*, Millard's father had once joked, *they're glad enough to take your money.*

The cemetery had in former times been three separate burial grounds. One of these, Beth-El, had been swallowed up long before Millard's first arrival, but he remembered Eden Gardens, previously separated from Mount Hebron by a service road, but now conjoined in a morbid economy of scale. Each cemetery claimed its own "street" grid—not perfectly aligned—so "Elm Lane" became "Locust Crossing" on his way to the older headstones. Millard knew the turnoff, opposite the four ledger stones of the Sinkoff brothers and their wives, precisely because his father had missed it without fail, regularly trekking all the way to the end of the row and back. Dear Papa, he thought—who'd introduced him as "my son, the doctor," from the day of admission to medical school. Millard stepped into the deep grass of the Salter plot, careful to avoid the stones. Coniferous hedges had overgrown several of the adjacent graves: Bernard Levinson, a devoted father and grandfather; Mollie Gruber, orphaned among Levinsons and Salters, who'd died at seventeen, "beloved and cherished," in 1932. He knew these neighbors like old friends, denizens of a district long filled to capacity; he still recalled when Grandma Minnie and the Levinson matriarch had been the only two residents, like housewives on opposite sides of an air shaft.

On his last visit, at Isabelle's unveiling, he'd taken a penknife to the yew shrub suffocating Mollie Gruber's headstone, pruning enough foliage to render her name visible. It was a start—even if Maia had discouraged his labors, afraid he might stab himself. Now, such efforts seemed futile. There was nothing left he could do for enigmatic Mollie Gruber, who had stood beside him, so to speak, during his life's harshest trials. As a teenager, he'd wondered: Had she been pretty? Later, as a medical student, he'd speculated on her premature death. In middle age, when he'd buried his own parents, he'd reflected on her grieving mother and father, if they had survived her—how cruel it must be to lose a child, and how fortunate he'd been to have his progeny outlast him. He thought of Jackie Kennedy mourning her infant, Anthony Quinn's toddler drowning in W. C. Fields's fish pond, Roy Rogers and Dale Evans losing their daughter to mumps, not to mention Art Hallam's granddaughter, who'd perished from a one-in-a-million dental complication, or Hal Storch's niece, who'd overdosed on a cocktail of barbiturates. Even an indolent directionless screwup of a son like Lysander—there, he's said it— was better than no son at all.

Millard paused for a moment before his aunts' graves: Fannie, shy and studious, who'd worked in a pharmacy, and Doris, stern but generous—and, he now recognized, queer as a wooden nickel. Let the associate dean hear him say *that*! But it was true, he sensed, and he loved the old spinster all the more for it. What characters his aunts had been—was there any other word for it? He could hear Doris warning, *Starve a cold, feed a fever*, and he could practically feel the soothing sensation of Fannie painting Mercurochrome on his scrapes and gashes. These were women who kept hats in milliners' bandboxes and warned against ptomaine poisoning, who whispered "cancer" under their breaths, even as it gnawed away at their loins, who called World War I "the Great War" well into the Nixon administration. After they died, he'd found a dozen double eagle gold pieces in their joint safe deposit box, wrapped in a velvet-trimmed case that also contained four silver mezuzahs and a pair of well-worn phylacteries. He never learned to whom the religious paraphernalia belonged. In addition, the dear women had preserved a deed—in Polish—to a half-acre lot in Lemberg that had once belonged to his grandfather's father; Millard had shelled out $20 translating the document.

Behind his aunts lay his older brother, Lester, who'd made a killing in the wholesale raincoat business and frittered most of it away on alimony and child support. One of Millard's nieces ran a tanning salon in California; the other was a tattoo artist turned organic wool farmer in northern Vermont. Alpacas, he thought. Or maybe vicuñas. He hadn't spoken to either woman since Lester's funeral—six years ago now—and they rarely, if ever, entered his thoughts; his sister, Harriet, touched base with them annually around Thanksgiving. For a while, in the 1970s, he and Lester too hadn't spoken—not estranged, merely distant—having little in common beyond shared DNA and a congenital proclivity for childhood ear infections. Lester had been an athlete: rugged, competitive. Able to launch a rubber Spaldeen two long city blocks with the swing of a broom handle. Also hot-tempered, capable of exploding over a late thank-you card, over an excess of salt in his consommé. A bit too much steam for Millard's kettle. But then Papa had died, a routine gallbladder procedure gone awry, and they'd reconnected over the memories of their lost, largely imagined youths. Millard retrieved a pebble from a cairn on a nearby marker—his back wouldn't let him pluck one from the ground—and placed it atop his brother's headstone. (The other fellow would hardly miss it, he reassured himself. What was one rock among dozens?) He vaguely recalled that he was supposed to place the stone with his left hand, although he couldn't remember whether this was an authentic Judaic tradition, or merely one of his aunts' many superstitions.

And then came his parents. Even at seventy-five, Millard couldn't help tearing up before the forty-year-old marker with its serpentine scalp. Papa had gone first, still at the tail of his prime. Millard and Carol had visited him at Beth Israel before the operation—he'd insisted upon a "Jewish" hospital—and he'd regaled them with stories about his recent sales trip to Arkansas and Missouri. He'd brought along a slide tray, hoping to display his inventory of knockoff mink coats and fox stoles to buyers in the Ozarks, but carousel projectors were still a novelty in the early 1970s, and his trip coincided with several high-profile hijackings to Havana, so "those dim-witted storm troopers"—that was how Papa described the airport security team in Little Rock—mistook his equipment for a weapon. He'd had to conduct a demonstration slide show with a heavy-duty flashlight before they let him board the plane. "Thank God for that," Solomon Salter had said. "Otherwise they'd be cutting my *kishkas* open in some backwater *goyish* hospital." But then Dr. Silverstein, the vice chair of surgery at the esteemed Jewish hospital, had accidentally nicked his bile duct. Ironically, Beth Israel was now St. Dymphna's-South, one of the many excellent community hospitals chewed over and swallowed by Millard's employer.

Millard's mother, Shirley, had lived another decade, but in a diminished widowhood where her social circle grew narrower and her forays outside the apartment increasingly rare. Her osteoporosis worsened. When she shopped, she carried the bag behind her in both hands, hunched forward, as though cuffed for arraignment; later, she'd loop her cane between the handles of the bag, dragging it like a plow. Eventually, her memory faded. He'd ask her the names of her *grand*children, and she'd say Lester and Millard. When he'd inquired who *he* was, if Lysander was Millard, she'd said—with remarkable confidence—"Grandpa Avram." By the end, she thought she was a seventeen-year-old pieceworker in Greenpoint again, and she kept demanding Millard bring her to the sweatshop so they wouldn't risk starvation. Death had come none too soon—not a blessing, but a painful necessity.

Millard stepped back and absorbed a panoramic view of the Salters. Or at least the few who'd made it across the Atlantic. Most of the deceased Salters—still Zarakowskis—lay somewhere in the Pale of Settlement, their corpses trammeled by Cossack hooves and panzer tracks, a heritage truncated and razed. Not that Millard had any romantic illusions about his forebears in their Ukrainian shtetl. Their lives hadn't been the quaint, quirky ideal depicted in Shalom Aleichem stories and *Fiddler on the Roof*. No, there was no Tevye the Dairyman among his ancestors. Rather, he came from a rigid, misogynistic, xenophobic tradition— people who survived on root vegetables and harsh punishments, whose law forced the husbands of rape victims to divorce their wives and forbid illegitimate children from marrying. His grandfa- ther, Meyer Wolff, had educated him on the ways of Haredi Juda- ism: how the women worked bone-crunching hours and the children went hungry while the men studied Torah all day in the bitter cold. And yet, in spite of all that, he'd sent Arnold and Sally to Hebrew school on Wednesday evenings and Sunday mornings. Lysander had refused to go—and he hadn't pushed. By the time Maia's turn came, he no longer cared.

"Farewell for now," Millard said to the stones. "See you soon."

He stretched his back—he could feel his spinal cord festering—and set off toward the newer portion of the cemetery, where Isabelle lay halfway up a sun-swept hummock. On either side, at his most recent visit, the plots had stood vacant, patches of lawn waiting to be filled. A few yards back, a family named Bloch had erected an enormous headstone for their father. *Out of proportion for the neighborhood* is what Carol would have said, one of her cherished objections to development when she'd served on Community Board Eight's zoning committee. But Isa- belle had remained calm and served up no objections. Millard re- called how, on the way to bury his wife, Grandpa Meyer Wolff had appeared jovial. At the time—Millard was only nine—he'd wondered how his beloved grandfather could laugh at a moment of sorrow. But when Isabelle had passed, he'd been seized with a desire to tell jokes at the cemetery. *Did you hear the one about the rabbi who goes golfing on Yom Kippur and hits a hole in one?* he'd said to Maia. *But who could he tell?* Only later did the grief—the icy permanence—sink in.

His stroll to Isabelle's grave took him past a festooned monument to the Jews killed in combat during the Second World War—not a grave, but a quixotic memorial commissioned by a former owner of the cemetery. The design was by Walter Hancock, cast in bronze. It was supposed to depict a brigade storming the beachheads at Normandy, but as a child, Millard had mistaken the soldiers for figure skaters, and the charging army still reminded him of the Ice Capades. He paused here for a moment, steeling himself for Isabelle. Visiting his wife's grave was always hard for him and he felt himself at a loss. No words seemed adequate for the occasion.

Talking to the dead didn't make rational sense. Either Isabelle was looking down upon him, omniscient, and he'd be telling her what she already knew, or she wasn't looking down upon anyone, because she'd long since become a clod of worm-pierced mulch. And yet he felt the compulsion to tell her things: *Lysander got himself booted from the Overlook this morning. Damn son of a bitch brought his dogs to lunch!* Or he might say: *Don't make dinner plans for tomorrow night. I'm on my way.* Or possibly: *I did what you told me to; I fell in love again. But Delilah is a supplemental blessing, not a replacement. You believe me, don't you?* He wasn't even sure that he believed this himself. How could he? He loved Delilah, after all. He'd even considered having Isabelle's body relocated to a plot that could accommodate three bodies. One of his former patients had done this so his father might be interred between his mother and stepmother. Yet somehow that had seemed a betrayal of Isabelle—that when she'd insisted they be buried *together*, she'd meant together *and* alone, not in a harem. Delilah, he knew, planned to be cremated, her ashes scattered over Point Loma at sunset, so the issue of eternal resting places had never caused conflict between them. Maybe love defied the laws of matter and energy: One could love two women completely, treasuring each conditionally without harming the other. Why not?

Millard felt his shirt matted to his chest, the bow of Isabelle's ring against his sternum. He'd grown so accustomed to the memorial pendant that, except when he showered, he noticed it no more than his underwear or socks. The ring, which featured three identical diamonds, had also been his mother's engagement ring, and he still remembered sliding it off the old woman's finger on the evening of her final stroke. His father's watch and cuff links had gone to Lester, and probably sat in the safe deposit box of one of his nieces—or under a mattress, for all he knew; Grandma Minnie's china had ended up in Tucson with his sister. (How strangely, how haphazardly property was ultimately divided!) During their marriage, Carol had insisted on keeping her jewelry in the freezer, as a safeguard against burglars. But his first wife hadn't wanted an engagement ring or a wedding band. (*For what? So the world can know I'm married? Why not just brand me with a hot poker?* she'd objected.) On that final autumn night in the hospice, as Isabelle's breath faded, he'd removed his mother's ring, but left in place his beloved's white gold wedding band and the opal-studded Hamsa amulet she'd worn around her neck.

A scorching stillness had settled over the cemetery. What heat! What a day to die! Visitors placed lilies at the base of the Hancock sculpture every Memorial Day—what his aunts had called Decoration Day—and their stalks now lay desiccated in the high grass. Overhead, a turkey vulture soared between patches of buttermilk clouds. Maybe a bad omen? But Millard had spent seven decades rejecting omens, so he wasn't about to start fretting over them now. That way lay madness: Today one worried about a circling buzzard, tomorrow one hired a haruspex to inspect the entrails of sheep or preached a second Star of Bethlehem. No, buzzards were rare in northern New Jersey, but not unheard of—and one had to situate this raptor in the context of things he hadn't encountered that afternoon: ravens on the telephone wires, owls in daytime, flickering lights at meals. His aunts had carried such nonsense with them from the Old World: covering mirrors during mourning, turning over the table and chairs on which a coffin had rested. Millard's childhood often seemed like one long taboo, his adolescence a series of apotropaic maneuvers. God forbid one lit three cigarettes off a match, placed hats on beds, drank water that had reflected the moon. Once Fannie had caught him rocking an empty chair, and you'd have thought he'd sent his allowance to Cardinal Spellman. Yet rational empiricist as he was, Millard occasionally rubbed his late wife's ring—not for good luck, not exactly, but for reassurance. He did so now, tracing the outline of the silver through his sweater. Who could fault even the most balanced of scientific minds for such a primal, uxorious gesture? He looked up again: The buzzard was gone.

Millard drew a deep breath and rounded the curve that led toward Isabelle's resting place, toward the eight foot by five foot by three foot patch of earth where he'd soon spend eternity. To his amazement—for his first reaction was shock, not horror—the soil in front of the headstone appeared freshly disturbed. In fact, a heap of excess earth lay nearby, scorched brittle in the heat, a shovel still protruding. On the headstone, a presumptuous engraver had even carved a date of death: June 12, 2015. Someone had usurped his grave!

On any other day, he'd have taken this error—for it had to

be an error, rather than some divine gag—in stride. But on the day of his suicide, such a mistake was, as his aunts used to say, "decidedly unacceptable."

Millard's watch read half past two. Konnie was waiting for him. But what did that matter? Let her wait—it was *his* dime.

He yanked the shovel from the mound and heaved it into a privet hedge. Why Millard did this, he couldn't explain. He'd often done the same with orange traffic cones placed prematurely beside his tires in anticipation of the ad hoc no parking zones created for VIP funerals and movie filmings. The motion sent a jolt of pain through his bad disc and into his upper thigh. On his hike to Mount Hebron's office, he found himself favoring his opposite leg.

The cemetery headquarters occupied a half-timbered Tudor-style cottage that seemed more suited for an English village than a Jewish graveyard. In a different location, Millard could have imagined charlatans hawking it as the birthplace of Milton or Bunyan, or a community theater using the structure to stage *Hansel and Gretel*. Orioles and grackles congregated at a birdbath out front; a flag hung limp above an eternal flame. The husk of a pay phone, sans telephone, stood to the left of the door, and to the right, adjacent to a louvered shutter, a sign listed regulations: *No fireworks, skateboards, etc.* Who in God's name brought a skateboard to a memorial park? But someone probably had, because rules stemmed from transgressions. (Similarly, ice-pick wounds, in addition to gunshots and knifings, were reportable to the New York State Department of Public Health, he'd once read—presumably because an epidemic of high-profile ice pickings must have occurred around the time that the regulations were codified.) When Millard crossed into the stuffy office, a tiny bell jangled above the door hinge.

A chubby woman of about twenty greeted Millard; when

she smiled, she exposed braces across both rows of teeth. "Good afternoon and welcome to Mount Hebron-Beth-El," she said. The atmosphere smelled of musty ledgers and unwashed carpets.

"I'm not sure if you're the right person to speak with," said Millard. "There seems to be a problem with a grave. . . ."

"Well, let's see how we can help you today," said the girl. "Do you know the row and plot numbers?"

"Grave G60-B #14 and grave G60-B #15," said Millard. "It's a double."

The girl plugged the numbers into an ancient computer. "Here you are. Millard K. and Isabelle Salter. Both occupied. What seems to be the problem?"

"The problem," said Millard, "is that *I'm* Millard Salter."

The girl glanced down at the computer screen and back up at Millard.

"Oh," said the girl. "Shit."

"So I'm not sure how I go about rectifying this, but it *does* need to be rectified."

"Certainly," agreed the girl—but there was nothing certain about her tone. "Excuse me for one moment, Mr. Salter."

She disappeared into a back room and he heard her phoning her boss. About three minutes later, she returned with a husky Russian woman. The supervisor sported a heavy cake of rouge from her ears to her chin—which she must have believed made her look girlish and attractive, but actually suggested the malar rash of lupus; her clump of hair—for there was no other way to describe her coiffure—matched the mauve pastels of her blouse. The woman's voice contained all the sympathy of the Kaiser authorizing an execution. Her underling retreated into a far corner of the office, like a chambermaid waiting for the royal bedpan.

"I hear a rumor," said the Russian woman, "that you are having some difficulty with one of our locations. . . ."

"It is not a rumor," said Millard. "Someone is buried in my grave."

"You are *sure* of this?"

"There's a mound of soil next to it," he said. "And there's a date of death on the stone."

"Then you are *not* sure of it. Maybe a misunderstanding."

"Maybe a lawsuit," answered Millard. "I'm telling you there's someone else in my spot. Ask her!" He hated to involve the office girl, but he had little choice. "She tells me I'm dead."

"You don't have the row and plot numbers, do you?"

"Grave G60-B #14 and grave G60-B #15."

The Russian woman punched the data into her keyboard. "Yes, it does say you're dead. You don't recall the date of death on the marker."

He held his composure. "June 12, 2015."

Again she punched away at her machine. Its innards wheezed under the exertion.

"Problem solved," said the woman. "We buried a Myron Slater on June 12. Similar name. Somehow, he found his way to the wrong location." She waved her hand dismissively. "See, just a minor mistake."

She frowned at him—her thin lips and painted eyebrows accusing him of raising a fuss over nothing, of wasting her precious time. Overhead, a ceiling fan swatted the stagnant air.

"But the problem is *not* solved. There is still someone else's body in my grave."

The supervisor didn't appear perturbed. "Not a difficulty. We can offer you an exchange—at a discount. I have some excellent locations near the mausoleum. Those are premium spaces on account of the quiet. We can cut thirty percent off the base price. . . ."

"I don't want an exchange," said Millard. "My wife is buried in that grave."

"Oh, your wife is already deceased?"

"Check your computer, dammit," he snapped. "Now I need you to take him out so that you can put me in. *Capiche?*"

"All right. We can do that."

She sounded grudging, as though he'd made an unreasonable demand.

"How long will it take?" he demanded.

"Usually only a few days . . . a week at most."

"I don't have a week. This is an urgent matter."

The woman nodded with indifference. "I understand. We'll take care of it."

"I don't mean to give you a hard time, ma'am," Millard said. "The thing is, I may not look it, but I'm critically ill. Dying. *Arrivederci. Sayonara. Auf Wiedersehen,* comrade." He did not know how to say goodbye in Russian. "Honestly, I could keel over at any moment," he added, snapping his fingers. "Poof."

"Poof?" she asked.

"Poof."

To emphasize his warning, he removed his handkerchief from his back pocket and feigned a violent cough—something between the bark of croup and the hack of tuberculosis. The Russian woman stepped back from the counter and shielded her face with her sleeve.

"I'll bump this work order up to priority," promised the supervisor. "We can dig them up fast if we have to."

"That's reassuring, I suppose," said Millard. "I'll be back tomorrow to check."

10

Konnie was waiting with the cab where he'd left her. A gust of cold air hit Millard's face as he entered—and he welcomed it—although it came with another dose of the girl's noxious music. His watch read 2:58. According to the meter, he was in the red for $140.50. She turned down the volume on the radio and said, "It took you long enough."

"I thought it was *my* dime," said Millard.

"Whatever. I was just afraid you'd gotten buried alive."

Millard considered revealing his switcheroo with Myron Slater, but he suspected the girl wouldn't care. "Not exactly," he said. "I'm sorry I kept you waiting."

"No worries. It gave me time to work on the Riemann hypothesis."

"The *what*?"

"The Riemann hypothesis. It's one of the six unsolved Millennium Prize Problems in mathematics. If you figure it out, you win $1,000,000."

"Bullshit," said Millard. "Whatever you're talking about doesn't exist."

"Excuse me?"

"Once bitten, twice shy," he said. "I'm done being a guinea pig in your experiment."

"It's not an experiment. It's an art project."

The girl retrieved her phone from the dashboard and her

thumbs whirled like eggbeaters over the tiny keys. An instant later, she handed the device across the divider. On the homepage of the Clay Mathematics Institute, the Riemann hypothesis was listed as an unsolved conundrum, immediately between the Yang-Mills mass gap problem and the Swinnerton-Dyer conjecture. "You win," he said, returning the phone. "Did you solve it?"

"No. I wasn't trying."

"But I thought you said—"

"I lied. I'm terrible at math. I can hardly balance my checkbook."

That was too much for Millard. He folded his arms across his chest—determined not to speak to the girl unless absolutely necessary. But the cab remained stationed in park, idling, beads of sweat forming on the windows. "Well? What are we waiting for?" demanded Millard.

"We're waiting," replied Konnie, "for you to tell me where to go."

"Back to the hospital," he ordered. Wasn't that obvious? But the girl hadn't even shifted into drive when another idea hijacked his thoughts. It was only three o'clock. He wouldn't be meeting Delilah until five. "Change of plans," he said, satisfied with the calculations in his head. "Do you know how to get to the Grand Concourse?"

"Not really," replied the girl. "But the magic lady does."

A moment passed before Millard realized she meant the GPS navigator.

"Can this magic lady get us to the Grand Concourse and One hundred and Seventy-Seventh Street?"

"She can get us *anywhere*."

Konnie activated the device and soon their guide was serving up commands: *Turn right on Bergen Avenue. Then take your second left onto Parkland Drive.* Millard remembered Maia telling him all about the corporeal form behind "the magic lady," who was actually in her late twenties and had lived in the same residential dorm with his daughter at Yale. Apparently, the previous voice—of a didactic middle-aged woman from Dayton, Ohio—reminded male drivers too much of their wives, so they ignored her directions.

Konnie turned on the music again, its volume low but menacing.

Millard cleared his throat. "Would it be all right if we kept the radio off?"

The girl responded with an exaggerated groan. "What is *wrong* with you, Millard Salter? This is my favorite band."

"You're kidding me."

"We Left the Puppy in the Microwave," said the girl. "I go to all of their concerts."

"*That's* the name of a band?"

Konnie ignored his question, but she did turn off the radio. He knew more about odd band names than she suspected: Maia had been a fan of Avocado Unicorn at one point, but at least they'd performed vaguely in the genre of folk rock. He'd listened to a CD once, at his daughter's insistence: the group sounded like Peter, Paul, and Mary on amphetamines. Also, years earlier, a patient had brought him a recording of her jazz quartet, oddly billed as *Hedy Lamarr Was a Communist*. He'd been so puzzled by the provocative name, which the patient refused to explain, that he'd actually gone to the branch library—this was in the pre-Internet era—to check out a biography of the actress. Miss Lamarr, it turned out, had been many things: a shoplifter, a pill popper, a plastic surgery addict—but *not* a communist. Konnie with a K, he realized, as he considered sharing this anecdote, had probably never heard of Hedy Lamarr.

"You know I used to be a musician," Millard said.

The girl looked up, mildly intrigued.

"I played a mean saxophone," he lied. "I did gigs with Frankie Valli, Jefferson Airplane . . . You've never heard of them."

"I've *heard* of them."

"The Rolling Stones. You've heard of the Rolling Stones, right?"

"You did *not* play with the Rolling Stones."

"I *opened* for them," said Millard. "Milwaukee Coliseum. 1965."

He had no idea whether this venue existed—but hopefully neither did she.

"Oh, you only *opened* for them," said Konnie.

She sounded rather underwhelmed by his fabrications—as though, in her world, opening for the Rolling Stones ranked alongside finding a prize in a Cracker Jack box. Initially, his goal had been to lure her into the same trap she'd sprung for him, making up bands and arenas until she claimed familiarity with nonexistent rock stars, but her lack of interest undermined Millard's own. Besides, he had no gift for this sort of deception. Soon he fell silent, leaving her with his trivial lies, and entirely forgot about their game. They crossed the George Washington Bridge again, following the whims of the magic lady, and Konnie pressed the front of the meter to halt the double rate. If the girl were duplicitous in some matters, she appeared scrupulous in others.

They approached the Grand Concourse from the Cross Bronx Expressway. Millard recalled when the majestic boulevard had been the Jewish Champs-Élysées, before Robert Moses sawed his six-lane highway through East Tremont. He'd lived in the penthouse of the DeWitt Clinton from the age of two until he turned fourteen—and never, he sometimes reflected, has a child lived such a life of sheltered innocence. There were distant calamities: Litvak cousins butchered by *Einsatzgruppen*, an uncle named Sam who was cared for at an asylum on Staten Island. Years later, following Fannie's death, and long after Sam's, Doris had told him about her brother's breakdown, which sounded like bipolar mania rather than schizophrenia—treatable today with an arsenal of mood stabilizers. But Sam had rarely been mentioned during Millard's boyhood, where his father preached mostly Democratic politics and an idealistic brand of Zionism. When they sang "Next Year in Jerusalem" at Passover, none of his relatives meant that literally. Why flee to a Middle Eastern desert when you already lived in the borough of milk and honey?

"I grew up in the DeWitt Clinton Building," he said as they exited onto Jerome Avenue. "This used to be one of the most expensive addresses in New York."

"Could have fooled me," said Konnie.

The neighborhood looked in better shape than he'd expected. He'd taken Isabelle and Maia to see his former haunts during the 1990s, when the storefronts had been boarded up and the sidewalks caked with crack vials. They hadn't dared to get out of their car—and he'd even insisted they duck to the floor until he returned to the expressway, fearful of stray bullets, although it was midafternoon on a Saturday. Now the streets teemed with children again: Latino kids purchasing snow cones, cavorting in the spray of fire hydrants. Yet these youngsters were chaperoned—sometimes by mothers who looked half Maia's age. In Millard's day, his friends had claimed free roam of the streets without supervision.

They turned onto 177th Street. Millard scanned the storefronts: an Ethiopian hair-beader, a check-cashing establishment, a bodega flying a Dominican flag. B'nai Yitzhak, the opulent, three-story synagogue where Millard had attended weekly Torah lessons and collected quarters to plant trees on kibbutzim now housed an Evangelical church. A banner hanging behind a baroque gate proclaimed: "Some Questions Can't Be Answered by Google." From a second-floor window, another canvas declared: "Salvation guaranteed—or we'll return your sins." At least the pastor had a sense of humor. What would Rabbi Kohlberg have said, Millard wondered, if the old man could see what had become of his sanctuary? (Rabbi Kohlberg, who'd insisted that Palestine had been empty before the Jews arrived, who'd refused to permit women wearing pants into the tabernacle.) But Rabbi K. was long gone, and a few years earlier, Millard had read an article in the *New Yorker* called "The Great Tree Fraud"—which reported that the *tzedakah* he'd raised for arboreal renewal in the Holy Land had largely been diverted. So let the fundamentalists have the place, thought Millard. Maybe they'd do some good with it.

Not that he wasn't saddened by the changes. Virtually nothing remained of the vibrant Jewish and Italian neighborhood that he remembered: Homberg's Groceries, Mrs. Rudnick's cigarette and candy shop, Plotnick's Eggs & Dairy. By the time his family had left for Hager Heights, there were already signs of incipient decline: blacks and Puerto Ricans encroaching north from Melrose and Mott Haven, entire blocks cleared for the pylons of the expressway. But it was a few years later that witnessed the collapse: the shuttering of the Art Deco movie houses, the Third Avenue El sold for scrap. And then Co-op City opened, offering holdouts the opportunity to own their own apartments, and that was the nail in the coffin lid. His aunt Fannie had used a more crass description, one that still made Millard cringe: "The *shvartzes* moved in and we got out." But who could blame the old woman for her prejudices? She'd been born in a shtetl and entered girlhood on Orchard Street; everyone she met, from the midwife who delivered her to the mortician who ultimately embalmed her, was an Ashkenazi Jew. All she knew of nonwhites came from listening to *Amos 'n' Andy*—and even they were white! In contrast, his mother had grown up in Yorkville, under the care of a black nanny, with whom she later exchanged cards at holidays, and whose husband she visited in the hospital. Dora had come to Millard's wedding, sporting a stylish lime hat. She'd given him a $50 check—quite a sum for a present in 1965—second only to his own father. He'd felt guilty for weeks. In hindsight, he'd realized that to his mother, who'd rarely social-ized outside her extended family, this frail old colored woman was probably her closest friend. Yet how much of a friend could she really have been to Dora when she sat politely in her over-furnished parlor and listened as her sisters-in-law described Dora's people as *shvartzes*? All of that now seemed so long ago.

They'd stopped in front of the DeWitt Clinton. The build-ing's Art Nouveau towers loomed over the avenue like barbicans, flashing the whiplash curves of its stonework. Jackalopes and sa-tyrs wandered the friezes. Gryphons roared in the cornices above the stately entryway, where a red carpet and white-gloved door-men had once greeted residents. Now a potbellied rent-a-cop sat out front on a beach chair; air conditioners buzzed in the win-dows above, dripping onto the pavement. The sight reminded Millard of a Thanksgiving dinner, many years earlier, when he'd reviewed his parents' wedding photos with Maia. The bride's fa-ther had splurged on a professional photographer. All of the guests were asked to pose, table by table, quite a novelty in 1937. Millard realized, as he had flipped through the pictures with his daughter, that every last person at the celebration was likely dead. Some—a dandyish young man in a striped blazer with peaked lapels, for instance—Millard could not even recognize, al-though he was clearly a relative, marked by the same sharp chin and ski-slope philtrum that distinguished all of his mother's kin.

(Everybody at the wedding, except the rabbi and Dora, was a relation or an in-law, even if the precise links on the family tree lay forgotten in the old country; friendship, outside blood and marriage, had been an alien concept to his grandparents' generation.) Alas, when Millard was gone—tomorrow—most of the remaining faces would fade into the ghastly oblivion of history. So too would his memories of the DeWitt Clinton: one-armed Eliezer, who overfed the furnace; Dr. Blatt, the optometrist, and his wife, renowned far afield for distributing licorice pipes and Choward's mints on Purim; primordial, German-speaking Mrs. Kugelman, who banged on her ceiling with a mop handle if he ran across the hardwood floors in his sneakers.

"Here we are," said Konnie. "Grand Concourse and One hundred Seventy-Seventh."

To emphasize their arrival, the magic lady announced, *The destination is on your left.*

He wished Delilah were at his side—not merely for her companionship, but so he might show her the streets that had formed him: the alcove behind Schnorr's Kosher Meats where he'd kissed tubby Lillie Balzer on a dare, the bench in front of the credit union where Great-Uncle Lou had dozed off, never to awaken. Carol knew all the corners and crannies of his history: she'd met his parents, his aunts, his medical school professors. He'd discovered, over the years, that as painstakingly as you described another human being, there was no substitute for actually meeting him. With Isabelle, it had been too late for introductions, but at least he'd taken her to the scenes of his triumphs and setbacks. But for Delilah, his past was as blank as a bedsheet, much as her history was for him: a few theatrical posters, some snapshots on a dresser, a niece in Tel Aviv he'd spoken to twice on the phone. None of this should have mattered to him—love was about the present, not the past—and yet it did. If only he'd met Delilah a few months earlier, when she'd still been able to travel around the city. . . . *If only your grandmother had possessed testicles*, he'd once heard his father say to a delinquent buyer, *she'd have been your grandfather*.

"I lived on the top floor," said Millard—as much to himself as to Konnie. "On a clear morning, you could see all the way to the Statue of Liberty."

"I went there once," said the girl. "My ex-boyfriend took me. He passed out on the climb up to the crown and the Park Service had to carry him down on a stretcher."

At least he didn't topple over the edge, thought Millard. Or get himself crushed to death like Shorty McTeague. McTeague did odd jobs for Eliezer, the one-armed building manager, and for the tenants of the DeWitt Clinton, running Papa's suits to the dry cleaner, polishing the bowling-pin newels and barley-sugar banisters, carrying Mrs. Kugelman's trunk to the curb for her annual flight to Miami. He'd been born in County Sligo and still spoke with a heavy brogue, almost a foreign dialect to a Jewish kid like Millard who'd thought *gupel* and *leffel* were English words until the age of eleven, when he'd wanted a fork and spoon at a delicatessen. McTeague was also, Millard realized years later, cognitively impaired. Back then, the neighbors just called him slow, or, if feeling less generous, dopey. One afternoon, shortly after Millard turned twelve, he'd run into Shorty McTeague on the twelfth-story landing, where the factotum was changing the dead lightbulbs in the chandeliers. The eighteen-foot ceilings made this a multifaceted process that involved lowering the chandelier frame, then standing on a ladder to remove each of the frosted glass shades that cupped the candle tubes. That day, one of these glass shades happened to be cracked and required a replacement. "Will you do me a favor, lad?" McTeague asked Millard, who'd been headed down to Carlton's for a shaved ice. "Keep an eye on this ladder while I go down to the cellar. It's rather bockety and we don't needs nobody snapping their neck." Reluctantly, Millard agreed. McTeague pressed the button for the elevator, and when the double doors slid open, stepped straight down to the bottom of the shaft. The car itself had jammed at the roof and the counterweight buffer had failed. Seconds later, the car dropped through the chute, unchecked, hammering the Irishman to pulp.

Millard had watched the fire department extricate the body. His first dead man. Had McTeague not asked him for assistance, or had he refused, *he'd* have become the macerated form gurneyed away beneath a cotton tarp. None of this was lost upon him—not at the time, not since. If a career in medicine taught one anything, it was that everybody from the cafeteria cashiers to the exalted President Bloodfinch lived at the edge of a cataclysmic precipice, only one errant bus or mutated cell away from a rapid and painful demise. He'd never told anyone—not even his brother—what he'd witnessed.

"Can you pull around the corner?" asked Millard. "Onto One hundred Seventy-Eighth."

Konnie did as instructed. The meter clicked through $170.00.

"Pull up a bit," he ordered. "To the far end of the building— by the cornerstone."

Sure enough, his engraving endured: MS + LM, surrounded by a cockeyed heart. He'd etched his romantic memorial during the summer after the sixth grade, on the night after they luted over several cracks in the masonry with fresh concrete. Lettie Moshewitz! How he'd worshiped the earth she walked upon—in the way that only a smitten twelve-year-old can. She'd developed early, but hadn't updated her wardrobe, so every curve of her Maidenform brassieres bulged beneath her sheer blouses. She had been the year ahead of him at Samuel Tilden Elementary, but they crossed paths in the corridors, and her family lived only two doors up the Concourse in the Centennial Arms. To Millard, it was like living a block away from Lana Turner or Jane Russell. His brother and her older brothers played sandlot baseball together on Saturdays, which is how he learned that the Moshewitzes would be spending their summer in Far Rockaway—which forced him to act, possibly prematurely. That June, Millard left a hand-written four-page love note with her doorman, and waited through July and August for a response that never arrived. By the time her family returned in September, he despised her.

Two years later, as his parents were packing for Hager Heights, he mustered the courage to telephone Lettie at home.

"You never answered my letter," he said. "That was a crummy thing to do."

She seemed genuinely surprised—flustered. She insisted she'd never received it.

"Oh, you left it with Jordi," she said. "That explains everything. Jordi quit and joined the merchant marine. Cleared out in the middle of the night." Lettie lowered her voice. "My dad says he owed people money."

"So you really didn't get it?"

Millard's fourteen-year-old heart swelled with forgiveness and hope. Here was a tragic miscommunication of Shakespearean dimensions. Never again would he dismiss the plays Mrs. Galynker assigned in English class as implausible.

"But it all worked out for the best," said Lettie. "You know I was going with someone. Still am. So I wouldn't have been interested."

"Oh," said Millard, deflated. And then desperation took hold of him. "But what if you *weren't* going with someone? Would I be your second choice?"

A long silence followed—like the hollow in the OR after a patient expires.

"I have to go," said Lettie. "My mom's calling me."

He ran into her again thirty years later at Gimbels. He was returning a pair of ice skates that he'd bought Sally for Hanukkah: Who knew that a girl's feet could grow two sizes between Thanksgiving and Christmas! To his wonder, and in a perverse way his delight, he recognized the zaftig, overly made-up woman behind the sales register. Lettie seemed delighted to see him— and although he was happily married to Carol, he'd still scanned her finger for a ring. All she wore was a pink sapphire on her right index finger. "It's so good running into you," she'd said. "And you're a doctor. We always knew you were a smart one." For Millard, the downfall of Lettie Moshewitz from glamour queen to counter girl was epic; he couldn't have been more shocked if he'd found Douglas MacArthur pumping his gas. But to Lettie, who'd never been on the pedestal where Millard imagined her, working the holiday season at Gimbels was merely the ordinary course of an extremely ordinary life. Somehow, after this encounter, Millard understood that she'd been lying about not receiving his letter.

"You see those initials?" Millard asked Konnie. "Above the cornerstone."

"Barely," she said.

"I carved them. Millard Salter and Lettie Moshewitz." He admired his handiwork, bold finger-scraped characters testifying to affection that had long ago dried up. "I wanted to write 'forever' but I ran out of room."

"Was she your girlfriend?"

"Sort of," said Millard. "Not really."

Konnie looked up with more interest. "Well, which was it? 'Sort of' or 'not really'?"

"It would take too long to explain," said Millard. "*On my dime.*"

The girl shrugged. "You done with memory lane?"

"In a minute. I'd like to get a bit of fresh air."

He wondered if anybody he knew still lived in the neighborhood—maybe some brave classmate who'd weathered the blight of the eighties. Not likely. Even the elderly couple dozing on the bench in the traffic median looked Latin American.

"Are you sure? This isn't a great neighborhood for a guy like you," she said. "You're basically walking around with a giant target on your back."

Now she really sounded like a girl from Scarsdale or Chappaqua. The Grand Concourse midafternoon wasn't exactly an alley in Hunts Point at four in the morning.

"I'll take my chances," he said.

He climbed out of the taxicab into the afternoon heat. Even the shade of twelve stories of solid Minnesota granite provided only limited relief; the sun gleamed off the cantilevered windows that wrapped around the high-rise across 178th Street. The Hotel Saint Claude had once stood on that corner, stomping grounds of Gene Tunney and Mae West and Al Jolson. Marilyn Monroe and Joe DiMaggio had occupied the honeymoon suite for a weekend in 1955—and Millard's brother stayed up all night, patrolling the side entrances, in search of an autograph. A few years later, Greer Garson toppled down the ballroom staircase and broke an ankle. City planners razed the entire structure for urban renewal in the 1970s. At present, many of the windows in the tedious development that had replaced the ornate hotel still displayed vinyl decals depicting curtains and flowerpots, distributed by the Commission of Housing and Development, at the borough's nadir, to create the illusion of occupancy. Closer by, kids hardly as tall as his waist played pickup basketball around a netless rim, their rib cages limned under dark, sweat-lacquered skin, competing boomboxes blaring from the sidelines. In Millard's day, the games of choice had been box ball and Johnny-on-the-Pony and Ringolevio, and you couldn't walk half a city block without stumbling upon the chalk outlines of a Skully board or a hopscotch course.

How Millard regretted Delilah wasn't with him! He had so much he wished to tell her—to show her. He'd even have considered dropping by his old apartment, or what remained of it, as he'd learned from a housing cop on his previous visit that the penthouse had been split into three smaller railroad flats. On that earlier excursion, he'd wanted to take Maia to see his childhood bedroom, but Isabelle had objected. "It's intrusive," she'd said. "It would be different if you grew up on Sutton Place, but these people will take it the wrong way. Honestly, I'd be insulted too if I were in their shoes." So that had been that. Besides, he'd consoled himself, the neighborhood was still too rough to explore with an eight-year-old. Yet today, if he'd been with Delilah, he'd have sought a brief glimpse. What harm could it really do to ask?

Millard ambled around the rear of the building, where enormous metal dumpsters collected the day's trash and recyclables. On his prior visit, he'd made a U-turn here in his Oldsmobile, interrupting what was most likely an act of prostitution; fortunately, Maia had been too engrossed in her biography of Clara Barton to notice. Now, the area stood quiet as a synagogue on a Sunday morning—nary a pimp nor a dealer, nor even an innocent bystander, in sight. What the occasion really called for, Millard reflected, was a bout of heroics. Since he was going to die in—he checked his watch—less than six hours, this was his once-in-a-lifetime opportunity to prevent a strong-arm holdup or a sexual assault. What did he have to lose? The worst that could happen was that he died a few hours prematurely, a hero's death on the streets of the Bronx. Under the circumstances, he figured, Delilah would certainly forgive him. Yet for all the violent crime in New York City, it seemed that none surfaced when you actually wanted it.

He looked up into the branches of the honey locusts, the patch of blue beyond as close as he might ever reach to the heavens. *Dear God*, he said, half in jest, *I'm not asking for the Great Train Robbery, but would a minor mugging cost you so much?* He put up his dukes and mimed his fighting potential, aware that he more resembled the Cowardly Lion than Rocky Marciano.

As though on cue, Millard glanced at an object charging at him in the corner of his eye. That "object" turned out to be a young African American male in an orange do-rag and sleeveless Knicks jersey. A woman wearing a sequined skirt chased after him on a broken heel, shouting: "Stop! My purse!" The thief was within yards of Millard before he noticed him—and then, with one swift motion, Millard tripped the fellow. The sound of the youth's skull colliding with the pavement reverberated across the asphalt and stopped Millard's breath.

He suspected that he had killed the man, but the fellow stumbled to his feet, disoriented, blood trickling from his temple down to the crook of his jaw. Before Millard had an opportunity to render assistance, other young men emerged—seemingly from nowhere—and surrounded him, encroaching as he inched backwards toward a wire fence. When the woman in sequins arrived at the scene of his heroics, she did not retrieve her purse. Rather, she tended to the wounds of the staggering perpetrator. "Are you crazy?" she shouted at Millard.

"I don't understand. He stole your purse."

"You fool," she cried. "We're filming a video. . . ."

Sure enough, one of the men who'd encircled him had a portable camera mounted on his shoulder and another carried a Lehman College athletics bag. They looked—at a second glance—like film students, not street thugs. "Call an ambulance," pleaded the woman. She'd knelt down beside her assailant, who'd once again sprawled out on the concrete.

For a moment, Millard considered apologizing and offering restitution—maybe if he paid the fellow's healthcare costs, they'd call it even. Then embarrassment overcame him. And downright shame. Sure, he'd made an honest mistake—but that's not how the media would portray it. No, he'd be categorized with those trigger-happy white cops who shot unarmed black civilians, which might not be so far from the truth. If he'd seen an identical woman running after a white teenager along Park Avenue, would he have stuck out his foot? He couldn't be sure. Not that these kids weren't partially to blame: How was he supposed to know they were filming a video? Nobody, he was sure, would give him the benefit of the doubt. And while dying a hero had its appeal, committing suicide with a cloud of violent racism hanging over his head was another matter entirely, not a fate he was willing to risk. One of the videographers advanced toward him—possibly to detain him until the police arrived. What made the most sense rationally, as well as ethically, was to identify himself as a physician and render first aid. Millard sensed the adrenaline coursing into his neck, his temples. On impulse, he made a break for it.

Millard ran and fell, scraping his palms and knees. He could feel tiny pebbles under his flesh, but he launched himself forward and continued running, as though charging the cliffs at Omaha Beach or the Union lines at Gettysburg. He dared not look back, but he sensed the film crew close on his heels. Then he heard one of the men shout—from a good distance away—"He's an old man! Let him go!" When he finally rounded the front of the building, his breath felt trapped in his lungs, as though his throat had been jammed with a stopper. Half-running, half-hobbling, he thrust himself into the waiting cab.

"What happened to you?" demanded Konnie.

"Drive," Millard tried to say. "Please, drive."

When he realized no comprehensible sound was coming out of his mouth, he pounded the back of the driver's seat. She peeled away from the curbside.

Slowly, Millard's breath returned, in harsh barks, as though he were recovering from whooping cough. He spoke from first-hand experience: He'd overcome pertussis, and scarlet fever, and German measles. Not to mention chronic bouts of otitis media. His brother, Lester, had suffered a bout of polio that left portions of his throat and uvula paralyzed; for his entire adult life, the man had been forced to carry a small bottle of ipecac in his trousers, to help him throw up in case of a poisoning or accidental ingestion. His second cousin—Great-Uncle Lou's oldest daughter—had succumbed to diphtheria at five. Now toddlers were vaccinated against chicken pox. Chicken pox! What a cozy life these kids led. But if he'd overcome whooping cough, he could handle a brief chase across a parking lot.

He assessed his wounds: some abrasions on his palms, a laceration below his left thumb; more concerning, he'd shredded his right pants leg and lost a patch of skin above the knee. On top of that, his bad disc was kicking like an infant. All of his limbs moved; he had full range of vision in both eyes. He'd survive. His sweater, a fisherman's knit that Sally had given him for his sixtieth birthday, appeared unsalvageable; he removed it and used the white wool of the cardigan to stanch the wound on his palm.

While he conducted this corporeal inventory, Konnie eased the cab to the curbside and shifted into park. A solid thirty seconds passed before he noticed.

"Why are we stopped?" he asked.

"Because I don't know where we're going," said Konnie. "I figured you didn't want me to keep driving straight ahead forever."

He nodded. Not unreasonable of her. They'd stopped opposite a FedEx warehouse, where a handful of uniformed workers smoked cigarettes on the exterior steps.

"So?" she asked. "Where to?"

Millard's initial reaction was to retreat to his apartment—to shower, disinfect his wounds, wrap bandages around his knee and hand. But on further reflection, he decided to return to his office for a final once-over: to make sure he'd left behind nothing of great personal value. Moreover, he wished to leave Miss Nickelsworth an early Christmas present, because he knew her well enough to recognize she'd feel cheated if he didn't, and also to pen a brief note to the chairman recommending Stan Laguna as his replacement. In addition, he had a handful of instructions for his colleagues on the locations of various documents, the timing of certain reporting deadlines, etc. Although Millard didn't plan to leave behind a tidy red notebook like Isabelle had done for him, he did wish to pass along some modicum of order.

"Just take me back to St. Dymphna's," he instructed. "Fast as you can."

They drove back to Manhattan in silence. Millard tried phoning Maia again, but her mailbox remained full—which was highly out of character. He almost started to worry, but checked himself: There'd be little he could do for her, even if she were in distress, and she was a brilliant, sensible adult woman capable of looking after herself; moreover, his subconscious reason for worrying about her was likely Hal Storch's so-called life instinct. He'd be looking for excuses not to hang himself, and he couldn't allow that. Konnie took him at his word and drove the vehicle at full throttle, wending between slower traffic with the dexterity of a fish. She covered half a block on the sidewalk to circumvent a wide delivery van. For a brief stretch of the Willis Avenue Bridge, she drove in the on-coming traffic lane. They pulled up in front of St. Dymphna's awning at 3:40. The meter read $205.85.

Millard reached into his wallet. A quixotic notion entered his mind and ricocheted around like errant grapeshot: He could write Konnie a check for $1,000,000. Didn't lonely old men do that all the time for their swan songs? Every night the evening news seemed to conclude with a tale of a truck driver who con-signed a homely waitress in Iowa his winning lottery ticket, or a college freshman from rural West Virginia who discovered the disabled miner next door, that harmless fellow she'd bought gro-ceries for a few times, had died and bequeathed her enough in savings from his Social Security checks to fund four years of tui-tion. So why not Konnie? With a few strokes of a pen, he could set her up for life.

But he didn't. Somehow, his sensible instincts kicked in— the same instincts that saw him save pennies by ripping napkins in half or shelling his own walnuts. He'd grown up with parents who'd survived the Depression. He was generous, but not de-ranged. Such an act of extravagance would raise too many ques-tions, even add an unseemly tinge to Millard's suicide. Besides, these acts of so-called selfless beneficence always rubbed Mil-lard's dander crossways, because he sensed something sexual, if not downright sinister, in such posthumous gestures. How could it be otherwise? You never read about lonely truckers and homebound lumberjacks giving their savings away to striving young men.

He tipped her $100 on a $205.85 fare. Forty-eight percent. "Go make some art," he said, winking.

"Thanks," said Konnie. The five crisp twenties did not appear to impress her.

Not too long ago, he wanted to tell her, $100 was a good month's salary—my mother furnished an entire kitchen for $150, including a Philco refrigerator with a monitor top. But he didn't. You had to have lived through something to truly believe it.

"Don't spend it all at once," he said, and shut the door.

11

Traffic currents ran heavily against Millard as he passed through the revolving doors and up the main stairs into St. Dymphna's resplendent glass-framed piazza. The nursing shifts on the medical units turned over at three o'clock, perpetuating a delayed but collective stampede for the exits—not as dramatic as at the post office or the Department of Motor Vehicles, but strong enough to generate a pedestrian tide. Millard strode quickly toward the service elevators, ashamed of his frayed trousers, hoping to make quick work of this office pit stop, when a familiar voice arrested his progress.

"Millard," called the speaker, in an idiosyncratic, patrician tone that Eleanor Roosevelt might have used to summon Franklin. "A word with you!"

Few sights could have proven less hospitable to Millard. Congregated around a café table opposite the hospital's coffee bar—once a mom-and-pop operation, now contracted out to Starbucks—sat the hospital's brass. Millard recognized most of these bigwigs: Kneeson, the chief information officer, whose round-rimmed spectacles recalled Joseph Goebbels; Nursing Director Edith Lane Kirk, wearing her gunmetal hair in a flipped-up bob; his own chairman, Van Doren, alongside the heads of medicine, orthopedics, and radiology; and, at their helm, Harvey Bloodfinch, president and CEO of St. Dymphna's, sporting his trademark handlebar mustache above his inscrutable, calculating frown. The council appeared to be breaking up; the Fates, or possibly the Furies, had scheduled Millard's arrival to facilitate an encounter with his boss.

Van Doren hailed Millard with a wave. The chairman crossed the lobby on his long, loping legs, nimble and stealthy as a gazelle, still holding his Styrofoam cup and the remains of a chocolate cruller in one hand, his breath strong from coffee.

"Ideal timing, Millard," said Van Doren. "But before that. Are you all right? Forgive me, old boy, but you look like you've been wrestling feral cats."

"There was an explosion earlier," replied Millard. "My son and I were dining nearby."

"Oh, that. I've heard. How unfortunate. Your son wasn't hurt?"

"Far from it," replied Millard.

"I don't believe you've mentioned your son before. Is he in medicine?"

Millard had in fact mentioned his sons, both Arnold and Lysander, on multiple occasions, but his boss registered nothing. Van Doren, he'd realized after numerous encounters, approached every human interaction as though it were an initial therapy session, posing heartfelt, nonjudgmental questions designed to build rapport rather than to glean knowledge.

"Not exactly. Not yet. He may apply to veterinary school."

"Nothing wrong with that. We can't all be psychiatrists." Van Doren chuckled at what had apparently been a joke; he placed his hand on Millard's shoulder. "Though I tell you, my wife took our new puppy to a behaviorist and the fellow charges more per hour than I do, so maybe we're in the wrong field, after all. Your boy might be onto something."

"Maybe," agreed Millard. He did not wish to discuss Lysander's career with his boss. "And you?" he inquired, diverting the conversation. "Dare I ask what nefarious purposes bring together the power brokers of St. Dymphna's?"

"Nothing nefarious," replied Van Doren.

He steered Millard toward the far corner of the pavilion, where a row of monuments paid tribute to former St. Dymphna's benefactors and board members. One of them, a lantern-jawed banker named Elihu Morton, had been the psychiatry chairman's father-in-law; another luminary, Lucinda Van Doren, had married a distant cousin. Above the parade of worthies, none of whom, Millard relished pointing out to the medical students, had been physicians, a monitor warned: ESCAPED LYNX. IF SIGHTED, PLEASE REPORT IMMEDIATELY. They'd even posted a feline mug shot. The cub didn't appear particularly menacing, but reminded him of the surly Maine coon that Maia's roommate, an acne-scarred physics major obsessed with quilting, had kept in their dorm suite one summer at Yale.

"I don't think there's any harm in me telling you this," continued Van Doren, as though delivering a fireside chat, "although it won't be public until the end of the week." He drew a deep breath and his eyes met Millard's with sympathy, as if he were about to reveal the death of a loved one. "They've decided to tear down the hospital."

"Which hospital?" asked Millard, dumbfounded. "Not St. Dymphna's?"

"Yes, I'm afraid. St. Dymphna's."

"They're closing St. Dymphna's? That's insane."

"Not closing. *Moving.*" Van Doren bowed his head slightly, a tonsure of hoary hair ringing his speckled scalp. "Four blocks north. They're planning to knock down a block of tenements and a parking garage between 103rd and 105th Streets and to rebuild the entire hospital up there—they already have a donor and permission from the city. Then they're going to take a wrecking ball to this place and sell the land to developers. It is park-front real estate, after all."

"Amazing," said Millard. "They're paving paradise to put up luxury condos. I didn't think even Bloodfinch was capable of that."

"It's not as bad as it sounds," replied Van Doren. "The plan makes solid financial sense. We're going to have state-of-the-art facilities. . . . Aren't you always complaining that your team has to meet in a visitors' lounge? Well, soon you'll have your own conference room."

"I doubt I'll live to witness the day. . . ."

"It's a five-year plan. You wait and see."

Millard wished he'd died in blissful ignorance. Soon his treasured St. Dymphna's—with its drafts, its wheezes, its cracked porcelain urinals and decaying spruce rafters—would disappear down the architectural vortex that had claimed the Ziegfeld Theatre and the old Produce Exchange, the Singer Building and the Hanover Bank Building. As a teenager, he'd accompanied his father to witness city work crews dispatch a wrecking ball through the gold-domed *New York World* headquarters, clearing space for the express ramps to the Brooklyn Bridge. To Papa, demolition was progress, architectural Darwinism—"history in the making." Papa, as only Papa could, had squeezed between two Jersey barriers, intended to shield onlookers from danger, in order to congratulate the demolition crew. He insisted on shaking each and every workman's hand. That night, Millard had curled up fetally under the bedcovers and sobbed himself to sleep. Even strolling past the soulless husk that had replaced Penn Station, or a photo of Ebbets Field on a steakhouse wall, proved enough to strum a dirge on his heartstrings. So he was grateful that he'd be long dead before they took their hammers and soldering irons to St. Dymphna's. Did

Thatcher Van Doren really believe that he could buy his support with a new conference room?

"Thanks for telling me," said Millard. "In any case, it's good to run into you. . . ."

He started for the elevators, but Van Doren detained him.

"That's not what I wanted to discuss with you, Millard," said the chairman. "It's another matter entirely. Something I'm trying to puzzle out." Van Doren rested his brow on the balls of his fingertips, as though actually trying to solve a riddle.

"I'm afraid to ask. . . ."

"This succession plan you proposed to Hecuba Yilmaz," said Van Doren. "I'll confess that I'm somewhat stupefied."

Van Doren's remark hit like a shank to the groin. "Excuse me?"

"I just don't see Hecuba as the right person for the job. Quite frankly, old boy, she rubs many people the wrong way. I was thinking we might do better with Stan Laguna. Or that young Oriental woman who's always on maternity leave."

"You mean Gabby Lu," said Millard. "She's absolutely excellent."

Millard felt entitled to joke about pygmies, or to call his dear Aunt Doris queer as a three-dollar bill, but he didn't appreciate Van Doren dismissing one of his most gifted attendings in similarly cavalier terms.

"Then forgive me, old boy, but why Hecuba?"

"Why Hecuba?" echoed Millard, throwing his arms in the air. "Forgive *me*, Thatcher, but I have no goddamn idea what you're talking about."

"Hecuba said you and she had agreed—"

"I'm going to stop you right there. Hecuba and I have agreed on absolutely nothing. I doubt we could agree on the color of the sky. Either she's delusional or she's lying. . . ."

"So you didn't tell her you were recommending that she take over as director of the consult service when you ultimately step down?"

"No, I did not," said Millard.

"Maybe she misinterpreted—"

"The woman did not *misinterpret* anything. And the fact of the matter is that if I were to step down—or if something were to happen to me unexpectedly—my vote would be for Stanislaw Laguna, although I wouldn't fight you if you preferred Gabby Lu."

"Well, I'll be pickled," muttered Van Doren. "It's hard to know what to make of this."

"I wouldn't make anything of it. It's just Hecuba being Hecuba," said Millard. "Now if that's all, I've still got miles to go at the office before I sleep. . . ."

"Don't mean to hold you up, old boy."

Thatcher Van Doren shook his hand vigorously. "A good egg," Millard's father might have called the chairman, or, more likely, "A good egg for a *goy*."

MISS NICKELSWORTH'S FLINTY eyes were capable of staring down a firing squad, or possibly a division of German tanks, so Millard did not relish having his secretary's full fury trained on his injured knee. "Hell's bells. First an explosion and now a purse snatching. Really, Dr. Salter, this is too rich," she observed, her fingers still resting on her keyboard. He'd edited the film crew out of his afternoon's adventure, leaving only a silhouette of his heroics. "You're far too old to be playing cops and robbers, if you don't mind me saying. You're going to get yourself murdered." Her genuine concern for his welfare, hectoring as it might be, touched him.

"Point taken, Miss N. It won't happen again."

"I should hope not," she said. "Oughtn't you see a doctor?"

He couldn't resist a bit of pushback. "I *am* a doctor."

Miss Nickelsworth uttered an indignant humph. "I'm glad you see humor in this—*this escapade*, Dr. Salter," she said. "Would you please do me the courtesy of making certain you don't have any hidden injuries? I had a cousin, you'll be happy to know, who was always poking his nose into other people's business. Do you know what became of him?"

"He was kidnapped by pirates," suggested Millard.

"He stepped on a nail and died of tetanus," retorted Miss Nickelsworth. "He didn't know he'd been wounded because he had the diabetes."

"I'll take that as fair warning," pledged Millard.

Ever since he'd known her, his secretary had spoken of *the* diabetes and *the* asthma, and she still referred to her back pain as *the lumbago*. How could you help admiring a woman like that? The only comparison he could conjure up was the reverence he'd felt for Winston Churchill as a boy, when on the radio, the British prime minister had cited the United States in the plural. Dear Churchill, the jolly warrior, that unflappable son of a gun, now *there* was a grammatical imperialist who intimidated even Isabelle with his *amongsts* and *whences*. As for Miss Nickelsworth's cautionary tale, Millard knew better than to question her reasoning.

"While you were away," his secretary reported, "Dr. Pineda from oncology telephoned. Three times. He said to please return his call before you leave."

She passed Millard a pink chit with a number.

"And you have two people waiting for you," she continued. "They're out by the elevator bay. Facilities management has carted off our benches because they're waxing the floors tonight."

Millard hadn't even noted the missing benches until then.

Gone too were the magazine rack, the low-slung wooden coffee table, the sprout floor lamp. He'd managed to avoid his visitors by taking the service elevator, and now he considered retreating via the same route—but even in extremis, he couldn't shake his Hippocratic superego.

"I told them you might be gone for hours, that there was a distinct possibility you would not return until the morning, but they insisted upon waiting," said Miss N. Her tone carried a disdain heavier than words, as though she'd pinched soiled clothing between her thumb and forefinger and was searching for a hamper. "Shall I retrieve them?" She might as easily have been asking: *Shall I order them guillotined?*

"No need," said Millard. "I'll do it."

He hobbled to the end of the corridor, favoring his good knee, his shredded trousers dancing at his ankle like a hula skirt. The two creatures seated in opposite armchairs, separated by a metal recycling bin, welcomed him with the warmth of Scylla and Charybdis: Hecuba Yilmaz, her unshaved chin jutting like the prow of a ship, and low-featured Jack Cappabucci, undisputed tsar of deceit, raja of fraud, suzerain of malfeasance, and heavyweight malingering champion of the world. Millard would have preferred a violent death on the Concourse.

"There you are!" exclaimed Hecuba. "I knew you'd try to sneak off."

She buttonholed him by the sweater sleeve before he could mount a retreat. Her breath, only inches from his nostrils, carried a sour, fermented odor that recalled the bowels of a brewery.

"Hey!" objected Jack Cappabucci. "I was here first."

Cappabucci had the audacity to appeal to Millard with an indignant look.

"I'm sorry," said Hecuba. "But Dr. Salter and I have urgent medical matters to discuss."

She pushed past Millard in the direction of his office, unstable on chartreuse pumps she'd somehow convinced herself were fashionable; he had little choice but to follow. As he passed his secretary's desk, he turned to her for aid, but Miss Nickelsworth refused to look up from her keyboard; she was punishing him for his reckless antics in the Bronx.

Hecuba entered the office ahead of him and settled onto the leather sofa—although he'd have been none too shocked had she circled behind his desk and kicked up her heels on the blotter. Millard remained standing.

"I knew you were going on vacation," said Hecuba. "I could just sense it. It's lucky for both of us I caught you before you took off."

Once Hecuba fixed upon an idea, no quantity of evidence could shake her. At first meeting, she'd decide that a junior resident was either "superb" or "unsatisfactory," often based upon how the trainee responded to her *frère et cochon* overfamiliarity—and she interpreted every future interaction with this individual through the lens of their first encounter. Nobody, to her thinking, was ever merely mediocre, competent, run-of-the-mill. Either her colleagues ranked somewhere between Gandhi and Raoul Wallenberg in the pantheon of virtue, or their very existence threatened to undermine the commonweal, and possibly all twenty-five hundred years of Western civilization, with such vices as "woeful ineptitude" and "treacherous iniquity." In Millard's nearly five decades in medicine, Hecuba remained the only physician he'd ever heard refer to a coworker—in this particular case, a social worker who hadn't processed a patient's nursing home application with sufficient speed—as "an enemy."

Nor was her clinical care immune from intransigence. One story, which had circulated among the house staff for years until it acquired an air of legend—although Millard knew several impeccable sources who swore to its veracity—involved a patient, a community college student, whom Hecuba, upon initial evaluation, determined to be faking weakness in her left leg. "Classic malingering," she'd announced to the medical team. "She's likely sitting for exams soon and she's trying to shirk." Two days later, when the patient's laboratory results came back with conclusive evidence of multiple sclerosis, including lesions in her white matter and oligoclonal bands along her spinal fluid, Hecuba refused to accept defeat. Her oft quoted defense had become a mantra among her detractors: "Just because the woman has multiple sclerosis *now* doesn't mean she wasn't malingering *then*." For months, Stan Laguna had entertained the consult fellows with variations on this theme: *Just because this patient has multiple sclerosis today doesn't mean he didn't have polio yesterday; Just because the heart sits on the left side this afternoon, doesn't mean it wasn't on the right this morning. . . .* Millard had shared the story with Isabelle, anticipating a laugh, but his wife, ever the nurse, had instead asked: *Why do you think she's like that?* He'd known enough not to reply, *Because she's a narcissistic bitch.*

The psychiatrist in Millard recognized that Hecuba's conduct stemmed from forces beyond the woman's control—possibly a traumatic childhood superimposed upon a genetic predisposition. Yet the same could be said, in one guise or another, for pedophiles and jihadi terrorists and the squad of SS officers who had gassed his mother's cousins at Treblinka and Majdanek. Comprehension wasn't the same as compassion. One of the conclusions Millard had reached, after far too many years of broad-hearted liberalism and nonjudgmental regard, was that when you opened your mind too much, you risked having your brain ooze out your ears. Ambling about in another fellow's shoes long enough, à la Atticus Finch, you could trick yourself, at least fleetingly, into sympathizing with *anyone's* conduct—Bull

Connor turning hoses and dogs on civil rights protestors in Birmingham, the Khmer Rouge bashing the heads of infants against Chankiri Trees, even Stalin and Hitler. If only Hitler had been loved adequately—hugged more as a child, encouraged as a painter, given sufficient praise for his carnal prowess—he might have embraced a humanistic impulse or, later, stepped back from the abyss. But that was a bullshit way of viewing the world. Bull Connor had been a thug and a troglodyte, Pol Pot a genocidal maniac. Hitler deserved to be burned alive, for eternity, on a pyre of human ash. No higher law of morals or decency demanded that Millard sympathize with everybody equally, or even at all. So what if Hecuba Yilmaz acted without volition, if she had likely cultivated her egocentric carapace to protect a vulnerable girlhood psyche! Her presence still made him want to retch.

"Could you give me a second?" he asked. "I have a pressing call to return."

Augusto Pineda, the chairman of the oncology department, wasn't a man to cry wolf. If he said his business was an urgent matter, you could take him at his word.

"I am sorry, Millard, but I really don't have time to spare right now," insisted Hecuba. She held her knobby wrist to her face, displaying the marcasite-encrusted sliver of her wristwatch. "You've already kept me waiting for two hours."

Millard dug his fingernails into his palms and said nothing. What was that pet expression of Lyndon Johnson's: *Don't wrestle with a pig because you get dirty and the pig enjoys it.* The same applied to arguing with Hecuba.

"I've taken the liberty of sharing a transition plan with Thatcher Van Doren," she said.

"It *was* a liberty," he replied.

"I figured that since we were both on the same page," continued Hecuba, "there was no reason not to get the ball rolling."

The plank that was Millard's restraint had buckled to the point of snapping. "I can give you one reason," he said. So high were his hackles, so inflamed his exasperation, that a tremor coursed through his arms. In spite of reason and good sense, he felt himself about to tell Hecuba Yilmaz how violently he loathed her—holding no punches. The words crouched somewhere between his frontal lobe and his glottis when, inches from Hecuba at the opening of the uncapped ventilation duct, he spotted a pair of inflamed yellow eyes. Two onyx pupils, arcane dilated ovals, pierced from the irises to the depths of hell.

The "baby" lynx proved far larger than Millard had envisioned: closer in size to an adult hyena than to a domestic cat. Spots dappled its coat, except for sock-and-mitten patches of black on its limbs and the crests of its pitched-tent ears. Whiskers sprouted rowdily from the hollows of the creature's nostrils. When it opened its slender lips—a threat? A yawn?—canines jutted from its upper jaw like alabaster stalactites.

Millard held up his hand to silence Hecuba, nodding in the direction of the cat. Then he spoke through clenched teeth as a ventriloquist might to empower a dummy. "If you make a sound, Hecuba, she'll rip your throat out," he warned. He had absolutely no idea whether this were true, but he issued the threat with conviction—a technique which usually worked. He'd learned this strategy from Horace Lardner, an otolaryngology fellow he'd met in residency, who followed the surgeon's creed of "sometimes right, but always certain." History brimmed with such confident falsehoods: Han van Meegeren's fake Vermeers, the diaries of Konrad Kujau, Titus Oates's fabricated plot against Charles II. Nixon denied a cover-up; Reagan "couldn't recall"; Clinton had "never inhaled" or "had sex with that woman." So Millard staked his safety on the certitude of his admonition. *And if she doesn't tear your throat out*, he thought, *I will*. Fortunately, even Hecuba had the sense to defer to a savage carnivore.

The lynx pawed the carpet as though she might charge. Millard suspected that one leap could take her across the room, into his chest. He dared not shout for help. By the time Miss Nickelsworth heard his cries and a security detail arrived, the feline could easily have eviscerated his abdomen. No, the only feasible approach to the animal was persuasion—a mild tone of voice, lulling gestures—in short, an attempt at lynx psychology. Not that Millard possessed any great insights in this arena. As he was always telling the vice president of his co-op board, Mrs. Lewinter, who pestered him about safe blood sugar levels for her Pekinese, he was a human psychiatrist, not a veterinary endocrinologist, but this particular occasion justified—in the language of his insurance company—a deviation outside of his practice area.

"Here, kitty, kitty," he said, inching forward. "That's a good girl. . . ."

He tried to channel what he knew of large cats—which derived largely from Tarzan films and Frosted Flakes commercials and a Siegfried & Roy show he'd attended with Isabelle many years earlier when the psychiatry meetings took place in Las Vegas. Across the room he tiptoed, careful not to show the creature the palms of his hands or the back of his neck—although he couldn't say whether this was myth or wisdom. "That's a good girl," he said. "Let's just slide back into that tunnel, all right? You just go straight in there and we'll leave each other alone. . . ." His technique appeared to be working: The lynx lowered her head like a penitent. "There you go," said Millard. "Almost done. Now turn around and climb into the shaft. . . ." He dared not glance at Hecuba, but he hoped she'd had the sense to dial 911 on her cell phone.

The lynx did not move, but her posture had turned submissive. He climbed down to the carpet, thinking he might give her a gentle nudge. "I'm just going to give you a little push, a *baby* push," he said. "Nothing unfriendly." Millard prodded the animal with the tips of his fingers, tenderly tapping her rump and left shank; she didn't budge. He tried a harder shove—firm, but not violent, and she stumbled toward the open duct. The blister of contact tingled through his hand. "Please, kitty," he said. "That's a good kitty."

And then the animal hissed—a fierce, guttural, sizzling hiss—and shot toward him, scraping her claw across his cheek. Her paws clung to his chest, while his arms wrapped over her back in a toxic hug. The beast's hostile eyes gawped only inches from his own. On instinct, Millard found himself squeezing the creature, deflecting, striking, clutching at hunks of fur. Most remarkable, for a man who planned to kill himself within hours, he found himself thinking, *God, don't let me die!* A boiling drive for life enveloped him, boosting his strength like a shot of absinthe or PCP, and in one herculean thrust, he staggered forward toward the ventilation shaft and shoved the beast backwards into the darkness. On the way into the chasm, the lynx ripped the pocket from his breast, and much of the underlying fabric from his shirt.

Millard shoved a metal filing cabinet in front of the aperture. A moment later, the creature started rattling the makeshift portcullis, keratin clawing against steel. What followed was a short cry, somewhere between a howl and a bark, not of pain—Millard was certain of that—but of mammalian frustration . . . and then silence.

Millard took a wad of tissues from his desk, always at hand for a sobbing patient, and compressed the talon print on his right cheek. He dared not look in a mirror. Hecuba Yilmaz, for her part, had scooted to the far end of the couch and held a Yoruba woodcarving—a souvenir of one of Hal Storch's forays into artistic imperialism—extended like an épée. She lowered the sculpture and returned it to its rightful perch atop the end table.

"Well, that was something, wasn't it?" said Hecuba.

Not: *Are you hurt?* Not: *Thank you for saving my life.*

Hecuba straightened out her skirt. "Now back to what we were discussing, Millard," she said. "I'm confident you'll be pleased with the proposal I sent to Thatcher. I can make you a copy, if you'd like, but if you trust me, we can just say that we're all in agreement."

Millard squeezed his eyes until his sockets throbbed.

"No!" he shouted. "Just no. No! No! NO!"

"Are you all right?" asked Hecuba.

"Am I all right? Now you ask that? Jesus, lady, I was just mauled by a lynx! I might have died. And you're babbling on about succession plans. Are you nuts?"

"No need to raise your voice," replied Hecuba. "I was trying to keep us focused."

That was enough to open the floodgates; he only regretted, in hindsight, that he hadn't recorded this speech for Stan Laguna's entertainment. "This is why nobody likes you," he shouted. "This, Hecuba, is why you're universally despised—why your approval rating around here would be lower than Saddam Hussein and North Korea and pubic lice. Are you hearing me? How anyone so narcissistic, so tone-deaf, so lacking in common sense or decency or compassion, could graduate from medical school, let alone practice psychiatry, is a mystery that no legion of Hibernian monks and Talmudic scholars could possibly unravel. So no, Hecuba, your plan is *not* okay with me. Not at all. You're the last person on the face of the goddamn planet I would let take over my division. I would sooner give the job to Attila the Hun or the

Son of Sam or Jack-the-fucking-Ripper. Now get out! Out!" He slammed a chair against the wall. "And never ever come back!"

Hecuba Yilmaz did not appear at all nonplussed. "I didn't realize you were so upset," she said. "You're still in shock, Millard. I know you don't mean any of that." She rose and walked toward the door. "No reason to feel guilty. I have a thick skin. We'll just pretend this never happened, all right? And I'll tell Thatcher Van Doren that we're all in accord—"

A knock on the door cut her short.

"Are you okay?" asked Miss Nickelsworth.

"We're fine," answered Hecuba. To Millard she added, "Have a safe vacation. I worry about you, Millard. You're under too much stress."

And then she yanked open the door and stepped past Millard's secretary, her heels drumming a staccato toward the elevators. Millard pressed the clumped tissues to his wounded cheek, hoping Miss Nickelsworth might not observe his injuries, but he felt the heat of his own blood trickling down his chin.

Miss N. shook her head—more disapproving than alarmed. "Gracious, Dr. Salter, I thought you were going to be more careful."

"I did the best I could. I wasn't expecting her to claw me."

"You should report her. I know it's not my place . . . but truly, you should."

How amusing, Millard thought. He'd unwittingly left Miss N. with the impression that Hecuba Yilmaz had carved a half-pound of flesh from his face—and he saw no reason to disabuse her of this inference. As a falsehood, his omission somehow seemed an honest one, as though attributing this attack to Hecuba accurately reflected her inner state of being. In addition, blaming Hecuba—at least for the day—absolved him of the need to report his encounter with the lynx to the authorities, which was liable to involve filing a police report and thoroughly mucking up his schedule.

"Let's get you bandaged up," said Miss N. "Before you run out of blood."

She departed for an instant and returned with a first aid kit. The oblong metal box appeared as though it dated from the start of Miss Nickelsworth's tenure, possibly military surplus of the Korean War. One side featured the lettering "Johnson & Johnson's VACATION FIRST AID" and a large red cross; the other read: "Manufactured in New Brunswick, NJ." Inside, the tin contained an elastic bandage, a glass bottle of rubbing alcohol and a set of swabs, enough Q-tips to rid an entire brigade of earwax, a spool of medical tape, several two-by-two cotton patches, and an assortment of tweezers, scissors, and clippers. Thankfully, no Mercurochrome. Miss Nickelsworth snipped off four strands of tape and dressed his wound.

"You should have been a nurse," he said.

"I *could* have been a nurse," she retorted. "But my sister was already a nurse, so my father sent me to Katharine Gibbs for shorthand. To diversify, he said—but the truth was he wanted someone to type his correspondence. He was in the women's hosiery business. But then he died and I ended up here." She placed the final band of tape below Millard's eye. "That's neither here nor there. *This* isn't nursing. This is basic first aid. Every girl in my high school class could do this when we graduated. We were taught tangible skills. Nowadays, these girls can't even sew on a button for themselves. . . . There you go. Let's hope you don't need stitches."

Millard's more serious medical concern wasn't bleeding, but infection—some exotic, lynx-borne relative of cat scratch fever. Fortunately, these tropical bacteria tended to have incubation periods of several days. "I'll be fine, Miss N.," he said, patting her handiwork.

Millard returned to his desk and wrote his secretary a check for $120. The same as the previous year. He slipped it inside a business envelope. "This may sound strange," he said, "but I'm giving my Christmas presents early this holiday season—for tax purposes. It's good for six months, so if you prefer, you can wait until December to open it."

Miss Nickelsworth stashed the envelope inside her blouse. "It's mighty odd to be getting a Christmas present in July," she said, yet objected no further. "I thank you for it. Now if you're all right, Dr. Salter, I'll be catching my bus. . . ."

"Better than all right," said Millard. "I could wrestle an ox."

He followed Miss Nickelsworth through the corridor and ducked into the adjacent washroom. His reflection belied his claims to health. While the laceration to his face was no longer visible, a second, shallower claw mark scored his neck at the clavicle, which had started to swell under his collar. Ugly hemorrhagic stains disfigured the flesh below his right knee. Little remained of his shirt between the plackets and the left shoulder. He buttoned all three buttons of his jacket like a schoolboy or one of those Internet millionaires—somebody who didn't know better. ("Sometimes, always, never," Papa had instructed of buttoning a dress suit. "*Never* button the bottom button.") The result concealed his damaged shirt, but made him look like a ringmaster at the circus.

Time to go home, Millard decided. He'd earned a shower and a shave. His Hippocratic oath be damned—he'd head for the service elevator and leave Jack Cappabucci to stew in his own deceitful juices. Why did he have any obligation to the fellow? Cappabucci wasn't a patient. Hell, he was the opposite of a patient. Millard returned to his office, delighted with his escape plan, and found Cappabucci seated on the Aeron chair across from his desk. The celebrated malingerer wore his shirtfront open, tufts of coarse gray hair sprouting from his chest. His aviator sunglasses perched atop his bold, glabrous crown.

"I thought you might have forgotten. . . ."

"I didn't forget you," said Millard. "But you really can't burst in here like this. . . . This is a private office, Mr. Cappabucci."

"I apologize," said Cappabucci. "Sincerely."

The man did sound sincere; that was his sociopathic charm at work. Ted Bundy had harnessed his allure to beguile and slaughter young women; Bernie Madoff tapped his charisma to swindle investors. Cappabucci's goals proved far more simplistic, even if he drew upon the same techniques: He wished to use the hospital as a motel. But since he wasn't actually undomiciled, merely renting an apartment for profit, he earned none of Millard's sympathies.

Most of the malingerers at St. Dymphna's proved rather inept. Either they feigned improbable symptoms (hallucinating in black-and-white, shaking hands with imaginary friends, hearing voices on only one side of their heads) or they proffered histories easy to debunk. Millard took pride in unmasking these impostors: watching a "deaf man" jump when he shouted a profanity in the next room, calling the Department of Veterans Affairs to ascertain that a "decorated combat pilot" had actually played cornet in the air force marching band. Someday, Millard joked to the medical students, he'd switch sides and run how-to workshops. Or publish *Malingering for Dummies* and sell copies for five dollars outside heroin treatment clinics and homeless shelters. But Cappabucci, through sheer audacity and force of will, had managed to con generations of headshrinkers. You had to give the bastard credit.

"I've come to negotiate," said Cappabucci.

Millard remained beside the open door, one hand firmly gripping the knob; his facial wound seared underneath the two-by-twos. He considered responding, *I don't negotiate with terrorists.* Instead, he waited for Cappabucci to exhaust his machinations.

"Look, buddy," said his visitor—as though speaking to a prep school chum. "I don't want to cause you any trouble. Let's have a truce."

"I didn't know we were in conflict," said Millard.

"Conflict? We're at war!" Cappabucci's cheeks flushed; his nostrils flared. "You wrote in a medical chart that I'm not mentally ill—that my schizophrenia is, and I quote, 'a tragicomic enterprise reminiscent of the best acting of Lon Cheney' and 'a farce straight out of the Marx Brothers.' Do you really expect me to take that lying down?"

"It's just one doctor's opinion."

"You've caused me a heap of trouble, Millard. But I'm willing to let bygones be bygones. You retract your accusations, make a few emendations to the medical record—you can say you had me confused with a different patient—and we'll chalk this up to a good old-fashioned misunderstanding."

Millard counted backwards from five in his head. "I'm not going to change my note," he replied. "Because that would be fraud. Something I imagine you are rather familiar with, Mr. Cappabucci. Now if you'll please leave my office. . . ."

The toggle in Cappabucci's warped psyche shifted instantly from flattery to menace.

"You don't know what you're getting yourself into, Salter," he threatened. "I've already filed a complaint with the Office of Mental Health. If we can't work this out today, I'll have no choice but to take the matter up with the Justice Center and the Office of Professional Medical Conduct. I have contacts in Albany. I swear I'll have your license for this!"

Millard forced a grin. "I'm an old man, Mr. Cappabucci," he said. "OPMC takes years to investigate these sorts of griev-ances. . . . I could be dead by then. . . ."

"You'll wish you were."

"You may be right," agreed Millard. "Now I'll have to ask you to leave. If you don't leave, our security officers will provide you with an escort."

The threat of force brought Cappabucci to his feet. "You're doing something stupid. . . ."

"That's because I'm a very stupid person," said Millard. "It's my nature."

He'd discovered over the years that agreeing with such de-nunciations always proved more effective than defending against them. Most assailants gave up on the spot, often sheepishly, as though they'd been caught boxing a deflated punching bag. Jack Cappabucci scowled at Millard and shuffled from the office with his hands in his trouser pockets.

At last! He was finally alone. The wall clock read 4:35 PM.

Millard fingered the pink memo sheet on which Miss Nick-elsworth had jotted the oncology chairman's name and phone number, crossing her sevens and zees. He knew Augusto Pineda casually from many years at the same hospital, but not well enough for a social call. Pineda was something of a legend. In 1968, a Latino street gang, Los Rebeldes—an offshoot of the Young Lords, modeling themselves after the Black Panthers—had occupied Lutheran Hospital in Spanish Harlem as a protest against substandard care. For nineteen days, armed with high-caliber firearms, they controlled access to the facility, managing everything from nursing schedules to meal orders. The gang even had patients fill out customer satisfaction surveys, a novelty at the time. (Art Rosenstein had been an intern during the crisis and claimed the hospital had never run better.) That was the era before SWAT teams and shoot-to-kill orders; a liberal mayor negotiated a settlement and the militants were granted immunity, on the condition they surrender their weapons. Several of them went on to prominent roles in the Puerto Rican Civil Rights Movement, others ended up junkies or drifted toward more commonplace offenses. Two committed a high-profile kidnapping and later fled to Havana. Augusto Pineda, touched by his work at Lutheran, enrolled in pre-med classes at the local community college and later transferred to Harvard.

Millard dialed the number and a receptionist answered on the first ring.

"Millard Salter for Augusto Pineda," he said. "I'm returning his call."

A moment later, Pineda's warm baritone greeted him. "Millard. Gusto Pineda here. Sorry to pester you, but I wanted to make sure we touched base about the rabbi."

"Not a problem," replied Millard. "What's going on?"

"I'm sorry to tell you this, but Ezra Steinmetz is dead."

"Heavens," said Millard—feeling surprised, even though he had expected this outcome ever since his secretary had mentioned Pineda's call. "I saw him this morning."

"How did he appear?"

"Exhausted. Uncomfortable. But not like a man at death's door, although he seemed pretty convinced he was done for," said Millard. "I suppose you can never tell with cancer."

Like suicide, thought Millard. The warning signs often emerged in hindsight.

"It wasn't cancer," said Pineda. "He slashed his own throat with a razor blade."

12

Millard hurried through the subterranean caverns of St. Dymphna's, black bag clasped to his chest, a pair of rubber bands securing his trouser leg to his calf. Two floors above, along the central arcade of the Luxdorfer Pavilion, his colleagues, weary, work-whacked, raced to catch commuter trains and theater curtains. Late afternoon witnessed a subtle power shift in the hospital—the senior attendings departing, replaced by over-tasked residents and petrified interns who made easy marks for demanding families and domineering nurse managers. Visiting hours ran from five o'clock to seven thirty, an opportunity for well-intentioned friends and relatives to undermine the pains-taking medical planning of the day. Narcotics and tranquilizers, declared taboo at noon, flowed like mountain springs six hours later. Parents smuggled candy bars to their diabetic children; love-blind companions trafficked malt liquor and miniature schnapps bottles onto the detox unit. Chaos, always present, shook off its latency. A schedule of the daily program was traditionally posted on every inpatient psychiatric unit in the hospital, and during Millard's own residency, a clever colleague had filled the space following "DINNER & EVENING ACTIVITIES" with the words "The Inmates Take Over." By contrast, in the sub-basement, the close of business hours saw the purveyors of so-called ancillary services revving up for real labor: cafeteria workers in mesh snoods pushing dinner carts, pharmacists preparing for overnight inventory, a trio of "engineers" struggling to steer a floor buffer. It was already a quarter to five. Millard darted from passageway to fluorescently lit passageway, under the Hapsworth Annex, past the linens stockroom, through the lower intestines of the medical student dormitory, planning to emerge only a block from the 96th Street subway station. After forty-nine years at the hospital, and numerous efforts to avoid his bosses, he knew every shortcut.

Millard's path carried him past the lounge where the students shot pool and along a corridor lined with banks of lockers. He nearly toppled a young woman toting a laundry basket as he rounded a corner, accepted a greeting from a buff kid in salmon club shorts and Birkenstocks whom he might have lectured in his "Brain & Behavior" course, but he couldn't be certain, because after a year or two, all of the faces blended together. Especially the men. A gangling, auburn-haired girl wearing only pajama bottoms and a sports bra—he recognized her as a fourth-year student—approached him on her trek to the recycling bins, and after a moment of recognition, looked away, mortified. Nobody expected to meet their psychiatry preceptor opposite their garbage room. While he felt badly for surprising the girl, it was not badly enough for him to travel at street level and risk another encounter with Hecuba or Denny Dennmeyer, or whomever those vindictive Furies had determined to inflict upon him.

The rabbi's death weighed heavily upon Millard. A young father's self-destruction under the duress of cancer was far different from an old man's premeditated suicide. Maybe that was a rationalization, but— He cut himself short. His decision had been made, a culmination of months of conscientious deliberation. No sound reason existed to reconsider it. Millard pushed open the reinforced door leading to the emergency staircase and the street beyond. Despite the red-lettered warning, he knew from experience that no alarm would sound. On the landing, he found a young woman snuffling into her drawn-up blouse. The sound of the heavy door scraping the cinder block drew her attention and she looked up in alarm. A second elapsed before Millard recognized the swollen eyelids and trickling liner as belonging to Lauren Pastarnack.

"Oh my God!" she exclaimed. "Dr. Salter."

"Excuse me," he apologized. "Are you all right?"

She nodded vigorously and attempted to speak, but lapsed into another bout of tears. The girl's white coat and stethoscope draped over the handrail.

Millard set down his bag. "There, there," he said. "You'll talk when you're ready."

Pastarnack refused to wait. "She was dead. . . ." she spluttered between sobs. "I thought she was only sleeping . . . but she was dead. . . . Oh God, you think I'm pathetic. . . ."

"I think no such thing," Millard said firmly. "You've experienced a trauma. This is a perfectly healthy reaction."

"I went back to her room," said Lauren. "I wanted to be helpful. . . ."

"Whose room?" demanded Millard.

"Ms. Noguerra's," said Pastarnack. "I thought she might want to talk."

Millard sensed his entire body tauten, each muscle tugging on its tendons—the human equivalent of a tortoise drawing its limbs under a shell. He knew this feeling well: his flesh braced for grave news that it already recognized, but had not yet been voiced. He would have no choice but to phone Dolores Noguerra's mother—Isabelle's dear friend Marta—even if that cut into his time with Delilah. Impending death offered no armor to common decency.

Lauren Pastarnack slowly composed herself; he patted her on the shoulder.

"So you went back to see Ms. Noguerra . . . to lend an ear," suggested Millard, "and you found her dead. . . ."

Millard saw no reason to mention that the visit transcended conventional medical student protocol. Dolores Noguerra hadn't been the girl's patient. Although her efforts were obviously well-intentioned, she really had no business stopping by the sick woman's room on her own.

Pastarnack shook her head. "No, I found her sound asleep," she said. "The *suicide minder* was dead." The girl's voice grew animated, her chest heaving. "I found her sitting in her chair. . . . Her name was Mary Catherine. . . . She wasn't breathing. . . ."

A flurry of relief passed through Millard. The suicide minder was a complete stranger to him—one of millions of strangers who died each day.

"I know what you're thinking," said Pastarnack.

"Do you now?" he interjected. "And what, pray tell, might that be?"

"You're wondering how I can possibly become a doctor if I fall to pieces every time someone dies. . . ."

The poor girl sounded so earnest, so desperate. Soon enough, she'd lose this purity—not all of the students did, but he could sense that Lauren Pastarnack would, on the way to becoming a gifted and compassionate physician. (The rare few that didn't proved a challenge for medical school administrators. Several years earlier, a third-year student had been expelled for repeatedly visiting oncology patients alone to reassure them that their prognoses weren't fatal, in spite of the morbid certainties of the senior clinicians.) The sad reality was that people died in hospitals. In a prior generation, that was the only reason patients checked into hospitals at all. His aunts, he recalled, had eschewed medical facilities like plague houses. "I'd rather drop dead on the street," proclaimed Fannie. When she'd ultimately sought care for the lump in her breast, after the agony grew too severe for indomethacin, the tumor weighed more than a cantaloupe and had ulcerated through the flesh below her axilla. Nor did the death of the minder faze Millard. In five decades, he'd witnessed an orderly suffer a heart attack in the radiology suite, visiting children seize in the cafeteria, a junior dietician choke to death on a chicken bone in the nursing station. The law of averages ruled that some people would die in their beds surrounded by loved ones and others would perish while transporting blood or reviewing bone scans. On his first overnight call as an intern—July 2, 1966—he'd admitted seven patients to the hospital; by sign-out the next morning, all seven of them had expired.

"You'll get used to it," said Millard.

"I won't. . . . I can't. . . ."

"You can't, but you will," he replied. "I wrote you a glowing recommendation, by the way. I meant every word of it then—and I still mean every word of it now. . . ."

His reassurance brought a faint smile to the girl's lips. Millard surveyed the landing for the first time: Someone had been smoking illicitly a few steps above, leaving butts and ash on the concrete. A patch of graffiti on the wall read: ST. DYMPHNA'S – BECAUSE LIFE IS OVERRATED. Footsteps—boots or clogs—traversed the tunnel on the opposite side of the fire door. Any other day, Millard would have been self-conscious about being alone in a shadowy stairwell with an attractive, twentysomething girl.

"Are you ready for another quiz?" he asked.

"Not right now," she said. "I can't think straight."

"Trust me. This one will be easier. I promise. *About psychiatry.*"

"Okay, I guess. . . ."

"That's a good sport," said Millard. "So here's the question—and this one actually might appear on your psychiatry boards someday. In 1950, before the discovery of medications like Thorazine and lithium, what were the six treatments, other than talk therapy, that psychiatrists used to treat patients with severe mental illness?"

His challenge served its intended effect. Pastarnack's grief gave way to the urge to prove herself; color returned to her cheeks. She crossed her legs, exposing a run in her stocking.

"Fair question?" he asked.

"Fair enough . . . but difficult."

Millard let her think. His evaluations from the medical students perennially accused him of answering his own questions too quickly.

"ECT?" she guessed.

"Yes, indeed. Shock therapy. That's one," said Millard. "But without anesthesia. My mentor at NYU began his career doing ECT during the afternoons in his home office. On his mahogany dining room table. His wife would scrub down the wood after lunch, they'd treat a depressive or two, and then she'd serve supper on the same surface. Every few weeks, a patient might fracture a long bone and require emergency pinning."

"That's surreal."

"It was a different world," said Millard. "Five to go . . ."

Lauren Pastarnack studied the backs of her pale hands, her brow puckered, an adorable dimple appearing in her chin. "Lobotomies?"

"Correct. Transorbital lobotomies. Egas Moniz won a Nobel Prize for perfecting the procedure. They performed twenty thousand in the United States alone." The image of the lovely but star-crossed Rosemary Kennedy, presenting herself at the court of King George VI, had haunted him ever since he'd learned of her fate. "That's two."

Gone was the girl's grief, supplanted by confidence.

"Insulin comas," she said—now a statement, rather than a question.

"Three for three," agreed Millard. "You're halfway there."

Even during his training, there had still been codgers who swore, despite overwhelming evidence, that using low blood sugars to induce coma or convulsions cured schizophrenia. To the current medical students, this seemed as bizarre as trepanation.

"Any more guesses?" he asked.

"I give up," said Pastarnack. "My brain is tired."

Unlike earlier, he chose not to hound her. "Three for six is impressive for a third-year medical student. You should be proud," he said. "For future reference, the other three are ice baths, malaria exposure, and the placement of baboon testicles under the skin."

"Baboon testicles?"

"Chimpanzees, too. And even gonads harvested from executed murderers. Crazy, no? You should read Voronoff's *Rejuvenation by Grafting*. Probably the strangest mainstream medical text ever published. The poet E. E. Cummings called Voronoff that 'famous doctor who inserts monkey glands in millionaires. . . .'"

The girl's smile dissolved into laughter. "Monkey glands . . ." she said between paroxysms. "Monkey glands in millionaires . . ." Millard couldn't explain why the quotation was particularly humorous, but he soon found himself laughing too. Pastarnack apologized for her frenzy through tears, then burst out laughing again.

"Oh, God, I'm sorry," she pleaded.

Millard bit his lower lip until he tasted blood.

"Well you should be," he said. "There was nothing funny about simian grafting therapy. It ruined the lives of hundreds of people."

"How?"

"Infection. Dashed hopes," said Millard. "Except for shock therapy, none of these treatments offered any benefit beyond placebo—and some, like lobotomy and insulin, killed or maimed lots of people."

Now he had Pastarnack's rapt attention.

"The point I'm making is that the greats of psychiatry— Meyer, Kanner, Sullivan—left a trail of dead bodies in their wake. Krugman and McCollum fed feces milkshakes to mentally impaired children to trace the natural course of hepatitis. *And these were the good guys*," explained Millard. "They thought they knew everything and now we know they knew nothing. In thirty years, someone else will come along and say, 'Salter, that crackpot, he treated patients with Prozac and Zoloft.' So don't be too hard on yourself. You're a talented young woman. You do the best you can. Nobody can expect anything more." Millard uncoiled the stethoscope from the handrail and passed it to her. "End of sermon."

"Thanks," said Pastarnack. "Wow. I feel better."

"Good. Now time for you to study and me to head home."

He waited for her to button her white coat and followed her up the stairs.

Outside, the bloated air held the promise of rain. Pea soup, thought Millard, recalling a favorite joke of his boyhood. *What is the difference between mashed potatoes and pea soup? Anyone can mash potatoes.* At seven, that had tickled him breathless. On the corner of 97th Street, a man in a derby hat and suspenders hawked umbrellas. Downtown traffic inched forward, unable to keep pace with the crush of pedestrians.

"Thank you for cheering me up," said Pastarnack.

"My pleasure. Now go ace that exam."

He waved to her, wishing her well. In response, she stepped forward and hugged him—her breasts pressing against his constricted arm. He patted her back gently. Over her shoulder, his eyes made contact with Stan Laguna. Lauren Pastarnack released her grasp and departed toward the medical library just as Millard's colleague approached.

If Stan Laguna appeared scruffy at the start of the workday, by quitting time he looked positively disheveled: coarse stubble varnished his nascent jowls; the residue of lunch—pasta sauce, cheesecake crumbs—clung to the wrinkles of his shirt. In one hand, he carried the paper shopping bag that served as his makeshift briefcase.

Laguna's gaze pointedly followed the girl's derriere down the sidewalk. "A date with destiny," he said, punctuating his comment with a whistle.

"I'm writing her a recommendation."

"Sure you are," said Laguna.

Millard didn't know whether his colleague was joking, but he no longer cared. So what if grubby minds drew sordid conclusions. He'd be dead. Yet he didn't want anyone connecting his suicide to his wholly innocent relationship with Lauren Pastarnack—or worse, Stan Laguna blaming himself for catching them in a moment of supposed intimacy.

Laguna wore a curious, live-and-let-live grin.

"One of the suicide minders died," Millard explained. "She found the body."

"Yikes," said Laguna. "I thought you were taking the day off. . . ."

"I did," replied Millard. "I visited Isabelle's grave."

That knocked the glow from Laguna's face. "I'm sorry."

"Did I miss anything?"

"Nothing to write home about. We saw that woman who blew up the building across the street. She's still out cold—but she's not going to be a happy camper when she wakes up."

"I imagine not."

"And the Royal Embellisher came looking for you. She kept babbling about 'changes coming to the service.' Should I know about this?"

"All of the changes are in Hecuba's imagination."

"A place where I'm glad I'm not," said Laguna. "All in all, a quiet day. Nothing stirring, not even a lynx."

"She'll turn up," said Millard.

The bells of the Russian Orthodox cathedral tolled the hour. Scotch mist had given way to ominous gobbets of rain.

"I have to run," he said.

"See you tomorrow," said Laguna.

"Yes, see you tomorrow."

But he wouldn't see Stan Laguna tomorrow . . . or ever again. As he hurried toward the IRT through the drizzle—a cab in rush hour traffic would take too long—the hard reality of his death finally took hold of him like a summer flu, pounding in his head, stanching his breath. He couldn't shake Lauren Pastarnack's intense despair at the demise of a stranger. How much worse for his colleagues, his friends, his children. Was there any crime, he asked, in postponing his plans with Delilah for a few more days? Choosing his birthday had been arbitrary, not based on any empirical evidence regarding her health or well-being. Surely, he might convince her to live a wee bit longer. Maybe he could meet Maia for dinner that evening after all—and bring her back to Delilah's apartment for introductions. What was the worst that the Compassionate Endings folks could do? Expel him? Exile him to Mexico like Trotsky? The more he considered a deferment, the less unreasonable it sounded.

The drizzle ripened into a steady, windswept shower. A man dashed toward a vacant cab with a newspaper braced over his head; nurses in turquoise scrubs and floral-print smocks huddled under awnings. Trash sopped and swirled in the gutters. Millard, buoyed at the prospect of longer life, of a few more days with Delilah, relished the rain. He'd buy more flowers, he decided. Maybe rent a movie—although he had no inkling how to rent a movie anymore, now that his corner video rental shop had gone the way of eight-track tapes and cathode ray televisions. (He remembered shopping with Carol for their first VCR, debating the merits of VHS and Betamax; they'd argued bitterly, but he'd gotten his way—and chosen wrong.) Nothing could dampen his mood, not even Denny Dennmeyer, who squeezed into the seat beside Millard on the southbound train.

"If it isn't the man of the hour," said Dennmeyer.

The accountant wore a bandage around his forehead and another that looped under his jaw; he reminded Millard of Boris Karloff playing *The Mummy*. Millard pretended to blow his nose, creating an excuse to shield himself from Dennmeyer's mortal breath with a handkerchief. He felt the fat of the man's thigh crushing into his own. A creature of his proportions, grumbled Millard, ought to pay twice the fare on public transit.

"I want to commend you for delivering your report, Dr. Salter," said Dennmeyer, at a volume fit for a crowded saloon. "You're a man of your word."

Dennmeyer's tone insinuated that he'd expected otherwise.

"Looks like you got beaten up pretty bad," said Millard, speaking into his sleeve. "I guess that post office wasn't there when you expected it, after all."

"Everything in a day's work, Dr. Salter. A prepared manager has to expect the unexpected . . . I didn't realize you'd been injured as well."

"Neither had I."

"I suppose we both should have ducked. In any case, I've got your report right here," said the accountant, slapping his attaché case. "It's my bedtime reading. I'm looking forward to it."

"May I see it?"

Dennmeyer removed a manila envelope from the side pouch. The sight of the report confirmed Millard's plans and he snatched it from Dennmeyer's grasp. If he intended to return to work for another week or two, there was no reason to antagonize the bean counters yet. "If it's all right with you," he said, "I'm going to hold on to it for another day or two. I just realized I've left out some key data. . . ."

Dennmeyer's narrow eyes bulged with alarm.

"You can always file an amendment," he pleaded.

Millard rose, using a pole for assistance. His knee ached; his cheek throbbed. "This is my stop," he said, inching his way toward the exit with the envelope tucked under his elbow. "Good to see you."

"But Dr. Salter. Really, I must protest—"

Luckily, Dennmeyer's protest was lost to the roar of the station and the closing subway doors. The platform bustled with anonymity. Millard slid the envelope into a nearby trash can and climbed the stairs into daylight. Sunlight greeted him in vibrant sheets. On 68th Street, steam rose off the asphalt; oil shimmered in puddles. All that remained of the brutal downpour were tidal pools around the sewer heads and flares of gray in the distant sky. A delicate sheen of rebirth hung over the city.

Millard snatched up a bouquet of tiger lilies at the nearest bodega and waited impatiently for the cashier to ring up another customer's lottery tickets. Now that he'd decided on extending his time with Delilah, he felt a deep yearning to see her. Already, he found himself planning their upcoming days together. They had still never listened to Christel Goltz perform Turandot or Antigone; he'd reserved the CDs at the public library, but another opera fan had dibs. Nor had they ordered in escargot from La Sirène. And why shouldn't he rent a private ambulette to show Delilah around the Bronx? He could certainly afford it. Paying for the flowers—Millard shelled out a ten and didn't bother to wait for change—he even wondered if he hadn't been wrong about marriage. He'd treated a federal magistrate for anxiety after a bout of bronchitis several months earlier; he imagined he could persuade the judge to stop by Delilah's apartment as a favor. Instinctively, his fingers reached for the ring suspended below his throat.

Yet as he hurried down the avenue toward her apartment, he checked himself: The whole purpose of rational suicide was to be *rational*—not to be swayed by hope or sentiment or love. Following your emotions is what landed you in the ICU, speckled in bed sores, with tubes and catheters protruding from all of your orifices. Millard valued his own dignity far too much to take such chances and he loved Delilah too deeply to play roulette with her future. No, he dared not fall into that trap. So that was that. The clock was still ticking. Subdued, he greeted the burly Montenegrin guarding his paramour's building.

"How's Miss P.?" inquired the burly doorman.

"Swell," replied Millard.

"Glad to hear it. We're pulling for her."

He rode the elevator to the sixth floor. One by one, he unlocked the deadbolts, and stepped into her foyer for his final entrance. As always, he called out her name. While he waited for two minutes to roll by, he found a second vase and arranged the tiger lilies. He set the vase on the countertop beside the toaster. She had already removed the helium canister and hood from the kitchen, as well as her lethal library and the anthology of Teasdale poems. His own footsteps reverberated in his ears as he followed the hallway into her bedroom.

"Sorry, I'm late," he said—and added, joking, "I hope you waited for me."

But she hadn't. He found her still, peaceful, the helium hood tucked neatly around her head and neck like a veil. Teasdale's book lay on her coverlet. In her hands, she clutched the cassette recorder. On a Post-it Note affixed to the machine, in a scrawling, hardly human hand, he recognized the letters P-L-A-Y. He had enough sense not to call 911.

The voice on the recording was the strongest he'd heard from Delilah in weeks; later, he recognized that she'd taped her final testament in advance:

If I know you well, Millard, you've been having second thoughts. You're going to ask me to hold out a few days longer. And I love you dearly, so if you asked, I'd probably give in. But I don't want that. Now is my time. I couldn't risk the chance of missing it. Please forgive me, as you are a lovely person and I truly adore you.

That was all. The remainder of the tape was blank.

PART 3

EVENING

13

Millard did not allow himself time to mourn.

Once he started grieving, he feared there'd be no stop to his anguish. Who could say what other emotions might also follow his heartache—fear, panic—to prevent him from fulfilling his pledge to Delilah and completing his own plans. Already, he sensed those malign, subconscious demons that Hal Storch had championed encroaching upon his psyche, the tickle of a "life instinct" laboring to disturb his curated death. But he refused to buckle. The circumstances called for action, not wallowing. How different from those minutes and hours immediately after Isabelle's passing, when the hospice nurses attended to every last detail, leaving him and Maia to watch their ministrations with a combination of dependence and awe. Eventually, he'd taken his daughter to the souvlaki grill across the street, where they'd wept and shared stories and laughed through their tears, while gorging themselves sick on baklava, until Isabelle's brother phoned to confirm the funeral arrangements. That had been a public death, a collective mourning. Cousins from as far away as Auckland and Johannesburg had sent condolences. With Delilah, he was on his own—nobody, other than doormen and delivery boys and her niece in Tel Aviv, even knew of their attachment. Except for the Compassionate Endings folks, sort of, but he couldn't exactly expect a sympathy call from his handler at Johns Hopkins.

Millard followed the organization's instructions step-by-step.

His foremost responsibility was to empty the helium canister, then secure both the cylinder and the hood inside an Acrilan duffel bag that he'd previously stashed beneath Delilah's bathroom sink. Arnold had once used the bag to stow the catcher's gear he'd schlepped to his sleepaway camp in the Berkshires each summer; later, it accompanied Lysander to Wesleyan and acquired doodles of rhinoceroses and peacocks. Millard had blotted these out with black marker. After snipping off the labels, he'd inspected the fabric—both exterior and interior—for any other identifying features. He intended to haul the bag to the locked storeroom in the cellar of his own building and to discard it among the unclaimed bicycles and forsaken appliances; years might elapse before the co-op conducted any meaningful spring cleaning, possibly decades. All of this effort to cover up a woman's rational decision about how and when to die. What a bizarre, priggish civilization, he lamented, that demanded such extremes of ordinary people.

Millard's postmortem responsibilities were, at least in the eyes of Compassionate Endings, as important as his role as a guide. The organization dreaded any material connection, however remote, to its dirty work. That was why Millard had chosen hanging for himself instead of asphyxiating on noxious vapors; there'd be nobody available to remove his used helium hood or his spent gas flask, so suspicion would inevitably have fallen, rightly or wrongly, upon the aid-in-dying group with their distinctive techniques. Not that he owed the suicide folks anything, but he didn't wish to sabotage their efforts. They were well-intentioned people, after all, despite their Stalinist streak. Candidly, he also worried that if the coroner's office did discover the moral fingerprints of Compassionate Endings on his death, his survivors might suspect coercion, and he wanted the world to know that he'd left the planet on his own terms.

Once he'd secured Delilah's paraphernalia inside its receptacle, which barely fit and required him to tug on the zipper with
the duffel bag braced between his thighs, Millard scanned the
apartment for other incriminating items. In the sitting room, he
found his lover's morbid, three-volume suicide library neatly
stacked on the escritoire; Millard stuffed these texts into his own
medical satchel. He slid the collection of Millay poems onto the
shelf in the study between a biography of Betty Comden and a
trio of George Bernard Shaw plays. Nearby, he found two dozen
business-sized envelopes, each revealing the underlying impression of a miniature cassette tape. Delilah had addressed these
months earlier, over the course of several weeks, while her hand-
writing had remained decipherable. The deterioration in the
quality of the penmanship from the first to the last stood as a
testament to her overall decline.

Millard recognized the names of several veteran Broadway
actors among the recipients, including one B-list celebrity he'd
thought to be long dead. Also several male names he did not recognize. He couldn't help wondering whether these men had
been her lovers. And how many of them, if any, had she actually
loved—to the depth that he'd loved her? Now *that* would be a
clever invention, he mused. A device to gauge degrees of affection, maybe based upon polygraph technology or measured
through implanted electrodes. While biotech companies
searched for the Holy Grail of a love thermostat, seeking aphro-
disiacs that might turn on and off affection or passion, what the
world truly wanted was a thermometer to assess the devotion
that had already been proclaimed. Salter's Yardstick for Love.
Devising and patenting such a device would almost be worth
surviving into his dotage. Almost.

At the bottom of the pile—in the most stable hand, as
though written first—he found his own name and address. *Mil-*

lard K. Salter, MD. So formal. So austere. These scraps were all
that remained of Delilah now: names scrawled across envelopes,
brief farewells preserved on audio tape, an apartment cluttered
with play scripts and bric-a-brac. And all that endured of Isabelle
were a terrycloth robe and a red notebook and a carton of expired cosmetics he kept forgetting to carry down to the curbside.
And all that remained of Millard K. Salter, MD, soon enough,
would be a black medicine bag and a few faded snapshots and
whatever other mementos Maia claimed from the apartment.
Also a lavish letter of recommendation and a conflict over his
job. And memories, of course, but memories were capricious and
fleeting.

Millard gave the sitting room a last cursory once-over, then
poked his head into the bedroom and the kitchen. On winter vacations to Fort Myers, Florida, as a child—the entire family
packed into a Pullman car for thirty-six hours—Millard had
watched his father scour their hotel room, on the night prior to
departure, investigating beneath the beds and behind closet
doors as though searching for a misplaced gemstone. (*Your Papa's
greatest fear,* his mother complained, *is that a chambermaid
should find a nickel.*) Sometimes, his father induced him and
Harriet to join in his labors, to make a family game of hunting
for loose change and misplaced toiletries; Lester, already too old,
found the enterprise demeaning. Now, out of habit, Millard
climbed down to one knee and peered into the dusty recesses
beneath Delilah's bed; the springs sagged nearly to the carpet.
He checked behind her ancient Kenmore sewing machine—a
make no more advanced than the devices his female classmates
had used in home economics at Hager Heights. He rummaged
through the medications inside the cabinet above the toilet—
calamine lotion, Vicks VapoRub, tinctures of iodine. Half-spent
bottles of amoxicillin and simvastatin stuck to the shelving

paper. What he was looking for, if anything, he couldn't explain. But in spite of himself, he sensed the tears welling. Never again would he complete a crossword puzzle to Delilah's directives, or argue with her over the merits of Lillian Hellman, whom he admired and she found doctrinaire. Never again would he—

Enough, dammit, he threatened himself. *Eyes on the ball.*

Millard plucked the duffel bag from the sofa and departed quickly, shutting the door to each room as though preparing for a fire drill. He left the air conditioner running in the sitting room to keep the corpse in good shape until the private nurse returned in the morning. When they'd find *his* body was another matter entirely: He hoped that his colleagues would have the good sense to send the police to his door, but knowing Stan Laguna, that might take days. Or maybe Carol would grow anxious if he didn't return her call, but that seemed farfetched. Such was the magic of the future—the future that he was forsaking: Anything might be possible. Virginia Margold could decide to pay him a visit, rather than phone, and persuade bull-browed Barsamian to let her into the apartment. That would certainly give her a story for the road. On a positive note, he reflected, he could now meet Maia for dinner.

Descending to the lobby, the elevator jolted spasmodically—nothing violent, but enough to remind him of Shorty McTeague's misfortune. Twice, the car stopped mid-floor without opening, and Millard was contemplating calling for help over the emergency intercom, when the plunge resumed. Travel by elevator was a testament to faith, after all, practically a religious act, although few thought of it in those terms. No different than flying in an airplane or crossing a bridge. You trusted—blindly—that someone had inspected the cables, that all of the sheaves had been lubricated. A strange, neurotic alarm seized Millard that he might die prematurely. Rationally, the consequences of keeling over in Delilah's lobby, or being hit by a cab outside the 33rd Street post office, differed little from hanging himself inside a bathroom closet a few hours later, but nonetheless, he suddenly dreaded those missing minutes and the implicit disorder they might bring. A genuine relief spread through him when the elevator landed safely on the ground floor and the iron grate slid open.

"Evening, Dr. Salter," said the doorman. "How's Miss P.?"

Millard was appreciative of this question for a change.

"Doing just fine," he replied. "Resting comfortably."

Outside, the recent squall had wrung much of the moisture from the atmosphere, leaving behind a pleasant late-day warmth. Downtown traffic glided swiftly on the avenue. Although he had more than a good hour left to drop off the cassettes at the post office, and still rendezvous with Maia at seven thirty, Millard decided to risk a cab. Why not? He could afford it.

The vehicle he hailed belonged to an umber-skinned man whose license, posted on the closed partition, identified him as Mouktar. He had no political slogans affixed to his dashboard, only a green and blue flag with a red star that Millard did not recognize. Reggae music pulsed through the change hatch in the divider. Mr. Mouktar repeated their destination—"Thirty-Third Street and Eighth Avenue"—and uttered not another word. Several times, Millard considered broaching a conversation, hoping to distract himself, but the driver's austere expression, almost a grimace, kept him silent, and by the time they reached Columbus Circle, Mouktar was speaking rapidly into his cell phone in French. Millard's linguistic skills were rusty, but he remembered enough to understand that the fellow was arguing with his wife over money.

They cruised through the theater district, fighting for ground between ripples of tourists. Millard had hoped for a chatty, offbeat driver like Konnie with a K, but the reality was that all cab rides, no matter who steered, were fundamentally the same. A passenger might have the most enthralling discussion about Renaissance poetry or African politics or even healthcare, as Millard had once enjoyed with a Cuban exile who'd previously worked as a transplant surgeon, but at the end of the ride, you paid your fare and the relationship was over. A one-time interaction—with no potential for a future social relationship with your chauffer. You didn't see him ever again. Unless, of course, he picked you up on a different occasion, which was statistically as likely as surviving two commercial jet crashes—except in European cinema, where it appeared to happen frequently. Funerals, Millard reflected, also shared a certain uniformity. No matter what transpired in the mortuary or at the graveside, the dead stayed dead. Maybe not in Irish folklore, where corpses had a pesky habit of arousing at wakes. But for Jews, at least, the dead stayed dead.

"Right side or left?" asked the driver.

Mouktar remained on the line with his wife, holding the phone away from his ear so that Millard could hear the woman shouting while he instructed the driver. For a moment, he considered leaving the duffel bag behind in the vehicle, but he feared the next passenger might panic at an unattended bag and phone the authorities. Everybody, it seemed, was seeing something and saying something these days, and the last thing Millard desired was to spend the final night of his life in a Homeland Security holding cell. At the same time, he didn't want to lug the duffel with him to meet Maia. She might recognize it and grow suspicious. He paid Mouktar, tipping exactly fifteen percent, and carried the bag to the sidewalk.

Millard considered leaving the paraphernalia at the curbside in front of a random high-rise—but feared a vigilant doorman or porter might spot him on a security camera. In college, Lysander's friends had "appropriated" a one-way sign that had fallen during a lightning storm, and the boy had brought the "souvenir" home with him for winter break. At first, Millard had insisted that his son discard the placard immediately, not wanting to be arrested for harboring stolen government property in his apartment, but ridding oneself of an eight-foot-high city traffic emblem proved—not surprisingly—rather a challenge. To Millard's knowledge, the object still stood in the co-op's basement storeroom, propped against a far wall behind a mutilated Suzy Homemaker oven that had belonged to a long-deceased board member. So he understood that divesting himself of Delilah's suicide contraband was no easy feat.

A municipal bus stopped opposite the post office, scooping up a file of commuters. Millard waited for the vehicle to pull away, then entered the Lucite enclosure. His only company was a teenage boy, eyes closed, catnapping in the crook of the artificial glass. A decal-encrusted skateboard rested on the boy's lap. Not exactly the sort to phone the FBI. They'd actually had a competitive skateboarder as a patient on the consult service a few months back, a professional who'd shattered his pelvis in a career-ending vault at eighteen and had contemplated suicide. Millard had assigned the kid to one of his younger colleagues; he still couldn't conceive of skateboarding as an occupation, any more than macramé or latch hook. Especially for a clean-cut white boy from Long Island. Yet at least he didn't have a shard of metal through his nose like Lysander. *And he'd had a job!*

Millard set the duffel bag down on the bench, then inched away from it, as he'd seen others do at weddings, discarding olive pits and leftover slices of cake on buffet tables. A moment later, two elderly women seated themselves in the shelter, but paid the neglected bag no heed. He'd read in *Psychiatry Today* about skilled nursing facilities that employed fake bus stops as decoys for demented residents, allowing escaped Alzheimer's patients to wait for nonexistent rides until they could be escorted back to the home by staff members. The article noted that the stops often displayed counterfeit advertisements dating from earlier generations, pitching products like Brylcreem pomade, Gensacol varnish, Calox tooth powder. In his day, Millard had used them all.

He patted his pockets dramatically as though he'd misplaced something, creating a pretext to depart before the bus arrived. "I'll be right back," he said. Loud. One of the women looked up briefly, then returned to her reading, some form of religious tract with a harp on the cover. Millard strode quickly toward the steps of the post office without looking back. His advance scattered a flock of pigeons, which recongregated nearby in the shade.

Millard couldn't recall the last time he'd visited the central post office—certainly not since he'd lost Isabelle, maybe not since his divorce—yet he found its very existence reassuring, the aura of permanence exuded by its towering Corinthian colonnade. Unlike Denny Dennmeyer's branch post office, a structure as flimsy as a house of straw, the Farley Building's pavilions of Brescian marble and hand-painted coffered ceilings had been built to withstand crowds of thousands, and jerry-rigged gas explosions, and even the tug of history itself. Of course, one might have said the same of Pennsylvania Station, whose matching colonnade had towered directly across Eighth Avenue, a protective brother looking after its younger sib, before the solons who ran the city traded in the landmark depot for a second-rate sporting arena and shipped the remnants to New Jersey for landfill. As a boy, Millard's Florida family vacations had started at Penn Station. Later, the Salters had gone to the terminus to see his younger sister off to a nursing school in New Orleans. His most vivid memory of the post office stemmed from the final days of the war, Papa sending money for the transatlantic passage to a Zarakowski who'd been reported alive in a displaced persons camp. He remembered the solemnity of the transaction—his father stoic, the female clerk businesslike—and the lecture his Papa gave him on responsibility as they rode the El back to the Bronx. With the fur business crippled by wartime restrictions, the ticket had cost his old man nearly a week's receipts. The displaced Zarakowski—probably not even a cousin—died on the layover in Le Havre.

"Yo, mister," cried a voice. "Your bag."

Millard turned to face the kid from the bus stop. He couldn't have been more than thirteen or fourteen—all bone and sinew—sporting an untucked crimson shirt with a popped collar and a pyramid-studded belt. One hand held his skateboard, SLEEP LESS, SKATE MORE emblazoned across the underside of its deck; over the opposite shoulder draped the discarded duffel. With a deft motion of his arm and torso, he set the bag down in front of Millard.

"You left it at the bus stop."

"Thanks," said Millard.

Thanks for nothing, he sniped to himself—but that was unfair. He had assumed the worst of this young man, banked on his indifference to a stranger's lost property, and the kid had responded with the benevolence of the best Samaritan. Similar episodes stood out in his memory, reminders that humanity was not beyond redemption: a churlish Vietnamese waiter whom he'd under-tipped, but who'd later returned a wallet left at the register—hand-delivering it after his shift; an ex-boyfriend of Sally's, an ad executive with a venal streak, who'd died trying to rescue an elderly woman from a houseboat fire. Isabelle had once dialyzed a homeless crack addict who'd later donated

$1000 to the renal clinic with money raised from salvaged soda cans. Yet these were the rare exceptions, low-frequency occurrences that might make one conclude—mistakenly—that one's cynicism was not a reflection upon the state of the world, but upon oneself. Years of consult psychiatry had schooled Millard otherwise: Leave someone an opportunity to disappoint, and, almost inevitably, they would.

The kid spun the wheels of his skateboard.

"Say, mister, you have any spare change?" he asked. "I could use some food."

So Millard hadn't been completely off the mark. *What you could use is a hard potch on the tuchus*, he thought, *or maybe a sound drubbing with a barber strop. Or some basic, old-fashioned parenting.* Since when did middle-class white kids start panhandling on the public streets?

"Not today," said Millard. "Sorry."

The boy scowled, bearing menace. "How about a reward?"

Millard didn't want trouble, so he reached inside his pocket and handed the kid the first bill he could find—an ink-stained fiver, the Lincoln Memorial discolored to a glossy blue. His fountain pen had exploded inside his pocket, tinging both his wallet and his slacks, another blemish on a day of disfigurement. At this rate, he'd hang himself with stigmata on his palms.

"That's one nasty bill," said the kid—but this didn't stop him from pocketing the cash.

Millard picked up the duffel and hauled it into the post office. The zipper hung open, he noticed; his Great Samaritan had clearly rummaged through its contents. Rather than irking Millard, the boy's greed delighted him—his faith in his own lack of faith was restored.

He joined the long line at the teller's window. (*Not a teller*, he could hear Isabelle reminding him. *A clerk. Tellers work in banks*.) Although early evening was likely a peak business hour, only one clerk was on duty: a mousy, elfin-eared woman who worked at the pace of a garden snail. Millard wondered how his father, a dyed-in-the-wool Democrat who believed deeply in the ability of Uncle Sam to overcome all of humankind's challenges, would have responded to a government that did everything ass backwards. Not just the post office—although FedEx could ship your package *faster and for less*—but the Department of Motor Vehicles, the IRS, the Veterans Administration. And the agencies his patients relied upon, those countless bureaucracies that meted out food stamps and disability benefits, proved even worse. A person could die of old age while waiting for their pediatric health coverage. No wonder they shielded the postal workers these days with bulletproof glass.

He inched forward—some customers receiving service, others giving in and leaving the line, a complex fugue that finally brought him to the counter. He placed each of Delilah's envelopes on the scale and waited for the clerk to assess them. With painful indifference, she weighed each package and affixed a series of stickers.

"They all weigh the same amount," he said, hoping to speed the process.

"We'll see," replied the clerk.

Millard sensed the impatience of the customers behind him; he wished he had a way of telling them that he was on their side. Yet the delay allowed him to formulate a plan for the unwanted duffel, one that hovered on the brink of wicked genius.

"Can I have a box?" he asked.

"What size?"

He patted the duffel. "Big enough for this."

The clerk broke off her labeling long enough to retrieve a large cardboard box.

While she deposited Isabelle's tapes in a canvas bin, he addressed the box to Harvey Bloodfinch at St. Dymphna's Hospital. And then came the pièce de résistance: Knowing that the post office wouldn't mail a package that large without a return address, he wrote in the name *Hecuba Yilmaz* on the lines for the sender. A sense of euphoria rose in Millard's chest—he felt like a mortally wounded field marshal celebrating news of victory on the battlefield. Let the Royal Embellisher explain *that* to the powers that be. "Nothing liquid, fragile, or perishable," he assured the clerk. She hadn't asked a word about lethal gases or asphyxiation hoods.

By the time Millard left the post office, it was a quarter past seven. He dared not risk a crosstown taxi again at that hour, so he hurried on foot toward Grand Central Station. His father's first fur outlet had been on 34th Street, but he no longer recalled the precise location—and those rows of low-slung shops had long since been razed for office towers. But he remembered hiding among the furs, nuzzling against stoles of fox and raccoon and beaver. Once, his father had received a shipment of coyote jackets—for men—that sold so poorly, the term "coyote jacket" became a euphemism at their dinner table for any terrible idea. On another occasion, unless his memory was playing tricks on him, Papa had offered a special on coats of Canadian lynx. That was in the 1950s, before wearing furs around Midtown put your life in danger.

He raced down the steps into Grand Central just as the hands on the four-faced brass clock approached the half hour. Maia waited for him on the concourse, sporting acid-washed jeans and a loose T-shirt that revealed her left shoulder. The girl took after her mother, full in the chest and the hips, what his own mama would have called a "child-bearing figure." She carried a backpack over one arm like a middle-school student.

"Fancy meeting you here," said Millard. "Small world."

"Small for some people. There are 1.3 billion Chinese peasants you'll never meet."

"Touché, young lady. Now what do you want to eat?"

"I was hoping to stop by the apartment first. . . ."

That caught Millard off guard. He hadn't planned on inviting his daughter upstairs, not tonight, and he wondered whether he'd left out anything incriminating that she might see. "Do you really want to go all the way uptown?" he asked.

"You are funny sometimes," replied Maia. "That was the whole point of this visit—or, at least, most of the point. I'm going to give Mama's nursing textbooks to my mentee from the Girls Club. . . . We talked about this last night. . . ."

"I guess we did," Millard conceded.

So this was how old age happened—encroaching, insidious. You'd forget a word here, a face there, and soon nothing remained but the void. He remembered his mother at seventy, pouring Softsoap onto her pancakes, trying to pick up Lawrence Welk on the toaster.

"I knew you weren't paying attention," said Maia. "I asked if you'd mind me giving Mama's old nursing books to Nancy."

"Nancy?"

"My mentee. The high school girl I'm tutoring."

"Oh," said Millard. "Won't they be out of date . . . ?"

"It's basic anatomy and physiology. How much can change? Besides, this is just to whet her appetite. . . ."

"Okay, I suppose. Let's catch the IRT."

She looked at him blankly; he might as well have suggested a stagecoach or a sedan chair.

"The *subway*," he said. "Let's take the train."

They crossed the plaza and waited on a packed platform. A few yards away, on a wooden bench, a young girl with a butterscotch ponytail sobbed against an elderly woman's shoulder, and for an instant, Millard mistook her for the child who'd played the piano so dexterously on the seventh floor of the Luxdorfer Pavilion—but then she looked up, revealing a disfigured jaw. On the train, a red-faced businessman offered Millard his seat. He declined. Did he really look *that* poorly?

"So I have a proposal for you," said Maia. "Before you say no, hear me out, okay?"

Millard smiled. "Why should I hear you out when the answer is no?"

He already anticipated the subject; his daughter was trying to fix him up again. All of his widowed friends, of which there were an increasing number, complained that their children resisted their efforts to resume dating—or, when they did, resented their new girlfriend with unreasonable bitterness. Alas, he should only be so lucky! Except for Lysander, each of his children had embarked on a crusade to find him a new partner. Arnold emailed him the names and phone numbers of mothers of colleagues in the beer business; Sally had opened a trial account for him on an Internet dating site—without his permission. In Maia's case, he sensed that the girl was projecting, displacing onto him her own desire for a husband and a family. For a twenty-seven-year-old with smarts and good looks, she boasted a dismal track record, a long cortege of self-absorbed, philandering boyfriends. Maybe he'd set a poor example. Maybe Lysander wasn't the only child to fall victim to his distractions.

"Trust me. She's great," said Maia. "She's a retired professor of comparative literature. And she loves opera. German and Italian. . . ."

"And you met her *how?*"

Maia looked away. "I haven't exactly met her yet," she confessed. "She's the mother of one of the temps in a coworker's lab."

"Nothing like thirdhand experience," said Millard.

He'd succumbed to Maia's pressure once before, so he knew the risks. That woman had been a librarian at a college in New Jersey, and quite attractive, with sharp black eyes and a regal nose that reminded Millard of a falcon. They'd met for breakfast on 23rd Street. He'd ordered eggs over easy. She'd ordered three Bloody Marys—all at the same time—and no entrée. Later, he discovered that Maia had met the woman on line at a liquor store.

"I'll think it over," promised Millard. "Good enough?"

"Good enough," agreed his daughter.

They climbed out of the subway at 86th Street. The last full rays of sunlight—orange, magenta—clung to the brickwork along the avenue. Couples in dinnerwear passed on the sidewalk, laughing, scurrying. An ambulance idled at the corner of 87th, where a cabbie and a limousine driver negotiated the aftermath of a fender bender. A wedding party snapped photos from inside the limo. Millard and Maia passed the 88th Street playground, heading north. Barsamian, the doorman, touched his cap as they approached.

"It's not even eight o'clock," said Maia. "Let's take a walk around the block."

Millard had no particular interest in an evening stroll—he was exhausted and increasingly anxious—but he also didn't want to raise his daughter's alarm.

"A quick walk," he offered. "And then we'll get a bite to eat."

They advanced toward Madison. Millard recalled when three-story town houses had lined the opposite side of the street, Italianate brownstones with projecting lintels and double-leaf doors dating from the late nineteenth century. Most of them had given way to a pair of glass-and-steel towers where yuppies and starter couples sojourned on their trajectory toward the suburbs.

Gone were the Sicilian cobbler who chalked your fee on the soles of your loafers and the brothers from Corfu who sold silver Judaica and religious garb. A twenty-four-hour Korean deli operated under a stone strut inscribed *First Bank of Manhattan*.

"It's amazing that it's still light out," said Maia.

"Happens every year," said Millard. "That's the amazing part."

When they finally circled back to Fifth Avenue, every bone below his pelvis throbbed like ten thousand blisters. In the lobby, Barsamian greeted them with a peculiar smile—almost a smirk, encouraging yet mischievous, as though he suspected Millard's intentions. But how could he possibly know? And did it even matter?

The elevator glided straight up to the ninth floor, a small blessing. Millard led his daughter around the corner toward 9-G, as he'd done countless times during her childhood, and unlocked both bolts sequentially.

He eased open the door. The apartment was dark and still, and yet—

The lights flashed on abruptly, followed by a chorus of gleeful, cacophonic shouts.

"Surprise!" The cries hit him like bullets. "Surprise! Surprise! Surprise!"

14

Millard's eyes adjusted to the light and the crowded parlor. Everybody he knew in life appeared to have congregated inside his apartment—or, at least, everybody he liked. Arnold, fresh off the plane from St. Louis, sporting a T-shirt that read *Beer Is My Friend*; Sally, resplendent with pearl earrings and a chiffon gown, accompanied by her dapper architect husband in his double-breasted Italian suit; his colleagues from the hospital—Art Rosenstein, Stan Laguna, Gabby Lu with a toddler on her shoulders. Also board members from the co-op, two of his fraternity brothers from NYU, even Isabelle's kooky girlhood friend Linda Blauer. On the whole, a geriatric crowd, a reminder of his place on the existential conveyor belt. His granddaughters raced from the maelstrom and hugged him around either leg, indifferent to his shredded pants and bloody knee.

"Surprise, Dad," said Maia. "Happy birthday!"

"We love you, Grandpa," cried Sally's daughters.

He had never been a fan of surprise parties, but he went with the flow. What alternative did he have? Many years earlier, practically a lifetime ago, his mother's relatives had thrown a surprise wedding shower for Carol—with disastrous consequences. His fiancée had returned home from a long evening in her physics lab to find thirty elderly, Yiddish-speaking women jammed into her dormitory suite, not one of whom she'd recognized. So she'd done the only sensible thing imaginable: She'd phoned the police.

But sorting out the confusion didn't mitigate his ex-wife's anger, which festered long after the guests had departed.

A romantic dinner at a French bistro had failed to assuage her.

"Is it such a big deal, darling?" he'd asked. "They meant no harm."

"You don't understand. It's a cruel trick," she'd replied. "Now I can't change my mind."

For Millard, the birthday gathering seemed designed to achieve the opposite effect: a ruse by the Fates to convince him that he was indispensable, that he was too well-loved to shuffle off his mortal coil so soon. Tears welled in his eyes, which his guests probably mistook for joy, but was actually grief, delayed but not forestalled, that he couldn't share this moment with Delilah. That he could never again share *any* moment with Delilah.

"Sorry about all the deception," said Maia.

"So *this* is what you were up to. . . ." He forced a smile. "We *didn't* have dinner plans."

"Nope. While I do have a mentee applying to nursing school, Mama's books are decades out of date," said Maia. "But we had to get you here *somehow*. Lysander was the one in charge of creating a pretext, but he forgot. . . ."

So at least he wasn't losing his mind. That was reassuring.

"Where *is* your brother?" asked Millard.

Maia snorted with disdain. "He probably overslept."

A whirlwind of greetings and congratulations followed. Someone offered him a glass of champagne, and he sipped gingerly, while guest after guest shook his opposite hand and wished him variations on "another fifty good years." Arnold apologized that his wife couldn't attend, but no amount of filial love or Xanax could lure her onto an airplane. Art Rosenstein introduced him to a shapely redhead in her sixties, his widowed sister-in-law, who managed to mention her Tony Award nomination twice in consecutive sentences. Nearby, Elsa Duransky had buttonholed Sameer Patel, her shrill voice filling the room with tedious anecdotes: *What my husband said was, 'I already have the only little minx I need right here.' Isn't that just delectable?* That nobody mentioned Millard's injuries—his rent clothes, his bandaged cheek—distressed him more than the wounds themselves, as though he'd reached the age where tattered attire and multifarious abrasions came with the territory. He jostled his way toward his bedroom. The air conditioner buzzed beneath the bay window, little match for the heat of the throng.

"Excuse me a moment," he said to nobody in particular. "I'm going to wash up."

Millard polished off his champagne and ducked out of the party, savoring the silence behind the closed door of the master bathroom. He doused his head in cold water and wrapped a fresh bandage around his knee. The laceration below his left thumb probably required stitches, but he was content to stuff the wound with tissues. His slacks went straight into the wastebasket beneath the sink. Sporting a fresh shirt and a pair of dark pants—he chose the cotton slacks with the pleated front that Isabelle had always complimented—Millard felt just refreshed enough to tolerate another round of hors d'oeuvres and pleasantries.

He braced himself and reentered the fray.

"There you are," said Maia, looping her arm around his elbow. "I was afraid you'd sneaked off on us. . . ."

While he'd been gone, his guests had rearranged the furniture. The sofa and upholstered chairs now faced a freestanding projector screen that had been set in front of the television; on an end table, mounted atop several books, rested a slide carousel. Across the screen, the text read: *The Life and Times of Our Father,*

Millard Salter. His daughter steered him through the crowd to an open seat at the center of the sofa.

"What is this . . . ?" he asked.

"We've prepared a little show," said Maia.

Arnold tapped his knife against a champagne flute to silence the room. "If you'll all bear with us, we've put together a tribute for the guest of honor." He dimmed the lights. Elsa continued braying her anecdote about the minx—this time to Sally's husband—until someone shushed her. A bowl of popcorn circulated through the audience.

The first image depicted Millard's parents, Solomon and Shirley, posing on the red carpet outside the Waldorf Astoria Hotel. Freshly married, obviously in love. He couldn't remember his mother so young, his father so full of vigor and promise. "Grandma and Grandpa," announced Maia. Then came Millard and Lester horsing around in the pool at Grossinger's Resort, sunbathing on the beach in Fort Myers, tossing a baseball across the sandlot at Van Cortlandt Park. Millard in a sleeved doublet with a neck ruff as Myles Standish in his elementary school's Thanksgiving pageant. Millard and Harriet dancing together at Lester's bar mitzvah.

"How on earth . . . ?" he asked.

"I found the photos in one of Mom's shoeboxes," whispered Maia. "Arnold wanted to convert them to PowerPoint, but I thought you'd enjoy an old-fashioned slide show. . . . Believe me, it was a royal pain in the ass, too. Nobody converts photos to slides anymore."

Millard wanted to ask: *Do you remember that time Papa brought his slide projector to the Ozarks and airport security mistook it for a weapon? It was cutting-edge technology back then!* But nobody in the room, he realized, possessed any memories of his father.

A candid of him and Lettie Moshewitz, lounging in the plush lobby of the Centennial Arms, popped onto the screen. How young she looked! A mere child. What foolishness, to have suffered so much for a girl in braces and knee socks. In a second photo, he and Lettie stood side by side, his arm draped over her shoulder, posing like a married couple. When had *that* been taken? Had she really allowed him to wrap an arm around her?

"Who's the hot chick?" demanded Stan Laguna.

"No idea," lied Millard. "Some girl from the neighborhood."

Thankfully, that was the last of Lettie, although he did have to endure a portrait of the Hager Heights drama club that included his high school heartthrob, Stella Vann, and, later, a group shot of him and Art Hallam in a booth at MacGregor's Pub with Art's fiancée and Judy Bell—*before* she'd urinated on his gabardine trousers. Next came sundry pictures of Carol: in jumper dresses, in a white lab coat, with and without her horn-rimmed glasses. And slowly a family emerged: Millard cradling Arnold; Millard, tongue plastered to his nose, hamming it up for Sally; all three children costumed as dental cosmetics for Halloween. Lysander, the Pepsodent toothbrush, already a towering gangle at twelve. The children fished off the dock at Hal Storch's lake house, cavorted on Millard's skiff, played Frisbee at Hyannis like the Kennedy siblings. Soon Arnold graduated college, Sally completed high school. The family was just starting to fragment— baby Maia claimed a place in Millard's arms—when Lysander entered the apartment with his usual tumult. Eyes turned toward the door.

"Sorry I'm late," he said. "Happy birthday, Dad."

"Grab a seat," ordered Maia. "We're nearly finished."

Yet they were far from finished. A series of work-related photos followed: Millard accepting the medical school's W. Feig Award for Teaching Excellence; Millard's induction ceremony into the New York Academy of Medicine; a photo from the psychiatry department picnic, when joyless David Atkinson had still been chairman and Stan Laguna was a first-year fellow, sporting sideburns and a bushy beard. And then the show returned to family once again: Millard with Isabelle, cruising the Seine on a *bateau mouche*; with Isabelle and Maia—maybe age fifteen—outside the Holocaust Museum in Washington. (Compared to Carol, Isabelle received short shrift on screen time, but he understood this was a sensitive subject among his children.) The final slide pictured Millard, alone, smiling, leaning over the side of the skiff with a snapper dangling on his line, above the caption: *Millard Salter, Beloved Father & Physician, Seventy-Five Years Young.* Fervent applause greeted the conclusion of the tribute.

"Speech!" called out Stan Laguna. "Speech!"

Millard waved him off. "The secret to living a long life," he retorted, "is not giving unwelcome speeches." That produced a sporadic chuckle. "Unless you're paid generously by a pharmaceutical company," he added. More laughter and cheers ensued.

"We have one more surprise for you," announced Maia. She handed him the telephone. "Someone very special wants to wish you a happy birthday."

For an instant, he'd anticipated that Virginia Margold had called. When his sister's voice came through the receiver, his first reaction was relief.

"Millard, is that you?"

"Yes, it's me. Harriet?"

"I'm not going to stay on the phone too long," said his sister. "I know you're having a big birthday bash and all. But I wanted to wish you a happy birthday. And say that I love you."

What Harriet meant was that she didn't want to keep him on the line, *long distance*, although he'd explained to her countless times that he paid the same rate whether he called her in

Tucson or Teaneck—or Tuscany, for that matter. But old habits perished hard: Papa never spoke on the telephone for more than thirty seconds, except for business matters, and kept sick calls at the hospital to a carefully timed fifteen minutes. *No need to overstay your welcome*, he insisted, when his primary thought was on his parking meter. How a man could shell out seventy-five dollars for a dinner at Lüchow's and fret over a five-cent meter had been one of the unresolved mysteries of Millard's childhood. When Millard had asked once—during their "parenting chat" at the Overlook—his father had replied, *At Lüchow's, I can enjoy my money.*

"I love you too, Harriet," said Millard.

He'd hardly hung up the phone when Sally entered with a chocolate cake. She'd forgone seventy-five candles for two large ones in the shape of a 7 and a 5. The designer had etched a stethoscope and a black bag onto the surface in frosting.

"Make a wish," urged Stan Laguna.

"Yeah, Dad," said Arnold, "make a wish."

Gabby Lu's toddler shouted an incoherent cry of enthusiasm.

"I already have everything I want," he replied.

Yet he ought to wish for *something*—even if it were only superstition. But what? A career for Lysander? A husband for Maia? A painless death. When he'd been in grade school, he'd solved these competing demands by wishing for "a lifetime of free wishes," which seemed a much better investment in childhood than in old age. What he desired, at the moment, was for his guests to leave, a request too frivolous for the occasion. And then Millard realized what he hoped for most, although he wasn't sure if one could wish retroactively: He wanted Delilah to have had a peaceful passing. Closing his eyes, he blew out the candles.

Sally took charge of distributing the cake. "And who wants coffee?" she asked. "Regular or decaf? Milk or cream?" She'd become quite the hostess since her days sketching gowns on paper napkins; Millard admired his daughter's poise as she navigated the room. "That's three regular coffees, six decafs, and a peppermint tea with lemon for Mrs. Duransky."

Millard retreated to a corner, where he chatted with his eldest son. Arnold's company had recently been taken over by a major soft drink bottler, creating both opportunities and risks, none of which Millard fully understood. He was also restoring a nineteenth-century farmstead on his own. "You come out and visit in the spring," said Arnold. "Lila and the boys would love to see you—and we'll get you working on the house. I could sure use some help. . . ."

"Please send Lila my love," said Millard.

Lysander approached, cradling a coffee cup.

"Since when do *you* drink coffee, baby brother?" asked Arnold.

"It's hot water," said Lysander.

"Your great-grandmother used to drink hot water like that," said Millard. "She'd suck it through a cube of sugar."

"No sugar cubes for me, Dad. Say, what did you do to your cheek?"

"Stray cat. Not a big deal."

"You have to be careful with strays," said Lysander. "What happened to her?"

At first, Millard was about to ask: *What happened to whom?* Then he realized his son meant the cat—that the boy's primary concern was not for his injuries, but for the fate of a random feline, an *imaginary* feline. So much for priorities.

"She ran off," said Millard. "Now if you'll pardon me for a moment . . ."

The alternative to excusing himself would have been to lash out at Lysander, which was not how he wanted their relationship to end. Fortunately, the party had started to wind down, and he was able to throw himself into the enterprise of farewells. He allowed Art Rosenstein's sister-in-law to kiss him on either cheek; he reassured Mrs. Lewinter that her Pekinese's potassium level sounded safe. One by one, the faces of his life disappeared.

Millard agreed to retrieve Linda Blauer's umbrella from the sitting room, principally because he needed another moment of respite. By now, a crisp darkness had settled over the city and he groped on the wall for the switch. This had been Isabelle's lair—and he could still picture her sketching at the window or reading an airport mystery on the divan. The aloe flourished in broad rosettes on trays beneath the window; he took pains not to overwater. With Linda's umbrella in one hand, he crossed the room and ran his fingers along the plant's fleshy leaves. Even the noxious smell of the yellow sap, like old scallions, made him miss his beloved.

"Hey, you. Now is no time for hiding."

Maia had followed him into the sitting room. She held a paper plate with cake in one hand, a glass of red wine in the other. So much like her mother, she looked—so beautiful.

"I was just thinking. . . ."

"You were just being antisocial," said Maia. "I know you."

"I suppose you do," he agreed. "Thank you, by the way. This wasn't necessary. . . ."

"Seventy-five is nothing to scoff at."

"I miss your mother," said Millard.

"I know," said Maia. "I do too."

He looked out the window at the traffic below. Beyond the awning, he could make out a cab unloading at the curbside, the top of Barsamian's red cap. Across the street, the neon lights flashed in the twenty-four-hour deli.

"Do me a favor," he said. "If anything happens to me, please be sure not to drown your mother's aloe. . . . It only needs watering twice each month."

"Nothing's going to happen to you."

Millard followed his daughter back into the parlor and dispatched the last of the guests. The apartment itself had seen better days: crushed popcorn stippled Isabelle's Berber carpet; crumpled napkins and icing-soaked paper plates perched on the bookshelves and the open breakfront like summer swallows along a cliffside. Not exactly the state of affairs Millard wished to leave behind, but it couldn't be helped.

Maia had started gathering the litter.

"Don't worry about that," he insisted. "I'll take care of it in the morning."

"Are you sure?"

"Yes, I'm sure. I'm not too old to clean up after myself."

He accompanied her to the entryway.

"I love you," she said.

"Me too. Now don't drown your mama's aloe."

Millard shut the door behind her and closed the latch. On the way to the bedroom, he retrieved a bottle of Courvoisier from the cabinet above the dishwasher. He'd received the bottle as a marriage present from Hal Storch; you couldn't exactly call it a *wedding* present, because he'd married Isabelle at city hall on a Saturday morning. For decades, the cognac had waited patiently for a fitting occasion. Millard downed a shot straight from the bottle, savoring the burn of liquid fire down his throat.

You've earned some rest, Millard, he thought. *You've done the best you could have.*

Lysander hadn't even bothered to say goodbye.

15

Millard unknotted his tie as he entered the bedroom: an act that announced a slumber well earned after a long workday, or in this case, a life well lived. Now that Delilah was gone, his death seemed neither necessary nor unnecessary, merely inevitable—a fact, like the day of the week or the number of dimes in a dollar. So he would be dead. He wouldn't know. Life would continue, his children growing old, his granddaughters marrying, humanity subject to countless vagaries and twists and revelations. Harvey Bloodfinch might dynamite St. Dymphna's, Hecuba Yilmaz could wrangle his job away from Stan Laguna, but the enterprise of loving and fighting, birthing and dying, would carry on just fine without him. What were those lines that a spurned Eliza Doolittle sings to dismiss Henry Higgins? "Without your pulling it, the tide comes in. . . ." Millard hummed the bars from *My Fair Lady*: "Without your twirling it, the earth can spin. . . ." How true it all was. His own tide was surging in for him—and he was okay with that.

Millard set the bottle of Courvoisier on the bureau. He didn't notice Lysander until he'd tossed his necktie over the nearest chair. His son was seated on the bedspread, arms splayed behind him to support his vast frame, shoeless feet dangling over the edge. The boy's hobnail boots rested close by on the throw rug. Beside him, atop the silk comforter—Millard was glad he'd made up the bed that morning—lay shavings of an orange rind and a carton of sugar-free breakfast cereal pinched from Millard's refrigerator. An empty wineglass stood on the nightstand; Lysander hadn't thought to use a coaster, which would have upset Millard on most occasions, except a dead man doesn't care if he leaves behind water rings on his furniture.

"Good God!" he exclaimed. "You could give somebody a heart attack. . . ."

"I didn't mean to surprise you," said Lysander. "But I was feeling bad."

As much as he loved his son, Millard instantly feared the worst: Did the boy need money? Had he gotten in over his head with loan sharks? Or knocked up a girl? How fitting that his son's crisis and his own should reach fruition on the same day. He'd help the boy, of course—even, he realized, if doing so meant forestalling his planned demise for the time being.

"Mom called me this afternoon," said Lysander. "She says you're worried about me."

So that was all. Millard could already imagine the tenor of his ex-wife's report: She'd downplay her own concerns and Lysander's shortcomings, pinning the entire impasse on the fanciful expectations of the guilt-soaked father. *It's how your dad was raised*, she'd say. *All he knew from his first steps was that he'd be a doctor. Everything else you do, even if you win the Nobel Prize while walking on the moon, is bound to disappoint him.* Which wasn't true, not the way Carol meant it—yet what was so wrong with another doctor? *Your dad's also a bit neurotic*, the boy's mother would say. *Impatient too. He takes after his own father.*

Damn Carol! That was a bridge too far. So he had high expectations like Papa: What parent didn't? Just because he had hopes for his children didn't mean he was prisoner to them. All he wanted, at least at this late juncture, was for his son to become a self-supporting, productive member of society; if that meant he'd be a veterinarian, or a trigonometry teacher, or even a cashier at the Bronx Zoo, Millard could accept his choice—although vending concessions at the zoo would obviously be harder to swallow. He still remembered how Hal Storch had suffered when his daughter quit UConn to train as a hairdresser, also the schadenfreude he'd felt when his niece opened a tanning salon in Laguna Beach. But even selling cotton candy outside a monkey house in the Bronx was *something*. Nothing, as Lear warned, came of nothing, and Lysander had mastered the art of nothing like nobody's business. How dare Carol cast the blame at his feet? It would serve her right when he didn't return her phone call in the morning.

"I *am* worried about you," said Millard. "I tried to tell you over lunch."

Lysander squinted—a sheepish habit—and examined the heels of his hands.

"How can I *not* be worried about you?" asked Millard. "You're forty-three years old. Art Hallam's son in Palo Alto is two years younger than you and practically retired."

That provoked a chuckle. "I'm practically retired too," said Lysander.

At least the boy shared Millard's wit. He sensed his own lips curling into a smile, but refused to be derailed. "You're *not* retired."

Lysander raked his hands through his unctuous hair. "No, I guess I'm not."

The boy's words settled over the bedroom like a miasma, and for the first time, Millard detected a melancholy in his son's voice, a disappointment, such a contrast from his usual defiant indifference. A tenderness took hold of Millard, an aching, much as it had earlier, when he'd recognized the desperation behind Virginia Margold's inane phone calls and visits. Lysander's failures weren't an act of rebellion, but rather a resignation to perceived inadequacy. The boy didn't try because, at some subconscious level, as Hal Storch would say, he feared that he wouldn't succeed. How had Millard been so blind? Comparing him to Art Hallam's kid, or even Sally and Arnold, only exacerbated his inertia.

"Maybe I've been too hard on you," said Millard.

Lysander gathered the orange peels into his palm. "What I wanted to tell you," he said, rising from the bed, "was that you should stop worrying. I'm going to be okay. Trust me."

They stood opposite each other, son and father, like reflections in a warped mirror. From the open window drifted the rumble of traffic on the avenue: the enterprise of life. A warm breeze ruffled the curtains, sent the lace valances line-kicking like chorus girls.

"All right," agreed Millard. "I will stop worrying."

Lysander took a tentative step forward, still cupping the orange peel, and wrapped his gangly arms around his father's diminished torso. Millard patted the boy affectionately on the wings of his back. He could not recall the last time he'd hugged any of his children. He'd only embraced his own father at graduations and funerals, and once, on impulse, before his draft board hearing; hugging wasn't the Salter way, at least, not until now.

"I'll see you soon, Dad. Happy birthday, again," said his son. Lysander shambled toward the doorway, his helpless languor visible in every step, and added, "I'd be an awful veterinarian, if you think about it. Can you really see me putting down injured puppies?"

A few hours earlier, Millard would have objected. He could hear his former self generating excuses, conditions: *Maybe you could have a partner who'd perform the euthanizing. You wouldn't have to put any animals down.* . . . Now, almost too late, he knew better.

"No, I guess I can't," he said.

And then he was alone.

The thud of the foyer door underscored his solitude. Millard returned to the parlor and rummaged inside the cabinet beneath the stereo for Isabelle's old cassette player. She'd saved recordings dating back twenty-five years: Maia as a toddler, Millard's brother singing in Yiddish, her own mother describing the family's escape from Horthy's Hungary on a Portuguese passport, sharing the same sleeping car with the Gabor sisters. At one point, before her diagnosis, Isabelle had intended to curate the recordings and burn them onto CDs. In a week or two, they'd probably end up at the curbside. (Millard considered writing a note to his younger daughter, emphasizing the importance of the audio tapes—but what was their importance, really?) His fingers struggled to untangle the power cords and headphone attachments from the assortment of obsolete devices that his late wife had stockpiled: his and hers Walkmans, remnants of their brief health binge after his cardiac scare; the monitor and keyboard of a discontinued Commodore computer; a Royal LetterMaster daisy wheel printer still in the original packaging, caked in a veneer of ominous, decades-old dust. How easily he might have passed the night reminiscing over these objects, but Millard refused to let his emotions distract him. When he finally had the cassette player plugged into the wall outlet, he unsealed Delilah's envelope and removed the tape.

The voice he'd anticipated had been his lover's. Instead, the lustrous mezzo-soprano of Christa Ludwig filled the parlor. Massenet's *Werther*. He recognized the piece instantly.

Millard hit fast-forward. The machine whirred. He released his thumb.

René Kollo in *Tannhäuser*. Delilah's favorite recording.

Astounding. She'd made him a mixtape. Clearly, Delilah had

been working on the project for months, because he couldn't en-vision her managing the editing during her final days. Millard knew all about mixtapes from the hours Maia had spent in her room, during those hot adolescent summers, copying niche hits by groups called Silver Limpet and Roomless Elephant to woo older boys; he'd made a point of learning the names of the bands, whose music sounded interchangeable and somewhat saccharine, as though the groups might earn extra cash singing backup on commercials for long-distance telephone service. Maia's idol at thirteen—a tambourine-toting, blue-haired Norwegian per-former named Kylling Skylling—sounded like Bobby Vinton, only drunk. Contemplating how the world had progressed from *Tannhäuser* to Hogtie and the Pentacoastal Five left Millard reel-ing. Maybe that was the cue for his curtain call.

He sat on the love seat, paralyzed, absorbing the music. The last aria, Leontyne Price channeling Don Giovanni, dampened his eyes. Somehow, the ornate hands on the box clock above the mantel approached midnight. He filled a pitcher at the sink and watered the African violets on the kitchen sill, but he under-stood that he was procrastinating. This wasn't *It's a Wonderful Life*; no guardian angel would emerge from the ether to alter his plans, to show him how life might evolve for the worse in his ab-sence. Nothing, no miracle or calamity, could change his course anymore. He'd best get the deed over with. What was there to be frightened of, really? Hanging, as he taught the medical stu-dents, year after year, was by far the most common method of suicide in the world. Old as Babylon too.

He retreated to the master bedroom and retrieved the shield-backed chair from beside Isabelle's writing desk, carefully removing the assorted neckties from its arms and re-draping them over the door of the chifforobe. Carol and he had received the chair as a wedding present from his mother's cousin, a peasant beauty who'd married into the furniture business; at one time, there'd been a second chair, but Lysander had splintered the legs while playing Batman. Most of the neckties were gifts as well: Yale Bulldogs courtesy of Maia; handmade silk souvenirs from his sister's trip to Italy, *all purchased duty-free in Milan*; a jazzy batik, rather hideous, designed by a former patient who ran a boutique in Woodstock. Millard carried the chair into the bathroom and set it down inside the interior closet, *Isabelle's closet*, where he'd cleared away a space beneath the central rafter; the heft of the solid oak reassured him.

Shortly after their marriage, Isabelle had carved the closet from the bathroom. She'd endured the mammoth walk-in closet off the hallway that she'd inherited from Carol for six months, then insisted upon an arrangement where she wouldn't have to traverse the drafty master bedroom to dress. Since his beloved had rarely asked for anything of value, Millard proved more than delighted to indulge her, insisting on the finest in both contractors and wood. Some of Carol's abandoned jetsam still gathered cobwebs on the upper shelves of the old closet, alongside Maia's stuffed walrus and Millard's spare fishing tackle. He'd seen his ex's wooden tennis racket up there too, caged in its trapezoid frame, now a testament to her fling with Howard Logan. (Who could say that she didn't have old love letters squirreled away in the crawl spaces as well?) In his fifties, he'd even installed a chin-up bar across the doorframe, hoping to improve his upper body strength. What a joke!

Once the chair was in place, Millard retrieved the Courvoisier from the bedroom; he seated himself on the toilet lid and downed two Valium, using the cognac as a chaser. Any more than ten milligrams and he risked falling asleep prematurely— waking up the next morning with a bad hangover and a bedroom chair in his closet. Many of his patients had betrayed themselves in this way. While he waited for the tranquilizers to kick in, he looped his spare belt over the rafter. *Almost done, Millard*, he urged. *Hang in there.* A bit of gallows humor.

Millard climbed onto the chair; he felt a twinge in his knee. A hint of his late wife's scent still clung to the red cedar boards, fighting through the naphthalene and Pine-Sol. Empty hangers drooped from the dowels, a hodgepodge of foam and wire. Vestiges of his former married life crowded the corners: Isabelle's ironing board and tailor's ham; their folded bridge table, host to countless nights of canasta with his in-laws; the carton of her cosmetics that he'd never managed to discard. Slowly, with systematic care, Millard secured the belt to the rafter and wrapped the other end around his neck. Through the haze of alcohol and Valium, he could feel the leather hot and tight against his neck, stanching his veins, the buckle biting into the muscle, yet his eyes focused on the box containing Isabelle's lipsticks and blushers, the name *Wanamaker's* fading from the cardboard. Leaving the used cosmetics behind bothered him—a sign of disorder, negligence. He would carry them to the trash chute, he decided, and then return to his endeavor.

Or maybe he would discard the carton tomorrow. Yes, that seemed an elegant solution to the cosmetics, and to Lysander, and to everything else that weighed upon him. *Tomorrow.* He cradled this final word on his lips, wistful, even as he kicked away the chair.

ABOUT THE AUTHOR

Jacob M. Appel is the author of many novels and short story collections, including *The Man Who Wouldn't Stand Up, Scouting for the Reaper, Phoning Home,* and *Einstein's Beach House*. His short fiction has appeared in many literary journals, including *AGNI, Colorado Review, Gettysburg Review,* and more. His prose has won many awards, including the Boston Review Short Story Contest and the William Faulkner–William Wisdom Competition. His stories have also been short-listed for the O. Henry Award and *The Best American Short Stories*. He has taught most recently at Brown University, at the Gotham Writers' Workshop in New York City, and at Yeshiva College, where he was the writer-in-residence. His essays have appeared in the *New York Times, Chicago Tribune, Detroit Free Press, Orlando Sentinel, Providence Journal,* and many regional newspapers.

MILLARD SALTER'S LAST DAY

JACOB M. APPEL

This readers group guide for *Millard Salter's Last Day* includes an introduction, discussion questions, and ideas for enhancing your book club. The suggested questions are intended to help your reading group find new and interesting angles and topics for your discussion. We hope that these ideas will enrich your conversation and increase your enjoyment of the book.

INTRODUCTION

*M*illard Salter's Last Day is the heartwarming story of a man who decides to end his life before he's too old—but then begins to reconsider when he faces complications from the world around him.

Rather than suffer the indignities of aging, psychiatrist Millard Salter has decided to kill himself by the end of the day—but only after tying up some loose ends. These include a tête-à-tête with his youngest son, Lysander, who at forty-three has yet to hold down a paying job; an unscheduled rendezvous with his first wife, Carol, whom he hasn't seen in twenty-seven years; and a brief visit to the grave of his second wife, Isabelle. Complicating this plan, though, is Delilah, the widow with whom he has fallen in love over the past few months. As Millard begins to wrap up his life, he confronts a lifetime of challenges during a single day—and discovers that his family has a big surprise for him as well.

TOPICS AND QUESTIONS
FOR DISCUSSION

1. Discuss the book's epigraph. Why do you think Appel chose to include that particular line from Larkin's *Aubade*? Read the full poem. What themes does it share with *Millard Salter's Last Day*? Did the epigraph affect your reading for *Millard Salter's Last Day*? If so, how?

2. Millard believes that "comprehension wasn't the same as compassion" (p. 181). Explain this statement. Do you agree with Millard that "open[ing] your mind too much" (p. 181) can be detrimental? Why does Millard hold this viewpoint? What are the dangers of sympathizing with every person equally?

3. Who is Virginia Margold? On Millard's birthday, she presents him with a box full of mementos. Why do you think that Virginia has held on to these items? Following the visit, Millard feels sorry for Virginia. What do you think has led to his change of opinion about her?

4. Given the circumstances under which Millard and Delilah met, were you surprised by how their relationship

progressed? After Millard confesses his feelings to Delilah, he apologizes, telling her, "It was a selfish thing to say" (p. 15). Do you agree with his assessment? How would you have handled the situation if you were Delilah?

5. As Millard tours his childhood neighborhood reminiscing, he chastises himself for wishing that Delilah was with him because "None of this should have mattered to him—love was about the present, not the past" (p. 159). Why do you think Millard wants to share this experience with Delilah? How might knowing someone's past deepen a romantic connection?

6. Late in his life, Millard comes to realize that "marriage— heterosexual marriage, at least . . . was a tortuous cat-and-mouse game of implicit contracts between the sexes" (p. 70). Describe Millard's marriages. Can you think of any examples of game-playing from his relationships with Carol and Isabelle that would have led him to have this viewpoint? Discuss them with your book club.

7. When Carol and Millard discuss their son, Lysander, Carol tells Millard, "You know Stanley and Livingstone, right? Well, Livingstone didn't consider himself lost, even if Stanley chose to find him" (p. 81). What does she mean? Do you agree with Millard's assessment of Lysander? Does Millard's opinion about his son change throughout the novel? If so, how? Did your opinion of Lysander change? Why or why not?

8. In Isabelle's final days, she tells Millard that she's filled a

notebook with lists of what he should do after her death, saying, "All *you* have to do is follow the directions" (p. 11). Why does Isabelle do this for Millard? How might it provide her with some solace? What is the effect of having Isabelle's instructions on Millard?

9. Despite its serious themes, *Millard Salter's Last Day* is a very funny book. Were there any scenes that you thought were particularly hilarious? What were they? How does using humor help Millard cope with mortality? Do you think it is an effective coping method? Why or why not?

10. In his youth, Millard believed that "true devotion was about breaking down barriers" (p. 24). Contrast this with his current view of love. What are the characteristics of "authentic love" (p. 24) in Millard's view? How does this impact what information he shares with Delilah? Do you agree with his decision to keep his plans from her?

11. Lysander's failure to mature and assume adult responsibilities gnaws at Millard because "Millard, embroiled in extraneous affairs, had let him" (p. 6). Is Millard being too harsh on himself? What responsibility do you think Millard, as a parent, has to his son? Do you think Millard has been a good father to Lysander?

12. Based on Millard's interactions with Lauren Pastarnack, did you think that she would make a good psychiatrist? Does Millard? Do you agree with Lauren that the quiz Millard gives her when she asks him to write a letter of recommendation is unfair? What's the lesson in the quiz

for Lauren? For Millard? Do you witness any other teaching moments that occur between Millard and Lauren? If so, what are they?

13. Ezra Steinmetz tells Millard, "There's nothing special about dying. . . . It's one of the few universals" (p. 61). Do you agree? In what ways is death universal? Are there any ways in which it is unique? What effect does each of the deaths detailed in *Millard Salter's Last Day* have on Millard?

ENHANCE YOUR BOOK CLUB

1. Millard believes that "maturity meant accepting the infinite expanse of existence, that there were many things one would simply never know or do" (p. 18). In contemplating his mortality, Millard begins to catalog these things, effectively making "a bucket list in reverse" (p. 18). Discuss Millard's list, then come up with one of your own. What sort of things have you wished to do? Pick one to attempt to accomplish and share reports of your progress with your book club.

2. On his way back from visiting Isabelle's grave, Millard tours his childhood home, remembering anecdotes from his childhood. Tell your book club about the place where you grew up, sharing some stories from your younger days.

3. *Millard Salter's Last Day* is filled with reminiscences, from Millard's tour through his childhood neighborhood to the slide show he's presented. If you were going to create a slide show representing your life, what would you include in it? Share your photographs and the accompanying memories with the members of your book club.

4. *Millard Salter's Last Day* has drawn comparisons to *A Man Called Ove*. Read both books and discuss them with your book club. Do you think the comparisons are apt? In what way, if any, are Millard and Ove similar?

5. To learn more about Jacob M. Appel, read more about his other books, and find out when he will be in a city near you, visit his official site at jacobmappel.com.